THE DARKEST NIGHT

THE DARKEST NIGHT

Jodie Larsen

HAWK Publishing : TULSA

Published in the United States by HAWK Publishing Group.

HAWK and colophon are trademarks belonging to the
HAWK Publishing Group.

Printed in the United States of America.

Library of Congress Cataloging in Publication Data
    Larsen, Jodie
        The Darkest Night/Jodie Larsen–HAWK Publishing ed.
        p. cm.
        Hardcover edition: ISBN 1-930709-44-7
        1.Fiction–Oklahoma
        I. Title
    [PS3563.I42145R4 2000]
    813'.54   80-52413
                                            CIP

HAWK Publishing web address: www.hawkpub.com

H987654321

For my wonderful, loving mother
Elizabeth Patricia Larsen

Special Thanks

Dee Wild's years of experience training dogs and working with both the National Association of Search and Rescue (NASAR) and the Louisiana Search and Rescue Dog Team (LaSAR) have given her the insight and knowledge to handle virtually any question I tossed her way. Her help and advice were an invaluable part of writing this book, and I deeply appreciate every minute of her time. Dee truly lives up to her team's motto, "Giving of ourselves to serve others."

Sgt. Ron Moulton with the Tulsa Police Air Support Unit is without a doubt one of the best pilots in the air. He generously shared his expertise on every aspect of helicopter flight, from basic physics to the most complicated questions about avionics, emergency landings, and rescue techniques. Because he is no stranger to treacherous wind currents and the tricks of long-lining in tight situations, his input made the technical aspects of this book possible. Without Sgt. Moulton, this story would never have made it off the ground.

R.T. Jones and Dennis Larsen of the Tulsa Police Department never fail to share their wisdom on every aspect of police work. I will always be grateful for their honest comments and eagerness to help.

Bill and Kirsten Bernhardt earned my respect and admiration years ago. Their continued support, encouragement, and advice is invaluable.

My family and friends continue to be a source of inspiration. Mark, Amanda, and Jonathan provide the laughter and joy that every writer needs. Joan Rhine never fails to bring sanity to the insane world of writing, along with great advice and a shoulder to cry on. Last, but not least, Ben, Julie, Chester, Brent, and Joy (also known as my running buddies) provide friendship and support on a daily basis.

Now what? Evan Newsome thought. *Sure, you heard a dog bark. Just like you saw that thick, juicy steak last night. The way my luck has been going, that's probably a wolf telling his buddies he's lined up a nice feast of human tartare.*

What felt like chunks of embedded glass made opening his eyes an ordeal, but Evan tried. A brief glimpse showed the same cruel world he seemed forever trapped in — a world that held little food in the sense that he had grown to know it, and more importantly, not a drop of water. At least he didn't think so. In truth, he didn't have a clue where he was, how long he'd been there, or why he had been left in the forest to die.

That's right. I'm going to die. Finding the thought oddly amusing, he would have smiled had his lips not been dry and broken. Even the salty taste of blood couldn't quench a thirst so pervasive that he was certain if he could just touch a drop of water it would restore order to the universe.

Struggling to sit, he tried to assess what was real. From bears to French silk pies, his mind had been playing tricks on him since the beginning. Somehow his starving brain created amazingly realistic images. Every sense, from touch to taste, would verify its existence before scrambling back into the recesses of his imagination. The horror of last night's crawl of a million willowy spiders had been harrowing, but dawn revealed the truth. Not a single crushed insect littered the chilled ground. The small shred of Evan's intellect that remained intact found the phenomenon fascinating.

As he leaned against a boulder near the edge of a jagged cliff, he remembered with fondness how easy things like swallowing, blinking, and breathing had been just a few days ago. Silently he vowed that *if* he survived he would never take anything for granted again. Never.

Several days ago Evan had lost count of how long the wilderness had been his captor. Using an arrowhead, he had planned to keep track of each sunrise by etching a mark on the side of his fine leather shoe. But the Cole Haans were hopelessly ruined — the result of endless wandering and an hour-long rampage against the inhumanity of God, Mother Nature, and the monster who had done this to him.

What had been a starched white dress shirt and navy suit were now in shreds. One hand rested on the remains of the red silk tie dangling loosely around his neck. Each evening when the sun abandoned him, he buried himself in leaves and thanked his lucky stars that the jacket was a warm, wool blend. Beneath the tattered clothing, taut skin stretched across every bone, but he didn't feel the slightest bit hungry. Just thirsty, and jealous — of trees.

Trees were everywhere. Tall, gaunt brutes loomed into the dreary sky. The scraggly, pathetic ones reminded him of himself — precariously clinging to life on the side of a rocky ridge. Evan was certain the trees were drinking all the precious water, purposely keeping him from finding it. If he had any strength at all, he would've tried to choke a few drops out of one. Rolling over, he started to chuckle. "Yes, your honor. I'm guilty of murder. I killed a tree to save myself."

Laughter consumed him. Everything he had worked so hard to achieve seemed utterly, completely pointless. A law degree. Busting his chops to make partner. Spending every free minute working. *For what? Money? What was I thinking?*

Rocking from the emotional high to an unbearable low, he thought of his wife. With two miscarriages in the last eighteen months, they'd been afraid to celebrate the positive home pregnancy test. Instead, they had vowed to keep it a secret, to wait four or five months before telling their friends and family to be certain they wouldn't have to share the pain again. The stress of his disappearance couldn't be good for her, and he felt certain she had lost the baby. If there had been a tear left to shed, the flash of guilt would've made them flow one more time.

Evan squinted to scan what little he could see of the horizon. It was either late morning or early afternoon. He couldn't tell because a line of thick, dark clouds were driving across the treetops, apparently planning to set up camp and stay for a while. As the last of the sunlight faded, he felt a sliver of hope. The sun had become his arch enemy in the daylight, and the long-lost friend he ached for each night. *What difference does time make? Either way, I'll be dead before I find a stream.*

"Jesus," he muttered hoarsely. "Come on. . .help me. Please!" As if expecting a reply, Evan tilted his head to listen. But the song of the forest didn't miss a beat. Life was all around him. Incessant life eluding inevitable death. And an imaginary dog who barked every so often as if to remind him that he had completely lost his mind.

For the millionth time he considered his predicament. *The meeting . . . They must have known something was wrong when I didn't show . . . Why didn't they send help?* A snip of anxiety danced across the fringe of his memory. Since the beginning, he'd only been able to latch onto fragments of what had happened, but this time a rush of fresh images hit him with nauseating clarity.

In the shadows of the parking garage, a call for help. He should have run when he heard that voice. Run and never looked back. The first glimpse of the man's face expressed it all. Cold and calculating, it was clear the beast's soul had been severed from his heart long, long ago.

Evan remembered now, but the man's haunting words still made no sense. "Retribution. You've been chosen to pay for the ineptitude of others. The innocent must suffer."

Why? Why me? Better yet, whose ineptitude? Evan let his eyes fall closed as he softly groaned, "He wanted me to suffer. His wish certainly came true."

For a moment he was sure the brilliant flash he perceived through closed eyelids was the beginning of the end, the bright light so fondly spoken of by those who had basked in its warmth while standing at death's door. But even as his anticipation soared, a low rumble of thunder shook the hard, cold ground.

The first drops of rain felt like explosions on his taut cheeks. Sprawling onto his back, he opened his mouth. Sweet, cool water!

Evan didn't care when the gentle sprinkles were replaced by torrential sheets just minutes later. The thought that he might be struck by lightning never crossed his mind, because a few feet away rainwater was transforming a depression in the rocks into a pool of fresh, beautiful water. As he watched, the pool joined with a rivulet flowing downhill, and together they gave birth to a tiny waterfall that cascaded over the lip of the cliff with an ease and grace found only in nature. Every ounce of his being listened to the serenade of the water splashing on the ground below, his heart pounding in reply.

With newfound energy, he mustered the strength to roll onto his stomach, to drag himself toward that angelic sound. When he reached the pool, he scooped handfuls of water until his thirst was finally quenched. As he pushed himself upright, the wind and rain abruptly died as though the heavy cloud needed to catch its breath. Finding himself precariously close to the edge of the cliff, he started to inch backward, but stopped.

Evan's raw hands clenched, his nails cracking as they dug into the wet rock. For a brief moment, he had seen the blaze orange hat and vest of a hunter, or maybe a forest ranger, on a trail in the canyon two hundred feet below. Waving, he tried to shout for help, but his calls were little more than raspy squeaks.

Another bolt of lightning snaked through the sky, striking a tree near the man in orange. As though a bomb had exploded, a loud *crack!* cut through the air, followed by an impressive display of splintered wood taking flight. The clouds opened again, unleashing a rain so intense that Evan wondered if the storm were trying to prevent a forest fire of its own creation. Unable to see more than a few feet, he leaned back and closed his eyes. In his mind, he pleaded, *I'm here! Please . . . If you're real, I'm desperate! Help!*

« « «   » » »

"Run, Stagga!" Max Masterson shouted, hoping his certified Search and Rescue, or SAR, German Shepherd would flee to safety instead of coming back toward him. In the blink of an eye, the bolt of lightning had transformed a benign tree into a weapon firing chunks of wood as lethal as any bullet. With savage precision, the bolt had split the trunk into two perfect halves. As if in shock, each side shivered in mid-air before beginning a cacophonous descent to the forest floor, crushing everything in their paths.

Although they needed to return to base camp, Stagga had darted in the opposite direction, toward the bluff. Max followed his lead, weaving through the brush as tree limbs slammed to the ground on each side of him. When he was finally clear of the debris, he slowed to a brisk walk and tried to catch his breath.

Before the lightning strike, Stagga had been using the scent carried by the wind to try to locate a man who had been missing for almost three weeks. A four-year SAR veteran, Stagga was also certified to do rescues using his track, trail, avalanche, and disaster skills.

Max had chosen the dog's name because it had perfectly captured the Shepherd's stubborn and aggressive traits. Watching Stagga bolt out of sight as if nothing out of the ordinary had happened, he smiled. His bet had paid off — the canine was one of the best in his field.

Finding Stagga wasn't a problem. Barking every few seconds, he stood at the base of the cliff where the falling water was rapidly transforming a dry creek bed into a stream. The dark tips of Stagga's ears were laid back and his brindled muzzle was pointed toward the sky. As loud as possible, the dog was proclaiming to the world that he had not only found the scent, it was so strong that even a human should be able to smell it.

Another streak of lightning slashed the ominous clouds as Max knelt at Stagga's side. Wrapping one arm around him, he ordered, "Hush, boy. I know the rain is knocking down the scent, but I'm already going to catch hell for staying. We should've turned around when they called us back an hour ago."

The dog whined, casting him a dejected look. In spite of the fact that his white fur was caked with mud and bits of tree, Stagga was eager to keep going. Max brushed chunks of green wood off his shoulders, then Stagga's back, before using his sleeve to wipe his eyes. Scanning the area, he knew the rain was too heavy to see or hear anything, much less spot a subtle clue left by a missing person.

Standing, he snapped the leather leash onto Stagga's collar and said, "I know we're close, but we'll have to come back after this passes." The dog's urgency was obvious. Straining, he pulled the leash taut to reach the base of the cliff.

Hopping vertically on his hind legs, it appeared that Stagga thought sheer willpower was enough to defy gravity and climb the ninety degree angle. With his front paws still high on the rocks, the dog looked back and whined. Another bolt of lightning made Stagga flinch, but didn't break either his drive or determination.

Rain stung Max's eyes as he tried to look up, wishing there was some way to follow Stagga's lead. "I know, boy. I know. We'll get back to base and have Cal take us up in his helicopter just as soon as this passes." Digging his GPS out of his pocket, he noted the coordinates so they could return to that exact location later before reluctantly ordering, "Heel."

Together, they backtracked through the forest. Had the rain and wind not swept them forward, they might have seen the red silk tie snag on a rock at the top of the cliff for a few seconds before it broke free. Flowing gracefully, it tumbled down the waterfall to sail the swift currents of the newly reborn stream.

« « «   » » »

Craig Sanderson sipped a cup of coffee in the café, his face partially hidden from the other diners by a copy of *USA Today*. Although he appeared to be reading the latest bestseller list, he had already learned the intriguing details two hours ago. The book he was tracking, *Vis Medicatrix Naturae*, jumped from #59 to #4 that week, an amazing feat for a title that had sold less than five hundred copies in the two years since its publication.

Seated next to the window, Craig was looking beyond both the newspaper and the meandering ribbons of rain trickling down the glass, his gaze focused intently on the motel across the street. One by one, he'd counted the members of the Search and Rescue teams as they had returned from another futile morning on the mountain. A single team was still unaccounted for, in spite of the thunderstorm. Could they have found him?

Touching the tiny earpiece wired to a device in his pocket, he wondered if it was still picking up their transmissions. It had been silent for thirty minutes, longer than usual in such hazardous conditions. Shifting nervously in his seat, growing anxiety made the coffee churn in his stomach.

For almost ten years he had closely studied the way emergency response teams worked. Taking into account the length of time Evan Newsome had been missing, and the prevailing weather conditions for the last few days, Craig was confident that the official search would be called off within the next 24 hours, probably sooner. The back to back storm fronts would likely be the last straw, since so much of the scent would be eliminated by the heavy rains and wind. That is, unless they had already found him. If so, then all the meticulous plans would have to be changed. The thought made his head ache, but he silently told himself that it didn't matter. Even if they fit the pieces of the puzzle together it was already too late. Their 20/20 hindsight wouldn't help them predict the pain their futures held.

A small pair of binoculars was tucked in his breast pocket, but he didn't need them. With relief, he watched a truck pull into the motel's parking lot, certain it belonged to Cal Stevens. At his side was the diehard SAR team, Max Masterson and his current dog, Stagga. Craig remembered Max's first dog, Oreo, an imperfect black Lab mix whose random white spots would have been more at home on an Appaloosa. He wondered if Oreo might still be alive, but it really wasn't important. Unlike their masters, dogs can't be held responsible for their actions.

The cell phone in the pocket of his jacket vibrated, and he answered it as he watched Cal, Max, and Stagga splash across the parking lot. Softly, he said, "I told you not to call . . . Either way, I'll be in Tulsa by sunset. Just leave my room key in the usual place and stop worrying!" After listening for a few seconds, he nodded. Without saying goodbye, he merely flipped the phone closed and slid it back into his pocket.

Tucking the newspaper under his arm, he dropped a ten dollar bill onto the table and casually walked out the door. As he dashed through the rain to his pickup, he kept an eye on the activity across the street. Once he was inside the truck, he used a towel to dry his face and hands, then tossed it on the passenger side floorboard. It landed atop two copies of the new bestseller, each carefully sealed in a plastic bag.

Craig couldn't help himself. Starting the engine, he slowly pulled out of the diner's parking lot and turned into the motel's entrance. The two men were laughing, trying to wash the mud off the filthy German Shepherd. As he drove slowly past, he waved a friendly Midwestern greeting, not at all worried that he might be recognized. After all, he was a ghost from the past, a reminder of injustice, inhumanity, and incompetence that was much easier to forget than to remember.

Driving away, he declared, "Enjoy your last days of innocence. Soon, very soon, you'll be in hell on earth."

« « «   » » »

Kaycee Miller snatched the phone before the ring had time to die. Pushing back her long, dark hair, she pressed the receiver to her ear and exclaimed, "It's early! Does that mean you have good news?"

"Hello to you, too," Max responded, the serious tone of his voice answering her question.

Sinking against the sofa's soft cushions, Kaycee tried not to let her disappointment shade the rest of their conversation. Back-to-back rescues had kept Max away for most of the last two months, and she cherished every second they shared each day, even though the fickle cell phone connections often made it challenging. "I miss you."

"Not as much as I miss you. I'm stuck in a thunderstorm in the middle of nowhere. I can't remember the last time I was this miserable."

"I seem to recall you repeatedly claiming that Search and Rescue teams have to be tough."

"Tough, yes. Invulnerable, no. For this time of year, it's been warmer than we expected. I only packed my winter socks and shirts, so I've been sweating up a storm. I've got blisters under my blisters, and even though I used the hair dryer on my faithful friend, he still smells like a big, wet fur ball."

Practicing the mental game that was rapidly becoming a part of her life, Kaycee closed her eyes. It was easy to visualize Max's long, lean frame stretched on a motel bed. With the phone cradled beneath one of his strong cheekbones, his green eyes would show the depth of his despair. Since his thick hair was probably still wet, it would be darker than normal — the color of a rich cup of coffee. She knew Stagga would be curled on the floor at his side, softly snoring. Like a kitten, his fluffy white tail would occasionally twitch upward for no apparent reason, although she suspected he had vivid dreams of chasing cottontails and tomcats.

The timbre of Max's voice conveyed his increasing frustration and exhaustion. She wanted to touch him, to hold him, but he was in the middle of Carlsbad Caverns National Park, and she was alone in her house in Tulsa, Oklahoma. Even though she knew the current crisis had stretched every volunteer Search and Rescue response unit to its limit, she wished he would stay closer to home. She not only missed him, she missed the time they shared on his ranch. In the few months that they'd been dating, she had grown accustomed to spending every free moment in the fresh air. Max was slowly, but surely, teaching her how to ride and care for his horses, but she still didn't have the confidence to try riding alone.

Under normal circumstances, envisioning Max would have lifted her spirits, but this time the image made her feel even more lonely and isolated. Trying to stay upbeat, she asked, "Speaking of Stagga, how's Supermutt holding up?"

"Kaycee says hello, boy."

Although she knew it was coming, Stagga's sharp bark in the background still made her flinch. Smokey, the large black Lab curled at her feet, reacted with a short whine, lifting one ear while cocking his head as if he wanted to talk, too. Smiling, Kaycee said, "Scratch behind his ears for me, then give him a big hug."

"Were you speaking to me, or Stagga?" Max joked.

"You, silly. Seriously, any leads at all?" she asked as she reached down to pet Smokey.

"Stagga was onto something today until a thunderstorm rolled in. Because the trail was so hot, we kept working longer than we should have."

Sensing he was leaving out an important part of the story, she coaxed, "And you stopped because . . . "

"A tree a few yards from us was struck by lightning."

"Max! You've got to be more careful!"

"I know. We'd been called back to base a little earlier, but Stagga was working so hard I just didn't have the heart to stop him."

"Even so, you know better. Lightning always calls off searches."

"Tell that to the poor guy who's lost out there."

"Getting yourself killed won't help him."

"True." With much more enthusiasm, he added, "In a strange way, I wish you could've been there. Being so close to a lightning strike was incredible. I felt the sheer force of its energy. It's true what they say about your hair standing on end, and the smell of ozone hangs in the air for quite awhile, even in the pouring rain. I'm amazed anyone could survive being hit."

"Please try not to find out for yourself. Are you going back out today?"

"Cal's glued to the Weather Channel. If the storm lets up, we'll do a fly by. The guy we're looking for is running out of time, and we were so close. I could feel it. I practically had to drag Stagga out of there."

"I'll bet."

"You should've seen him. He was covered with mud from the tip of his muzzle to end of his tail by the time we got back to the pickup point. Cal insisted that I wrap Stagga in a blanket before he'd let him inside the new truck. Water was flying everywhere when we hosed him down in the parking lot. He's still a mess, and his rescue vest is in dire need of a long soak."

Kaycee laughed. "Can't say that I blame Cal for wanting to keep his latest toy clean. It's still hard to believe he flies to rescues in his helicopter *and* has one of his guys bring a truck."

"Jet A fuel isn't easy to find. Without it, the helicopter is useless."

"Sounds very expensive."

"I'm sure it is. But money isn't a concern for Cal. Since he never married, he only has to worry about himself, and he'd be happy sleeping on a cot in a storage room if that's what it took to keep doing rescues. He started R.R.M. a long time ago and it does very well. He's probably got ninety percent of the helicopter and small plane maintenance contracts within five hundred miles of Tulsa. His house makes mine look like an ice-fishing shack."

"What does R.R.M. stand for?"

Max chuckled. "We always joke that it's Rescues Require Money, but it's actually Reliable Repairs & Maintenance."

"He's a very generous guy."

"That's putting it mildly."

"Be sure to give him my best."

"I will. He's still mad at me for not letting you tag along. Besides the fact that he likes to flirt with you, he claims he wants you to analyze his handwriting again."

She laughed. "If that's what he considers flirting, then it's no wonder he's single. Hopefully you'll both be home soon, and we'll have something to celebrate. I'll whip up a batch of my famous Hawaiian Surprise, then delve into his deep, dark secrets."

"After all the takeout food we've had lately, that's sure to cheer him up. Besides, if there's a way to Cal's bachelor heart, it's a good, home-cooked meal."

"What happens if the storm doesn't cooperate today?"

"Day or night, as soon as the weather clears we'll start at the section of dense forest near the cliff where Stagga alerted. We'll work there, then head toward where Joan and D.C. were at the top of the mountain. We've been warned that tomorrow is our last try. They're calling off the search."

Feeling guilty for being relieved, she softly replied, "Which means you'll be home soon no matter what happens."

"Good point. I guess there's always a bright side."

Sensing he would rather talk about something else, Kaycee said,

"I ran across an interesting article last night that seemed slightly relevant to the recent disappearances."

"Let me guess. You stayed up searching the Internet again. You know, you've got to get more rest."

Closing her eyes, she nodded. "Easier said than done. I found a story called, "The Ancient Forest — Suicide Magnet or Peaceful Haven?"

She had obviously piqued his curiosity. "Go on," he urged.

Picking up the page, she paraphrased, "It says that hikers who stray off the forest trails have consistently been finding dead bodies for years. Often they hang themselves from tree limbs or take poison, nestling in the underbrush until it takes effect. The forest is one of the most common destinations for the suicidal, and growing more popular every day."

"Interesting. Which forest was the article written about?"

"Well, that's what makes it such a longshot. The original story was written in the late 1990s, but it was recently reprinted because the phenomenon still applies. This particular article was referring to the forest at the base of Japan's Mount Fuji, but the author added some statistics that indicate a slowly rising level of suicides in U.S. forests in the last few years."

Max sighed. "Why did you get my hopes up like that? I thought you might've stumbled onto something to explain the current rash of suicides. Somehow I don't think Japanese people committing hara-kiri has anything to do with the crop of middle and upper class Americans who keep wandering off in our national forests."

"The article goes on to explain that while suicide currently carries a stigma in Japan, their society has traditionally viewed it as an honorable way out of a shameful situation. Samurai warriors used to disembowel themselves to atone for failure."

"So you're suggesting that these people are so shamed by some incident that they're killing themselves? I might buy that if they were teenagers, but, so far, we're talking about two established businessmen and an average mother of three young children. Certainly not the type of personalities to make rash decisions."

"The Extreme Alternative — Suicide by Nature is the relevant chapter in the book that keeps turning up in the victim's belongings. It describes several methods of graceful worldly departures, including one of a woman dying of cancer who listens to the music of the trees and feels the sunlight on her face as she slowly slips away after taking an overdose of barbiturates."

"Not one of these deaths has been peaceful. Starvation and dehydration lead to dementia, and I won't give you nightmares by describing some of their last, desperate acts."

"Rational or not, people do kill themselves after suffering personal or professional setbacks. Surely you see the connection. Maybe the people you're searching for were at the end of their ropes. They found, or were given, the book at a time when they were vulnerable. I'm sure the FBI has checked into it."

"The book!" Max growled. "It always comes back to that stupid book."

"Actually, it's a compelling read. Did you know that the media coverage of the disappearances has pushed it to onto the bestseller lists of both The New York Times and USA Today?"

"So I've heard. Just what we need — a few more nut cases getting crazy ideas. As it is, we've stumbled across several news teams filming in the middle of nowhere. I'd bet it's only a matter of time before one of them wanders off and we have to stop the search we're working on long enough to find them, too."

Kaycee sighed. "You sound so tired."

"And frustrated."

"I wish I could be there." She leaned toward the coffee table, running a finger along the book's glossy jacket. "Max, maybe you should at least read the chapter on suicide. It's actually a very spiritual interpretation of how human life is tied to nature and vice versa. I don't agree with the premise, but I can certainly see how someone who is terminally ill or in great pain could easily be drawn in by the idea of a peaceful, serene death."

"No thanks. After finding the emaciated bodies of a few of the people who believed its garbage, I think I'll pass. Besides, not one of the people we've found has been terminally ill. They're middle-aged, apparently in the prime of life. The autopsies have found lots of bumps and bruises, but in the end, the cause of death has always been exposure, starvation, and dehydration."

"Suit yourself, but as a psychologist, my professional opinion is that these people must have left behind some clues as to their confused mental state. Rational people don't just drive to a forest, totally unprepared, then wander aimlessly around until they die."

"I couldn't agree more. We're having another meeting with the FBI in a few minutes. Maybe they've found something unusual in the profiles of the victims, some connection that will tie them all together."

"I know you think I'm busy enough without wrapping myself around your job, too, but I'd really like you to ask them something for me."

He sighed. "Kaycee, if I didn't care about your future, I wouldn't worry about you working twelve hours a day."

"I know."

"What do you want me to ask the FBI?"

"I'd like to have a chance to analyze the handwriting of the victims. It would help if I could have some samples from a few months before they vanished, then one as close as possible to when each person was last seen. I know it isn't much, but maybe it could help."

"You constantly amaze me."

"There's nothing amazing about it. If these people really were headed toward suicide it will show."

"Good point."

"Oh, and could you ask them one more thing for me?"

"Sure," he replied.

"I'd like to know if there were fingerprints from the victims, not just on the covers of the books they recovered, but inside the books, especially on the chapter on natural suicide. If the books were never read, then we're dealing with an entirely different reason for all the disappearances."

"Excellent point. Then again, you're always thinking outside the box."

She laughed. "I wish. Right now I feel like the box is rapidly closing in on me."

"I take it the programming isn't going as fast as you'd hoped?"

"That would be putting it mildly. There are so many variables. Every time I get ready to send you all the specifications that I think will finish one handwriting characteristic, I think of a dozen more to add to the list."

"Keep the faith. Someday soon the two of us will have developed the premier handwriting analysis program. You just have to realize that there's a lot of knowledge in your head that you use automatically— "

" — And even more that's intuitive. I'm really having my doubts, Max. Every sample of handwriting is so different, so unique. What made me think that we could create a computer program that could recognize all the variables?"

"Because it's possible. Okay, not every variable, because to a certain extent I believe your intuition and perception are very important factors. Even so, the base knowledge is groundbreaking work. In the last ten years you've made true scientific advances in a very tough field. I won't let you give up on this. Got it?"

"Yes, sir." In the background she could hear a loud rapping.

Max quickly said, "I'm sorry, but I've gotta go. Someone's at the door and I still haven't updated the Internet site with today's search results. I'm looking forward to seeing what progress you made on the program."

"It isn't much."

He laughed. "No one ever said this was going to be easy. In fact, programming and rescues have a lot in common. They're both long, hard roads to follow, but every once in awhile the perfect combination of luck and skill come together to bring an awesome result."

With a broad smile, she claimed, "It's no wonder I can't resist you."

"Ah, the truth at last."

"Be careful, okay?" she sighed.

"Always. I'll call you tomorrow. Promise you'll get some sleep tonight."

"I'll try."

"And shift finding an assistant to the top of your To Do list. It might take some time to find a person you can trust."

Kaycee nodded as she said, "I know."

"I miss you, Kaycee."

"Miss you, too. Bye."

Cradling the phone, Kaycee knew he was right. She had placed an ad in the paper and had been accumulating resumes. Since the doctors couldn't predict how quickly her *retinitis pigmentosa,* or RP, would advance, she needed to prepare for the worst. Even so, losing her eyesight was something she preferred to push to the back of her mind. It was much easier to pretend it wasn't really happening than to face the truth.

After sliding onto the floor next to Smokey, she picked up the book, *Vis Medicatrix Naturae,* more certain than ever that it held the answer to the mysterious suicides. With a sigh, she shook her head at the irony of the title, then pulled the large black Lab close to ask, "How do you suppose reading about nature's healing power could make perfectly responsible people think the answer to their problems lies deep in a forest?"

Smokey rubbed his muzzle against her neck in reply. Stroking his soft, warm fur, she finally allowed herself to get excited. Max and Stagga would be home very soon.

At four o'clock that afternoon Cal was pounding on Max's door, demanding that they resume the search. Suppressing a yawn, Max gruffly called, "Coming!"

Stagga barked, then sat with his tail softly sweeping the cheap hotel carpet as he eagerly watched Max assemble their damp gear. Throwing open the door, Max took one look at Cal's serious expression and stepped up his pace. Together they crossed the parking lot, then jogged across the field to where the helicopter was waiting.

After the emergency response teams had met with the FBI to discuss their progress, Max had managed to squeeze in a two-hour nap. It had been a welcome escape, and he could tell that Stagga was energized, too. Scanning the area, Max asked, "Aren't Joan and D.C. joining us?"

Cal shook his head. "Joan ran into town for supplies. She should be back any minute, but we don't have time to wait."

"I thought the meeting this afternoon went well. Do you think the FBI will really act on Kaycee's suggestions?"

With a shrug, Cal replied, "They're grasping at straws right now. This is a tough case. The families are all screaming kidnapping, but the evidence keeps pointing toward suicide. Besides, the FBI has everything to gain and nothing to lose by tapping Kaycee's skills." With a sly grin, he added, "That whole *death stroke* performance in New Mexico certainly made a believer out of me, and I know Randy's convinced Joan, too."

Roughly shoving Cal's shoulder, Max said, "You'd better not let Kaycee hear you say things like that. She's constantly fighting to keep handwriting analysis from being classified with tarot cards and voodoo dolls."

"Then she needs to dye her hair blond. Right now, she's got that dark, mysterious look going for her."

Max laughed. "I'll tell her next time I see her."

"Nah. It wouldn't do any good. No matter what color her hair is, there will still be those eyes."

Wondering how Cal could possibly know about Kaycee's vision problems, he asked, "What about them?"

With a shrug, Cal replied, "It's hard to describe. There's just something special about them. Kind of a sexy, sultry thing. I can easily see why you fell for her."

The discussion made Max miss Kaycee even more. Although he didn't agree with her logic, he had promised to keep the fact that she was slowly losing her eyesight a secret until she decided to tell the world.

When Max didn't answer, Cal added, "You know, if you've decided she's too much for you to handle, I'd be happy to step in."

"No way! Hands off. And quit flirting with her."

"Flirting? Me?" The innocence in his voice was betrayed by the twinkle in his eyes.

"Yes, you. She thinks you're cute — too cute to not be married. In fact, any day now I expect her to start setting you up with her friends."

Rolling his eyes, Cal groaned. "That's what they all do. And why is it that hot women always have such doggy friends?"

Max simply laughed. In spite of their relaxed conversation, he knew from Cal's hurried pace and the furrow creasing his brow that he was still very concerned about the weather. Glancing over his shoulder, he searched the western sky, where the sun was playing hide and seek with a handful of scattered clouds. Turning his gaze to the menacing skies pushing off to the east, he commented, "Good call, Cal. Looks like the worst has passed."

His reply was a slight shrug, a move that confirmed Max's suspicion that the break in the storm was probably nothing more than a small window of opportunity. Knowing Cal's lack of aversion to risk, it was more likely a porthole than a window. Max doubted if anyone else knew they were making a quick run back to his search sector. Even so, with a life hanging in the balance, he was more than willing to take the chance.

Since Max had already fastened Stagga into his lift harness, the dog was eager to be back on the job. At the ripe old age of four, his loyal companion had been on so many missions that he knew the routine well. With a wagging tail, he ran ahead to frolic beside the helicopter.

Max reached into the oversized pocket on the thigh of his drab olive utility pants to double check his walkie talkie and be certain that he had extra batteries. Taking a deep breath, he tried to still the nervous energy that was pulsing through his veins. Even after years of doing rescues, the rush of adrenaline just before going into the field still made his fingers tingle.

As they approached the Bell 427 helicopter, Max admired its sleek design. Although the front was a polished black, the rear was painted a metallic gold that sparkled in the sunlight. Atop the gold on each side was a red cross behind large black letters that read "SEARCH AND RESCUE." Below each door were the most important words of the mission statement of the National Association for Search and Rescue, " . . . that others may live." No matter how many times Max read those words, he always felt a surge of pride.

Cal ran through the pre-flight routine and started the engine as Max climbed aboard and prepared both himself and Stagga for the ride. Sensing the urgency, the moment they were ready Max gave Cal a thumbs-up. Without wasting a second, Cal expertly lifted off and headed for the exact location Max had pinpointed earlier.

Under normal circumstances Cal would have lowered them and returned to base to wait for pickup instructions. Instead, since Stagga's lead was so strong, they had agreed that Max and Stagga would search on the ground while Cal did a visual inspection from the air. If he could find a spot to land in the forest, he would, otherwise, he would stay airborne.

Leaning his head against the vibrating window, Max watched the landscape sweep past. The mountainside looked substantially different than it had when they'd hurriedly left a few hours earlier. The downpour had created shimmering puddles and numerous transient streams. Beams of late afternoon sunlight gleamed on the raindrops still clinging to the leaves, gracing the forest with an almost magical quality. Even though the rain had stopped their progress, it was a welcome relief to those who lived in the area. The entire region had been unseasonably warm and dry through the winter, which had increased the risk of fires to a dangerous level.

The familiar rush of altitude and nerves pushed Max's senses to their highest state, while fear blended with rising hope to intensify the anxiety. Through his headset, he heard Cal ask, "Is that the bluff ahead?"

Shifting so he could see out the front windshield, Max confirmed, "That's it. Try to get us as close to where the water is running over the edge as you can."

"There's no place to land around here, so it looks like you'll have to hike back a few hundred yards. The wind is starting to kick up and I don't think it would be wise to try to long-line you and Stagga down too close to the edge of that bluff. Mountain air currents are always tricky, and on a day like this you might end up getting really friendly with a few branches or rocks."

"No problem." With a quick glance to the west, Max confirmed what he suspected. On the distant horizon, well beyond the sprinkling of broken clouds, was another dark line that looked like thunderheads. Even though he knew the answer, he pushed the intercom button on his headset to ask, "How long do you think we have before the next line of storms hit?"

"I wouldn't waste a second if I were you."

Max stroked Stagga's back and shifted into position. "March is certainly coming in like a lion. Don't stay too close, or you'll kick around the air. The rain will have knocked down most of the scent, so Stagga will have to work on what little fresh scent is being carried by the wind."

"I know. Be careful, buddy."

Once Max had snapped both himself and Stagga onto the cable

they would use to descend, he signaled they were ready. Using the helicopter's swinging arm and winch, Cal began to lower them into a small clearing in the trees. In a matter of moments they were safely on the ground. Max released the line and Cal retracted the cable as he whisked the helicopter away.

Silence descended on the mountain as Max squatted at Stagga's side and readied him for the search. After giving him a quick rub, and a whiff of Evan Newsome's scent, he was satisfied that they were both ready. Standing, he commanded, "Search, Stagga! Find him, boy!"

At first, Stagga moved slowly, inhaling the humid air as though it held all the secrets of the universe. For several minutes, his paws seemed glued to the damp ground and Max wondered if they were wasting their time. Reacting to a slight gust of wind with an affirming bark, Stagga shot into the woods, heading in the direction of the part of the bluff that had been directly above them earlier in the day.

As if Stagga understood the urgency, he would occasionally stop to focus on the wind's subtle secrets for a few moments before starting again. Moving with more confidence each time, Max knew they were back in business when a strong breeze kicked Stagga into high gear.

Max had to move fast, practically jogging to keep close enough to maintain verbal control of the dog. Less than ten minutes into their search, he was thrilled to hear sharp barks, indicating that Stagga had accomplished his goal. Breaking into a run, he followed the familiar sound. Confronted by a thick layer of brush, he shouted, "Good boy, I'm coming," as he worked his way toward the small clearing twenty yards ahead.

Once in the open area, the music of rolling water made him certain he was near the place where the stream flowed over the bluff. Cal's voice on the radio broke the tension as Max heard, "Rescue One, come in."

Digging his radio out of his pocket, Max continued to jog along the water's edge as he replied, "Rescue One. What's wrong?"

"The lion's getting ready to roar. We've probably got fifteen minutes to clear the area before the next line of storms pushes through."

"Stagga's on full alert. He's just up ahead." With the victim in sight, Max reported, "Cal, we found him! He's under a pine tree less than ten feet from the edge of the bluff. His legs are partially submerged in water. Stand by."

After stuffing his radio into his pocket, Max rushed across the slippery rocks and mud, fully aware that the man wasn't moving. The old fear of being too late wrapped around his heart like the stinging lash of a bullwhip. As much to himself as to the victim, he muttered, "Hang on, hang on . . . "

Sliding into the mud at his side, Max pressed against the taut flesh of Evan's neck to check for a pulse. The moment he leaned close, a pungent odor made his eyes water. He recognized it from the previous victims — as potent as the stench of death, but with a distinctive smell unlike anything he had ever experienced.

Max held his breath until the weak rhythm of Evan's heartbeat beneath his fingertips declared that he was still clinging to life. Relieved, he gauged the depth of the movement of his chest while digging out his radio. Keying it, he said, "Cal, he's alive! Pulse is thready, breathing shallow. We've got to get him out of here now. How soon can you be here with the rescue stretcher?"

"I found a spot to land. I'll rig it on the winch and be there in under two minutes."

"Strap on a couple of extra blankets."

"Will do. Looks like the gusts are picking up. There's no time to move him away from that cliff, so the wind currents are going to make the ride up a little wild."

Max instinctively cringed. Translating *wild* from Cal's daredevil terminology into normal language put the impending lift somewhere between treacherous and suicidal.

Even though Evan appeared to be unconscious, Max spoke calmly to him. "Evan, you're safe now. We'll have you out of here in no time at all." After checking for broken bones, he slipped on a neck brace then gently pulled him out of the water. Careful to keep Evan's back as straight as possible, Max dragged him to the open area nearby where there was enough room between the tree limbs for Cal to lower the Bell rescue stretcher.

Digging deeper in his pack, Max took out a blanket, wrapped Evan tightly inside, and prepared everything for their ascent. As he was working, Cal radioed, "Max, this is going to be tight. I think you should all three come up at once."

Under normal circumstances, Max would've made two long-line trips from the ground to the helicopter — one with the victim, the other with Stagga. Keying his radio, he confirmed, "I understand. I'll have Stagga ready, too." Grabbing the lift harness, he called Stagga and prepared him as well. As he worked, he felt the brisk transformation of the wind — it was bold now, reaching out to rattle the trees with cold, damp hands.

As the whisper of the helicopter grew louder, Max tied a piece of hot pink, lightweight marking tape onto a tree limb to help Cal gauge the winds. Long before the downdraft from the helicopter's rotors had time to influence the ribbon of tape, it had started churning as if it were confused. It would snake to the south, then to the east — rise, then fall, before backtracking over its original path. Cal was an experienced pilot, but Max's instincts were screaming that it wasn't a good day to pit human technology against Mother Nature.

The Bell 427 was equipped with a bubble window on the pilot's side, which allowed Max to see Cal whenever he leaned over to watch what was going on between the helicopter and the ground. Cal maneuvered into place to hover and Max stared at the descending stretcher as it swayed, staying out of its way until it was on the ground. Rushing to it, he unfastened the carabiners and dragged it next to Evan.

Max folded down one side of the stretcher's deep basket so that he could easily shift Evan into the center. After wrapping him in the extra blankets, he snapped the side back into place and pulled Evan as far to one end as possible to leave enough room between his feet for Stagga. At his command, Stagga crept into place at the end of the stretcher. Over the roar of the helicopter, Max ordered, "Down, boy!" Stagga reluctantly lowered his belly between Evan's legs and Max added, "Stay!"

In what felt like record time, Max buckled and cinched both Evan and the dog firmly down with the safety straps, then clamped the rig back onto the long-line. After slipping on his own gloves and helmet, he connected his safety line and grabbed the cable. Straddling the stretcher, he gave Cal a thumbs up. For good measure, he shouted, "Stay, boy!" one last time.

As the cable tightened, the rush of adrenaline that always accompanied leaving the ground pulsed through him. The downdraft from the rotors invariably makes the ride back up to the helicopter tough, but the journey is usually predictable. Not that day. Gusts of wind played with the litter like a cat toy, batting it to and fro as the winch worked to haul the shifting load. Just before they cleared the treetops, an impressive blast slapped the stretcher into the bough of a sturdy pine, so hard that Max lost both his footing and his grip. His right side rammed the branches, embedding pine needles from his shoulders to his knees.

Still dangling from his safety line, Max took a deep breath. Like trying to walk in a hurricane, he battled the swirling winds and fought to regain his footing. When he was finally standing back on the stretcher, he signaled Cal with another thumbs up and tried to reassure Stagga by calling, "Stay, boy! We're okay."

Having ridden with Cal through similar dicey conditions, Max was certain a string of cuss words were filling the cabin when another gust started swinging them like a pendulum. Since the ride was so unstable, it took Max a little while to realize that they were no longer hovering directly over the pickup location or being reeled in by the winch. Cal had apparently decided to try to find a spot where the winds weren't quite so dangerous. Looking down at Evan's peaceful expression, Max was almost glad that he was still unconscious. If he'd been awake, the ride might have induced a heart attack.

It didn't take long for Cal to try one more time. After circling a relatively flat location for a few moments, until they were no longer whipping around, Max felt the cable begin to inch upward again. Glad to finally be within reach of the skids, he struggled to get the stretcher positioned right, then hauled it onboard. Once they were all

safely inside, he disconnected the cable, slid the door closed, and signaled Cal. Without wasting a second, Cal sharply banked and headed toward town.

Tugging off his gloves, Max pressed three fingers against Evan's
neck. At first, he couldn't feel anything. Trying not to panic, he
checked the other side and sighed when he detected the faint rhythm
of a heartbeat. Trading his helmet for a headset, he keyed the intercom so he could talk to Cal.

"How bad is it?" Max asked.

"Not enough fuel to try the next town, so we'll be heading straight
into the heavy rain. You buckled in?"

To save time, Max left Stagga with Evan on the stretcher. After
threading the two shoulder harnesses through the safely latch and
shoving them together, he declared, "I'm set. Have you called in the
find?"

"Tried. Too much interference from the storm. They're not picking
us up. Need to switch to a different frequency, but haven't had a free
hand."

Rain began pounding the cabin, followed by the sickening sound
of hail pummeling the craft's lightweight skin. Flying a helicopter
requires the coordinated use of both hands and feet while keeping an
eye on the panel of avionic gauges. Leaning to where he could see
through the front bubble, Max instantly realized that the rain had
reduced Cal's visibility to a few feet, if that. He knew all too well that
without visual references, a pilot can easily become disoriented and fly
the aircraft into the ground. "Any way I can help?" he asked.

"There are too many helicopter catchers between here and the hospital to safely try this. We're close enough to town to be near some
county roads. Keep looking down. If you see an opening, let me
know. We'll ride out the storm on the ground. If we can establish
radio contact we might be able to get an ambulance to respond."

"Will do," Max replied, knowing that helicopter catchers were
radio and microwave towers and electric lines. Since Cal would never
give up unless the situation were critical, Max began scanning what
little he could see of the surface.

Although he was a seasoned flyer, Max found himself nauseated by the combination of vibration and the lack of a visual horizon. He almost didn't believe his eyes when the clouds broke enough for him to spot the trees, then a stripe of brown. "Cal, take it down! There's a dirt road."

Cal began to descend as he replied, "How wide?"

"No way to tell."

"Get a good look at the trees?"

"Sorry. Just that there were lots of them."

"Okay. I've got a visual on the road. We're going in."

"Smooth or rough?"

"Rough. Hang on and say a prayer."

CHAPTER **3**

Max wrapped one hand around the safety grip at the top of the door and rested the other on Stagga's back. Twice Cal started to land, only to pull up at the last second when he spotted a tree too close to the side of the road. Finally, the skids slapped the ground and Max heard the relief in Cal's voice. "Looks like we're still in one piece. I'm going to skip the cooldown to speed things up. Let's secure the blades ASAP so the wind has less of a chance of flipping this bird."

Zipping up his coat, Max replied, "No problem." They both hopped into the pouring rain and worked together to slide the end caps onto each blade, then secured them to the fuselage. Once the blades were anchored, they climbed back into the cabin, soaking wet. Shouting to be heard over the storm's rumble, Max said, "I'll start an I.V. Any idea how long we might be here?"

"I'll find out. Give me a couple of minutes."

Max pulled open the drawer of medical supplies and quickly found the things he would need. He considered having Stagga move, but decided that the dog's body heat was beneficial since Evan was still in his wet clothes. By the time he established the I.V., Cal had contacted the control tower at the local airport. Calling over his shoulder, Cal reported, "There's a break in the storm headed our way. In about fifteen minutes we'll have a narrow window. Think he can last that long?"

"His pulse is still pretty thready. I'm going to put him on the Biolog just to be sure he doesn't slip away."

The family of a girl they had helped had donated a pocket-sized Biolog electrocardiogram unit that could be placed directly on the patient's chest. The small electronic device not only recorded the patient's information for a doctor to use later, it also displayed the heart rhythm on an LED screen and had an alarm in case the rhythm was interrupted. After folding back Evan's blankets and clothes to expose his chest, Max positioned the device and watched the first few blips register.

Inside the small cabin, the nervous energy was almost tangible. Max sensed that if it were possible, Cal would have been pacing. Instead, he sat nervously at the controls, checking every adjustment twice as he focused on the task still ahead. While they rode out the storm, Max calmly explained what was going on to Evan, even though the rescued man had shown no signs of regaining consciousness. Each second dragged, until finally Cal shouted, "Three minutes until show time! Let's free the blades and start the warm-up."

Although the winds were less violent, the rain still pummeled them as they removed the end caps and tie downs. Once they were back inside, Cal started the engines and the blades began to slowly turn. From his seat in the back, Max could see the timer on the instrument panel as it digitally clicked off each second in the two-minute pre-flight routine. The moment the clock hit 2:00, Cal flipped on all the avionic controls and announced, "We're good to go. You set back there?"

"Ready, here."

"The minute the rain lets up, we're off. Should be any second now."

Max took a deep breath and adjusted his headset. The whine of the engine had drowned most of the storm's angry voice, but every few seconds he could still feel the cabin rock from a gust of wind. He had been intensely watching the rivulets snake down the bubble windshield when Stagga barked. Glancing down, he saw the warning light on the Biolog and realized that he couldn't hear the alarm because of the storm. After double-checking that the unit was still seated properly on Evan's chest, Max knew that Evan had gone into cardiac arrest.

Keying his intercom, he declared, "Cal, we're losing him! I'm setting up the defibrillator."

"Rain is tapering off, so our window is here. Do you want to hold this position until you get him stabilized?"

As he pulled out the portable machine, Max exclaimed, "No! He'll be better off in the hospital. I can work while you fly. I won't be buckled in for a few minutes, so take it easy at first."

The roar of the engines revving almost overpowered Cal's reply. "I'll try to keep it smooth, but buckle up ASAP. There's no way to predict the up and downdrafts in weather like this."

"Will do." Max flipped on the machine, and set it to the right level. After unfastening the strap that had secured Stagga to the stretcher, he patted the seat on the opposite side of the cabin and ordered, "Stagga, come!"

The dog obeyed just as the defibrillator's green *charged* light began to glow. Placing the paddles on each side of Evan's chest, he made certain he wasn't touching any part of the basket before he pushed the button. Evan's body violently jerked in reaction to the powerful shock, and Max traded the paddles for the small Biolog unit to see if his heart had started beating again.

Max anxiously waited for the rhythm to register, but the line stayed flat. Removing the Biolog, he shocked Evan again. On the third try, the Biolog's small screen finally showed a steady heart rhythm.

After taking a deep breath, Max shut off the defibrillator and took a seat next to Stagga. He buckled them both in, then pressed his intercom to say, "He's stable for now. What's our ETA?"

"Three minutes."

With a sigh of relief, Max responded, "Thank God."

« « «   » » »

Kaycee observed the FBI agent as he took a seat in the wingback chair in front of the desk in her new home office. Between his classic navy suit, rigid demeanor and ultra short grey hair, she got the distinct impression that he was a strictly business, no nonsense type man. She had instantly known from the tone of his voice when he introduced himself that he considered his current assignment to be little more than a wild goose chase.

"Will this take long?" Agent Hite asked.

"That depends. How many writing samples did you bring for me to analyze?"

Reaching into his suitcase, he handed her three envelopes. "There are a few papers for each person. Apparently you requested a variety — some several months old, as well as a recent sample from each case."

"Are they originals?"

"As far as I know. Why?"

Kaycee shrugged. "It's only been a few hours. How did they collect them so quickly?"

Raising one eyebrow, he replied, "I've spent most of the day gathering them and running through airports trying to get them here as fast as possible."

She pulled the samples out of the first envelope and replied, "I'm impressed that the agency acted so promptly. These will be very useful for comparison purposes."

"This is a top priority case. Every second counts."

Kaycee didn't miss his insinuation that she was wasting valuable time. Settling into her chair, she smiled and declared, "This will only take a few minutes per person, but you're more than welcome to leave if you're easily bored." Looking toward the large digital clock on the corner of her credenza, she added, "It's four-thirty. I'll have everything ready by five o'clock sharp."

Without a glimmer of anything that could be classified as a facial expression, he snapped, "I'll wait."

"Fine." Kaycee considered asserting her case for the dependability of expert handwriting analysis, but quickly decided that there wasn't enough evidence in the world to convince Agent Hite that it was anything more than a circus trick. Instead, she withdrew the samples from each envelope and placed them in the order in which they were penned. Although normally, to be polite, she would have walked through the analysis aloud, another glance at the man's stoic face convinced her to keep her findings to herself until the end of the process.

Gently running her fingers over the samples from the first subject, she took out a magnifying glass and began jotting notes as she worked. *Female. Long heavy loops on y's and g's indicate emotional involvement, most likely with children or family. Physically fit. Energetic. Slight right inclination of slant indicates good judgment, sympathy, and compassion. All three samples are similar. Virtually no changes in rhythm, slant, use of zones, or pressure. This subject is of sound mind and body and would not be considered at risk of suicidal behavior.*

The other two samples were from men. The second sample indicated a man with a strong temper who tended toward overreaction. Even so, his writing distinguished him as intelligent, intuitive, and most likely a person who enjoyed reading and outdoor activities. His samples did not change over time and showed no indication that he was in any way unstable on the date of his disappearance.

While she worked, Kaycee could feel the intimidation of Agent Hite's unwavering glare, but it only served to make her want to prove herself and her profession. Turning her attention to the last set of samples, she found them to be the most interesting. From a personally signed letter to his wife, Kaycee knew that she was examining pages written by Evan Newsome, the man Max and Stagga were trying to locate at that very moment. A flash of anxiety for their safety crossed her mind, but she quickly pushed aside the nagging suspicion she'd had all afternoon that they were in trouble.

Focusing on her work, she began jotting: *Male. Firm upward thrusting strokes indicate brilliance and a determination to prove himself to the world. Driven. Creative. Zone usage displays forward-looking personality traits, doesn't dwell on the past and is realistic about the future. The change in loops on the middle sample from several months ago indicate he was under stress or emotionally upset at the time he wrote the note. However, the loops return to the previous range in the last sample. No other indication of significant changes in style or pressure. This man shows no signs of depression or instability.*

Kaycee looked up at Agent Hite as she placed her pen softly on the desk. For a moment, they simply eyed one another. He was the first to break the silence. "Are you finished?"

"Yes. Am I supposed to report my findings directly to you, or should I submit them in writing to Agent Collier?"

He handed her a business card. "Both. You can tell me, then I'll contact Special Agent Collier. As you know, she's coordinating the efforts on a national level. It's possible she may want written documentation, but there will be plenty of time to worry about the details later. Right now, we're just trying to determine the cause of the disappearances so that we can effectively handle the investigation."

Kaycee made an effort to remain friendly, but professional, to see if she could change his mind. "Fine. From the handwriting samples I've just examined, I can give you a conclusive profile of each of the individuals involved. They're all balanced, normal people. Not one of them could be classified as emotionally or physically unstable at the times of their disappearances."

He hesitated, waiting for her to continue. Narrowing his dark eyes, he asked, "That's it?"

Kaycee shrugged. "I could give you a long list of specific details about their various personality traits, but I really don't see what good it would do. The first two were found dead, and the search teams are rapidly losing hope of finding the third. The question at the root of my examination was whether these people were candidates for suicide at the time they went missing, as was implied by the presence of the book *Vis Medicatrix Naturae* in their personal possessions. The answer is a resounding *no*. I'd stake my life on it."

"So you're saying that all three were kidnaped, hauled to a different national park, then just left to die?"

"I'm saying that none of these individuals were in the state of mind to intentionally do anything that would end their own lives. I suppose it's still possible that they accidentally wandered away from their vehicles dressed in unsuitable clothing, but that's highly unlikely. These were smart, dependable people who had healthy relationships with their loved ones. No signs of mental illness, no aberrant behavior patterns."

He shook his head and slowly stood. "Sorry, but that doesn't make any sense. If you want to kill someone, there are a million better ways to do it than leaving them alive and well in a national park. What's to prevent them from simply walking to safety?"

"Since none of them have managed to do that, there must be some reason it hasn't happened. Possibly the place they're dropped is too remote, or they've been drugged."

"Autopsies on the first two have come back clean — no drugs."

"Some drugs don't show up on the usual toxicology screens. Plus, since the victims all wandered for a long time before they were found, they may have cleared the drugs from their systems naturally. As you know, I'm not an expert on criminal behavior, but I am a licensed psychologist. It seems obvious to me that the method used to commit these crimes is rooted in some event in the criminal's past. The victims are either tied to a common incident, or they were randomly chosen to die in places the criminal finds meaningful."

Nodding, Hite stood and began pacing as he added, "We can't discount the significance of the book, either."

"True. But its sole purpose could have been to throw off the authorities, to make suicide appear to be the cause of death."

"Do you think there's any chance the authors are behind all this?" he asked.

Kaycee paused, taking the book and turning it over so she could see the photo on the dust jacket. The book had been written by a middle-aged married couple. "Is there some reason to believe they might be?"

His eyes met hers. "They're directly profiting from the publicity."

"So has their publisher, but that doesn't mean they're tossing people in the forest to draw attention to their work. I think you're grasping, Agent Hite."

"Maybe. I've been in this business for a long time and am constantly amazed at what people will do when large amounts of money are involved. Plus, I've learned to look at the big picture. Assuming you're right, we're hunting for someone capable of kidnapping an individual, transporting them deep into a national park, abandoning the victim's car within a few miles from where they will eventually be found, and planting a clean book at each scene — one that only has the victim's fingerprints on it."

Nodding, Kaycee agreed, "Which in itself could be a lead. Lots of people handle a book before it finds a home, whether it's bought at a local store or on the Internet. And you're saying that all the books were wiped clean?"

For the first time, he almost cracked a smile as he slipped back into his seat. Leaning forward, he declared, "Exactly. Now carry it further. How does *one person* pull off such a crime? Each of the victims' cars have been abandoned at a designated parking area for campers, and getting an uncooperative person to hike deep in the woods would be very difficult to do. Not one of the search teams has noticed any sign that the people were dragged or left an obvious trail."

Kaycee replied, "Which means the killer either had help transporting them, had already left a vehicle at the site, or carried something like a bike or motorcycle to get back to his own car. Even so, once he had his victim in the parking lot, how did he get them so far into the woods?"

Hite's eyes lit up. "You may be onto something. He could be using a four wheeler — an ATV. If he pulled it on a trailer, then he could use it to haul the people up the mountain." As quickly as his excitement had arrived, it departed. "The only problem is that no trailers have been recovered in the area, or reported by people who noticed the abandoned vehicles."

"He could've left the trailer somewhere, then retrieved it with his own car later."

"True."

"Were all the victim's cars capable of towing?"

He nodded and abruptly stood up. "All SUV's. Nice ones. I'd assume that they all have standard towing packages, but I'll have the lab guys double check. Plus, there could be evidence near the ball hitches that has been overlooked so far."

Realizing he was declaring the end of their meeting, Kaycee stood and said, "I'm sure you know that serial killers are almost always white males. They're usually loners."

As he walked toward the door, he replied, "Yes, they are, and any multiple homicide case is intriguing, complex, and pressing. We need to stop this guy before he kills again."

Kaycee reluctantly followed him, wishing they had more time. Handing over the samples and her notes, she said, "I hope this helps."

Agent Hite extended his hand. "I'm sure it will. If you think of anything else that might be relevant, please be sure to contact us."

"I will."

"By the way, you did a nice job on this place. What was it before you renovated?"

"A formal living room and a small bedroom." Cocking her head, she asked, "I just finished converting it to an office last week. How did you know?"

"Fresh paint, new carpet, practically no clutter or knickknacks, a stack of resumes on the credenza, and there's not a speck of dust. But mostly it's the way you slightly hesitated when you needed something — like you weren't comfortable here yet and had to think of where to find things."

"Very impressive."

"Will you be working here all the time or do you have another office?"

"All the time. It was a tough decision, but I gave up my office in the Warren Building last month."

"Why?"

She hesitated, remembering her last conversation with Ellen, her RP mentor. *Even though you're not ready to tell the world, it can help to talk about it. It's a disability, nothing else. Some people need wheelchairs, others have crutches. Your impairment won't be visible to the general public, but it will impact how you interact with them. For a long time you're going to be able to hide it, but the time will come when you'll need to rely on the kindness of strangers.*

Kaycee stiffened, then stated, "I'm slowly losing my eyesight. Right now, I can still drive in the daylight, but that may change soon." Reaching down, she patted Smokey's neck and added, "So I decided to move my practice here. My clients seem to love it — no parking hassles."

Glancing at Smokey, who was at her side, he asked, "Is he a seeing-eye dog?"

Kaycee laughed. "No, but he is very special. He was a Search and Rescue K-9 until he was critically injured a few months ago. Since he's almost seven and will always have a limp, his owner won't be able to do rescues with him again." Giving Smokey a hug, she added, "Which works out well for me because he's such a great companion."

"Sounds like he's the lucky one. I hope you have a good evening." Watching him walk down the sidewalk, she wondered why he felt the need to put on such an authoritative front when he first met people. The psychologist in her found his chameleon personality intriguing, and she wished she could get to know him better.

Since it would be getting dark soon, she closed the door, locked it, and began her evening ritual. Going from room to room, she flipped on every light as Smokey padded softly at her side. When she was done, she said, "Well old boy, looks like we're alone for dinner again. How does leftover pasta salad sound?"

Smokey simply followed her into the kitchen and settled onto the overstuffed cushion in the corner of the breakfast nook. When her phone rang, she grabbed the receiver before the new talking Caller ID had time to finish announcing Max's cell phone number. It was odd having the phone report who was on the line, a mixed blessing of modern technology. She answered, excited. "Hello, handsome."

Max proclaimed, "We found him! He's alive!"

Kaycee's heart pounded. "That's fantastic! What happened? How did he end up in the forest?"

"We don't know yet. He hasn't regained consciousness, but they think he's going to be okay. I'm still at the hospital. We've only been here about twenty minutes. He went into cardiac arrest in the helicopter, but we brought him back and made it just barely within the golden hour."

"The golden hour?"

"As a rule of thumb, if we can get a person stabilized and at a trauma center within an hour, they usually make it."

"That's fantastic!" Wiping tears from the corner of her eyes, she replied, "I'm so proud of you! Did you and Stagga make the find?"

"Yes. Cal flew us back to the place Stagga located this morning. We ran into some more bad weather, but nothing Cal couldn't handle."

In the background, she clearly heard Cal grumble, *And my 427's got the hail damage to prove it.* Kaycee said, "Sounds like his helicopter took quite a beating."

"Let's just say it has a few character marks now. Besides, it'll give his employees a chance to show off. That is, if he can stand to wait that long before trying to fix the dings himself. He's already asking where he can come up with some dry ice to pop the small ones back out."

"But they aren't bad enough to ground him, are they?"

"No. The rotors are fine and the dings are cosmetic. I'm sorry, Kaycee, someone's coming. Can you hold on for a minute?"

"Sure." While she waited, she called to Smokey, "Max and Stagga are coming home!" As if he understood, he rushed to her side with his tail wagging furiously. Tossing him a dog treat she whispered, "Don't tell Max or Randy that I'm spoiling you, okay?"

In a few moments, Max was back on the line. "Sorry. Evan Newsome's wife wanted to say thank you. She said the doctors are optimistic that he's going to make it, and promised to keep us informed of his progress."

"I can only imagine how grateful she must be."

"Especially since she's pregnant. Apparently they've been trying to have a baby for a few years. I sure hope he makes it."

"He will. I know he will."

"This one was touch and go. An hour later and we probably would've been too late."

"It was meant to be. By the way, thanks for setting up the handwriting analyses with the FBI. I just finished and they were very interesting."

"Great. What did you find?"

"I don't see any possibility that these cases were suicides."

"I knew it! Could you tell anything else?"

She took a deep breath, saddened by the death of the first two victims. "Yes, but nothing that would help find the reason this happened to them. Do you think Evan is still in danger?"

"It's very possible. I'll ask the agent in charge if she plans to post a guard. I'm sure they're gonna catch the guy who did this. It's just a matter of time."

"When will you be home?" she asked.

"We've got the final review meeting with the emergency response teams in an hour. Looks like we'll easily be back in Tulsa by mid-morning tomorrow."

"Do you think Cal would mind dropping you off in my back yard?"

"I'm sure he'd be happy to, but then my 4-Runner would be left at his place, and I'm afraid he'd be tempted to try to set a new land speed record in it. Besides, it's only twenty minutes from R.R.M to your house. I'll drive straight there. We'll do wherever your heart desires for lunch."

"I can't wait!"

"Then it's a date. See you tomorrow."

"Congratulations, Max. Take care and be careful on the way home."

"Always. If the meeting doesn't last too late, I'll call before I go to bed."

"You know it doesn't matter how late you call. I'll be waiting."

"You need your rest."

"I can rest anytime. I'd rather talk to you."

"That's very flattering. I'll see you in the morning. We can talk for a week if you like."

"Promise?"

"You bet."

« « «   » » »

The small conference room was already packed when Max, Cal, and Stagga squeezed through the door. In addition to the other SAR teams, the local sheriff was chatting with several police officers, and a group of civilian volunteers had gathered toward the back of the room.

A tall woman they didn't recognize sat next to the mini-buffet, giving her full attention to a laptop computer. In another setting, she could easily have passed as a model, but the harsh lighting and complete lack of makeup did little to emphasize her femininity. Suppressing a yawn, she self-consciously smoothed the auburn hair that was pulled tightly back into a pony tail. In spite of the professional statement made by her FBI raid jacket, she still appeared to be young and vulnerable.

Max and Cal spotted Joan and slid into the seats she had saved for them. Making himself at home, Stagga curled up under the table next to D.C., Joan's brown boxer.

Two pieces of apple pie topped with melted cheddar cheese were sitting on the table in front of Joan. Max grinned and asked, "Are those for us?"

"Of course. The desserts were going fast and I promised Kaycee I'd take good care of you." To Cal, she added, "And I'm smart enough to be nice to the guy who's going to fly me home in the morning. After all, we wouldn't want you to faint from hunger."

Patting his slight middle age bulge, Cal declared, "I don't think you have to worry about that."

Max asked, "So, did you have to call out the National Guard, or did you finally track Randy down?"

Joan pushed back her chin-length black hair as she shook her head. With a mischievous grin she replied, "He had forgotten to charge the cell phone, and left the computer's modem tying up our home line, then somehow managed to turn off the answering machine without realizing it. Sometimes I wonder how he survives without me."

He chuckled. "That's because you've spoiled him."

"True." Her eyes softened as she added, "But right now I feel sorry for him. He wants to be here so badly he can taste it. After all these years, I think this is the first time he truly appreciates how hard it was for me to wait at home with Courtney while he did rescues."

"It's nice to have someone to hold down the fort," Cal commented-ed.

"Holding it down is probably all he's doing. I'm almost afraid to see how high the dishes and laundry are stacked. It's a good thing Courtney is old enough to take care of herself."

Cal replied, "You should have him teach the new mutt how to wash clothes. It'd be a great time saver."

"They'd both love it. Unfortunately, Courtney inherited her father's dislike of housework. She'll do it, but only if I twist her arm."

Seriously, he added, "How's Randy's physical therapy going? Is he still on crutches?"

"No, he's been off for almost a week now. The doctor says he's making great progress. He'll be back in the field driving us all crazy as soon as he and Prince learn to work together. He sure misses Smokey, though. Bonding with a new dog is hard, especially when the last one helped save your life."

"Smokey was a special SAR K-9. He'll be a tough act to follow. But he's in good hands. Kaycee really loves having him around."

"It's a match made in heaven. Randy needs to be alone so he can bond with Prince, and Kaycee doesn't need to be alone all the time."

Max shook his head. "You'd never convince her of that. I have to remind her every day that she needs to hire a new assistant so that she can delegate some work."

She laughed. "And they say opposites attract. The two of you couldn't be more alike."

"Are you accusing me of being stubborn and independent?"

After rolling her eyes, Joan lifted her Styrofoam cup of coffee to toast the two of them. "Of course. Oh, and I almost forgot. Congratulations on a great find! I can't believe I missed the best part."

Max tapped his cup against hers. "Thanks, but remember it took *all* of us to narrow the area. Stagga just happened to be in the right place at the right time. If D.C. had been working our sector, then the find would've been yours."

Joan simply grinned, then turned her attention to the slender FBI agent with auburn hair who had stepped to the front of the room.

"Good evening, everyone. I'm Special Agent A.J. Collier. I've been assigned to coordinate the investigation on the recent disappearances. I see that everyone has filed the reports we requested, and on behalf of the FBI, I'd like to thank you for the extra effort, and for doing such a great job with this latest search. I spoke with the hospital a few minutes ago. Mr. Newsome hasn't regained consciousness yet, but he's holding his own and his doctors are optimistic. Thanks to each and every one of you, and especially to Mr. Masterson and Mr. Stevens, our search was successful and we may finally have a chance to discover the nature of these disappearances."

After a hearty round of cheers, Agent Collier continued, "We hope that when Mr. Newsome is able to talk, he can shed some light on this puzzling case. I've received word that both the profilers in Quantico and an independent psychologist have confirmed there is a high probability that the three cases tied to the book, *Vis Medicatrix Naturae,* are the result of criminal actions. As a result of these recommendations, the Bureau has decided to increase the team of experts working on the investigation. In addition to reviewing the previous cases, these agents will respond to any alert issued by the National Park Service. Employees of the Park Service have been put on high alert and are being asked to check public parking areas at least once every twenty-four hours for abandoned vehicles. Of course, we hope that Mr. Newsome will be the last, but without an apparent connection between the victims or an established motive, there's no way to tell."

Max barely noticed the man who quietly slipped into the back of the room and tipped his hat to the FBI agent. She smiled and said, "Mr. Newsome's father, Richard, would like to say a few words at this time."

As Richard Newsome walked to the front of the room with a distinctive limp, Max realized that they had met before. He wasn't quite sure when or where, but he definitely recognized the man's rugged face. With a broad smile, Richard said, "I'm sorry I couldn't be here sooner to help coordinate things. I just want you all to know how much our family appreciates your hard work." Looking toward Max and Cal, he said, "I've worked rescues with a couple of you before, but it's been a long time. My arthritis dictates most of my life now, and it keeps me from doing what I love to do the most — rescues. Again, I'm eternally grateful for all your help. May God bless each and every one of you, and your extraordinary dogs, too."

Once the applause died, the young FBI agent opened the floor for questions.

Joan raised a hand. "If these people were purposely left to die, then could Evan still be in danger?"

"We have a guard watching his room. Right now, he seems to be our only hope of solving these cases and we have no intention of letting anything happen to him."

Max asked, "Is there any other way we can help?"

She shook her head. "I'm afraid not. My best suggestion is for everyone to go home and get some well-deserved rest. I hope we won't need your services again for a long, long time, but I'm afraid we probably will. Thank you again for volunteering. It's good to know that there are people like you who are willing to put aside their personal lives to help others in their time of need. I hope you all have a safe trip home."

Although Joan and Cal both decided to go to bed early, most of the workers mingled for another hour before calling it a night. Max stayed to reminisce with Richard about the two rescues they had worked together. One had been Max's first time in the field, an unsuccessful search for a boy lost in the Ouachita National Forest, the other had been an even more depressing time when they had traveled to Mexico after a major earthquake. For two weeks, they had helped recover bodies from the rubble. Richard filled him in on Evan's life, and thanked him again for his persistence.

Nothing could've made Max feel better than to know that they had successfully located a fellow SAR colleague's son. Thoroughly content, the moment he walked into his motel room Max realized he was so tired that he could hardly keep his eyes open. As though the weight of the world had been lifted from his shoulders, he plopped on the bed, kicked off his shoes, and closed his eyes. Thinking he would merely rest his eyes for a few minutes before taking a shower, he dozed off.

Several hours later, the ringing of the cell phone roused him from the depths of a dreamless slumber. Disoriented, it took him a few moments to realize that the phone was still in the pocket of the jacket he had tossed across the back of the chair. As he fumbled, Stagga cocked his head and wagged his tail, staring at him as if he were trying to understand a strange new game.

The clock read almost one a.m. "Hello," he answered gruffly.

Kaycee spoke in a rush. "Are you okay? When you didn't call I got worried."

Still groggy, Max rubbed his eyes, hearing barking somewhere in Kaycee's house. "I'm fine. Must've dozed off. What's wrong? Why's Smokey barking?"

"That's actually why I called. I really didn't mean to wake you. It's just . . . I . . . I wasn't sure what to do. He's scaring me."

"Smokey's not barking *at* you, is he?"

"Of course not. Something outside. He started by the balcony doors in my bedroom, then ran downstairs. He's been at it for a couple of minutes."

"Have you called the police?"

"No. Do you really think that's necessary?"

"Probably not, but call them anyway. Then ring me back as soon as you get off the line."

"Max, don't hang up! I'm on my cell. I'll dial them on the regular phone."

Fully awake, Max began pacing as he listened to her place the call. He felt powerless and guilty for not being close enough to help. When she was on the line again, he asked, "Is your alarm set?"

"Yes."

"Where are you?"

"I'm still in the master bedroom upstairs. It sounds like Smokey is running back and forth between the front door and the French doors that lead to the back patio."

"If it were Stagga, I'd say that he's trying to tell you that there's something out there and he wants to go check it out. Could just be a raccoon or a possum."

"Or a person?"

"Probably not. Did you look outside?"

She hesitated. "Max, it's dark."

Feeling foolish, he said, "I'm sorry. I forgot. Call Smokey, tell him to come and see if he obeys." Max listened, amazed at how much he could ascertain just by listening. He heard Kaycee shout, quickly followed by the sound of Smokey's huge paws bounding up the stairs.

"Okay, he's here."

"How's he acting?"

"He's looking at the doors that lead to my balcony." Her voice raised a bit and he could tell she was fighting hard to sound calm. "Max, the hair on the back of his neck is standing up and he's baring his teeth."

"Do you have a panic button in there?"

"Yes."

"Hit it." Sirens began to wail. "Kaycee, do you have a gun in the house?"

Raising her voice to be heard, she replied, "I've been holding it ever since this started."

"Is the safety off?"

Kaycee snapped, "Yes! I know how to shoot. If someone actually came in, what would Smokey do?"

"It's only a guess, but I'd say he would attack."

Her other phone rang. "Max, it's the alarm company. Hold on."

Eavesdropping, he heard her explain what was going on. When she came back on the line he asked, "Any sign of the police? Can you see the street from your bedroom door?"

After a brief hesitation, she declared, "No sign of them yet . . . Wait! There they are!"

"Great. I think it's safe to turn off the alarm now." Once the din of the sirens died, he was able to speak softly again. "How's Smokey acting now?"

Kaycee sighed. "He's much better — just sort of pacing. Do you think he'll be okay with the policemen?"

"I think so. He'll sense that you're not afraid of them."

"They're coming to the door, so I guess I'd better go. Thanks, Max."

Relieved to hear her at ease again, he replied, "Make sure they thoroughly check the backyard and look for signs of forced entry. Are you positive you don't want me to hold on?"

"I'm sure. You need to rest so you'll be alert and enthusiastic on our lunch date."

"Hmmm . . . Sounds like you're craving attention. Come to think of it, that would be a win-win situation, wouldn't it?"

"You bet. I hope I can get some sleep soon. Tomorrow's a big day. I set up an interview for a new assistant at eight a.m. At least on paper, she's a perfect candidate."

"Great! I can't wait to hear all the details. Promise to call me back if you need anything."

"I will. Good night."

"Good night."

Max hung up and sat on the edge of the bed. Still fully dressed, he was wide awake and knew that it would be impossible to go back to sleep before unwinding. Ruffling Stagga's hair, he asked, "Want to go for a walk?"

Stagga replied by prancing to the door and sitting down. Max put on his shoes and jacket, snapped on the dog's leash and opened the door. As they slowly circled the perimeter of the parking lot, he looked at the moon and stars, wondering if he were destined to spend the rest of his life with Kaycee. Max couldn't imagine his life without her, a thought that made him both ecstatic and nervous.

After Stagga finished eradicating the latest scents with his own, they walked back under the sidewalk's awning. Trying not to disturb anyone, they stepped quietly past the windows of the downstairs motel rooms. Since the lights were on in Cal's room, Max stopped at his door and listened. Certain he heard the muffled sound of his friend's voice, he knocked softly.

Cal peeked out the window, cast Max a curious look, then opened the door. As he waved Max inside, Cal continued talking on the phone. The anguish in his eyes spoke volumes. Something was terribly wrong.

Cal motioned for Max and Stagga to make themselves at home while he wrapped up his phone conversation. Max felt a little uncomfortable listening to the end of what appeared to be a very strained discussion. "Promise me you'll get some rest. I'll be there by first light. Don't worry, I'll handle everything and I promise that Aubrey is going to be all right. Try to get some sleep. Bye."

Hanging up, Cal turned to Max. "What are you doing roaming around at this Godforsaken hour?"

"Kaycee just called. Smokey was going crazy barking at something outside and it freaked her out."

Shaking his head, Cal replied, "Can't say that I blame her. There are days when you have to wonder if the forces of evil are capable of converging. Is she okay?"

Max cast a wary look at Cal. "She's fine, which is more than I can say for you. Since when are you a believer in anything that isn't supported by rock hard science?"

"You gotta admit, there are some things in life that are pretty tough to explain."

"True. Have you gotten any sleep?"

He shook his head. "That was my mother."

"At three in the morning?"

"Actually, I've been talking to her on and off most of the night." Yawning, Cal stretched and added, "After the meeting, I had an urgent message to call her. She's worried sick about my sister."

Max had known Cal's sister for years. He sighed. "Is something wrong with Aubrey?"

Cal nodded. "Apparently she hasn't been seen since day before yesterday."

A knot began to form in the pit of Max's stomach. "Have they called the police?"

"Yes. But it hasn't been long, and there's no clear sign of foul play. Technically, she can't be classified as a missing person yet, but they're still working with us."

"Just local police, or have you brought in the FBI?"

"So far, just the local guys."

"Is her car missing?"

"No. It's still in the garage. My mother was holding up pretty well until my brother-in-law called to say that he'd found Brey's purse and keys on the shelf in the laundry room. Mom's sure that means she didn't leave willfully, since she would never even go for a walk without her keys. I've tried to convince her that she could've taken a garage door opener, or just left the house unlocked since she didn't plan to be gone for long, but Mom won't buy it."

"Does she still live in Colorado?"

Another nod. "Estes Park. Her place backs up to the Rocky Mountain National Park."

Their eyes met and held for a fleeting moment. Based on their mutual experience with searches, it was clear that they both feared the worst. Max offered, "You just said that her car wasn't missing, which means this isn't like the recent cases we've been handling. Besides, every one of those people lived a long way from the park where they were eventually found. It's probably just an eerie coincidence. We both know how much Aubrey loves to hike. She could've twisted her ankle, or stumbled and bumped her head — "

"Which would mean she's been stuck on a trail somewhere between twelve and forty-eight hours. Max, the terrain isn't like it is here in Carlsbad. That far north, the temperature is probably still dropping below freezing at night. In March, most of the higher elevations in the Rockies are still snow covered."

Max said, "Aubrey is well-trained, athletic, and level-headed. When she used to tag along on rescues, she never had any problem keeping up with the rest of us. Plus, she's well versed in survival techniques. If she is lost or hurt in the forest, she knows exactly what to do until help arrives. Unlike the others, she won't wander aimlessly."

Cal looked exhausted as he shook his head. "A few months ago, I would've agreed with you, but everything has changed. Max, she's been diagnosed as diabetic. So far, she hasn't been able to get it under control. They've been experimenting to find the right balance of insulin and diet, so she's been carefully monitoring her blood sugar so that she can take appropriate action when needed."

The gravity of the situation made Max pause to think. "Okay. What do we know for certain? She was last seen two days ago, which means she could have gone missing any time since then."

"When her husband left town day before yesterday, she was fine. Apparently, she's been working a lot of overtime, so he didn't think anything of it when she didn't answer the phone the first night he was gone."

"What made him suspect something was wrong?"

"She's a certified morning person, loves to fix a cup of cappuccino and watch the sun rise every single day. When he called at six a.m. yesterday and she didn't answer, he started to worry. When he checked with her office, they said that she never came in the previous day and hadn't called in sick, either. By noon, he contacted their next door neighbor and asked her to check the house. At first, the neighbor didn't notice anything out of the ordinary, but when she looked in the garage, she was sure something was wrong."

"Because the car was there in the middle of the day?"

"No. Because the side door was open and there was an elk inside the garage, eating right out of the storage bin where Brey keeps the food she puts out for them. Her husband claims that it was like Aubrey vanished in the middle of feeding them because she would never have left the container open. She always sealed it tightly to keep it fresh."

Max nodded. "That's right. The last time I was there, an elk walked right up to the window on the back door and looked in the house. Scared me half to death."

"Virtually everyone feeds them and since they're protected in the national park, they haven't learned to fear humans. Brey loves to watch them. She's even named all the regulars."

"Did you already send Bruce ahead with the R.R.M. fuel truck?"

Cal nodded. "He left around midnight. I'm getting ready to file a flight plan. Aubrey lives at roughly 13,000 feet, so I want to arrive before the sun generates enough energy to kick up a lot of mountain turbulence. Luckily, Colorado is sitting in the middle of a stationary high pressure system so the weather conditions have been good. Unfortunately, it doesn't look like that will last long. The next front should pass through in about thirty-six hours."

"That's not long. So when are we leaving?"

He shook his head. "*I'm* leaving in about an hour. Max, you need to get back to Kaycee. You said so yourself. Your priorities have changed. Doing rescues 24/7 will jeopardize another relationship, and this one is too good to lose. We both know you've been gone way too much lately."

The fear in Kaycee's voice was too fresh a memory for Max to ignore. He bit his lower lip. "You're right. It's not just my decision anymore." Glancing at his watch, he paced for a few seconds. "On the outside chance that she's asleep, I don't want to call her right now. I'll fly to Colorado with you, then ask her in the morning how she feels about it. If I sense even the slightest reservation on her part, I'll hop on a commercial flight back to Tulsa."

Cal shook his head. "That's a big risk, buddy. She's not the type to complain."

"I really believe that Kaycee will be fine with this. If it were possible, I think she'd be the first to join in a search for Aubrey." Placing his hand on Cal's shoulder, he added, "I fell for her because she's got a heart of gold, just like the friends I've made over the years. Friends don't let friends down in their time of need, or any other time."

"Okay, thanks. I need all the help I can get, but I'm going to want to talk to Kaycee myself," Cal replied.

"Deal."

"By the way, we'll be making a quick stop at the Boulder Police Department on the way."

"Why?"

"An old buddy of mine is head of their Aerial Support Division. Their department just upgraded to a new model, so he's going to secretly loan me their old FLIR for a day or two."

"Which is?"

"FLIR stands for Forward Looking Infrared. It's an infrared aerial camera with magnification and thermal sensitivity. I'm sure you've seen them in footage of police chases. With it mounted on the bottom of the 427, I'll be able to see images from the air of anything warm on the ground."

"Sounds expensive."

"The new ones are well over a hundred and fifty thousand bucks. Normally, thermal imaging in a national park would be a waste of time because the canopy of trees is so thick and there's too much territory to cover. Plus, the sheer number of elk and deer will make progress relatively slow."

"Because . . . "

"Because they can be roughly the same body mass as a human, especially if the person is curled up on the ground. The FLIR will reveal anything that's warmer than its surroundings. Depending on the foliage, we may be able to tell from the video image if it's an animal. If not, I'll have to fly low and spotlight the area. If Aubrey really did hike from her house, there's a slim chance we can find her using the FLIR."

Puzzled, Max said, "Assuming nothing has disturbed her scent, Stagga should be able to track her right from her house."

Cal nodded. "Believe me, I'm not challenging the effectiveness of using a dog. Now that you've agreed to tag along, the two of you are going to be our first line of attack. The FLIR is a backup, in case Stagga can't get a fix." Cal pinned him with a heartbreaking look. "Besides, you have no idea how hard it is to sit on the ground for hours, waiting to hear from you guys. This way I can be working while you do." Shrugging, he added, "It couldn't hurt, and we've got nothing to lose."

Max had never given much thought to what Cal did while they were in the field. He didn't think it was possible, but realizing what a lonely job the pilot had made him admire Cal even more. Smiling, Max said, "I think the FLIR's a great idea. Aubrey is lucky to have you for a brother."

"I can't believe I haven't taken the time to be with her more. We used to be so close. I haven't talked to her since Christmas." He took an envelope out of the pocket of his jacket. "Then out of the blue, I got this letter from her the day before we left for Carlsbad. I tried to call her, but got the answering machine. Instead of leaving a message, I just held onto the letter, hoping it would remind me to try again. I can't believe I never took the time to get in touch with her."

"You've been really busy."

He shook his head. "Even so. She's my only sister and I should've been more conscientious."

"Does the letter say that she needed help?"

With a shrug, he replied, "Actually, it really doesn't say much at all. That's why I wanted to talk to her. It gave me a weird feeling, like something bad was going to happen." Looking at Max he added, "*Deja vu*, huh?"

Patting his chest, Max replied, "There are a lot of things that you can only feel here. Always trust your instincts."

Cal shook his head and snapped, "She needed me and I ignored her."

"Don't be so hard on yourself. She's married, lives in another state, and has a high pressure job. You've kept in touch as much as you could. You have a pretty busy schedule yourself, even without the flurry of rescues we've responded to lately. Listen, I know you're tired and it's tough being on the other end of a search. Even so, I'm not going to let you pull a negative attitude on me. We both know that clinging to hope is imperative for success. It's way too early to give up. Aubrey is alive and in a few hours, we'll have her back where she belongs."

Cal nodded. "You're right. There's a lot to do and not much time to do it."

Max asked, "You *are* planning to take along Joan and D.C., aren't you?"

He shook his head. "You heard her tonight. Randy and Courtney need her."

"Are you crazy? Joan's already packed and ready to go, and she'd be royally ticked if you didn't let her come help. Besides, you're obviously not thinking very clearly. If you left us behind we'd still find a way to get to Estes Park. We might have to hitchhike, but either way would end the same. Joan and I will be searching for your sister. One way's just a little faster than the other."

Biting his lip, Cal shook his head.

"Judging from the circles under your eyes, I'd say you need to get a little rest before we head out."

With a weary smile, he said, "I'm too wound up to sleep, plus there's so much to do. I don't want to waste a minute."

"I'll wake up Joan, then start downloading the contour maps while you handle the flight plan." He held out his hand, "We're all in this together. Deal?"

Cal took his hand, then pulled him into a brisk hug. "Deal."

« « «   » » »

Applying a light layer of powder to the puffy skin beneath her eyes, Kaycee carefully scrutinized the last touches of her makeup, no longer able to trust a simple glance. Even though the police had reassured her that there wasn't any reason to worry, she had tossed and turned the rest of the night, hearing every creak and gust of wind. Normally at seven-thirty in the morning Smokey would have been at her side, but he was softly snoring, still curled up on his bed in the corner of the room. Apparently, his midnight madness had taken its toll on both of them.

Since Max would be home soon, Kaycee stood in front of the full length mirror to double check the sleek line of her burgundy slacks, then turned to be certain the delicate rose blouse was buttoned all the way up the back. Confident that she looked her best, she quickly snapped her fingers and called, "Come on, sleepy, let's go downstairs."

Smokey yawned and stretched, in no apparent hurry to leave his warm bed. Even so, by the time her foot touched the first floor, he had bounded past her to wait at the back door. Opening it, she took a deep breath of fresh spring air as he dashed outside.

Kaycee noticed Smokey dart toward the fence, but stopped

watching him when the phone rang. The moment she realized the Caller ID was announcing Max's cell phone number she hurried to answer it. "Hello!"

"Hi, beautiful. I take it the police said that there was nothing to worry about."

"They checked every nook and cranny. I think they added me to their list of crazy single women."

"Single, yes. Crazy, no. Did you get any more sleep last night?"

"Not enough. How about you?" she asked.

"I'm good. Did Smokey have any trouble settling down after the police left?"

Kaycee smiled. "Not a bit. In fact, he wasn't thrilled about getting up this morning. You sound tired. Max, I'm really sorry that I woke you. Next time I'll just call the police first. After all, they're paid to help crazy single women."

"Always call me first. It's flattering to know that you thought of me when you needed help. It means you trust me."

"Of course I do!"

"Amazing. Even after analyzing my handwriting, you still trust me. Come to think of it, you may not be as clever as I thought."

"I knew everything that I needed to know about you long before I saw your handwriting. Anyone who would be friendly to a person who had just run them off the road has got to be a pretty special guy."

Chuckling, he replied, "For someone who was up chasing ghosts all night, you sound like you're full of energy."

"Well, most of it is because I'm looking forward to seeing you in a couple of hours. But I have to admit, part of it is that I'm really nervous."

He hesitated for a breath, then asked, "About what?"

"Remember, I've got my first interview this morning. She should be here in twenty minutes."

Max laughed. "It's the interview*ee* not the interview*er* who's supposed to be nervous."

"I can't help it. My last assistant was like my right arm. I'm afraid I'll never find anyone like Cheryl again."

"Maybe she and her husband will hate Tacoma and they'll move back to Tulsa."

"Right. When I talked to her last week, she was practically doing back flips. This is the first time they've been able to afford for her to stay home with the kids and she's loving every minute of it. The kids love their new school, they're all playing soccer, and Cheryl even has time to do some volunteer work while they're in class."

"Good for her. Speaking of which, how do you like being a stay-home psychologist?"

"It's okay. A little weird, but I think I'll get used to it." Sensing he had changed the subject to postpone telling her the real reason he had called, she asked, "Are you still going to make our lunch date?" In the time it took for him to sigh, she knew the answer. Slumping onto a stool in the kitchen, she said, "It's okay, Max. Really. Where are you?"

"Fueling up in Boulder."

"Boulder? As in Colorado?"

"Cal's sister lives on the edge of the Rocky Mountain National Park just north of here. She hasn't been heard from since day before yesterday."

"Oh my God! You don't think — "

"We don't know what to think yet. Right now, Cal's having a special infrared camera mounted on the bottom of the helicopter so that he can search from the air at any time during the night or day."

"Max, he's only human. He has to rest sometime."

"Then you don't know Cal. Besides, there's a complication. She's diabetic."

Kaycee groaned. "How long has she been gone?"

"There's no way to know for certain, but we think about two days. Her husband cut his trip short and hiked her usual trails last night but there wasn't any sign of her."

"That can't be good."

He sighed. "Kaycee, I really miss you, and I'm very sorry that I won't be able to make our lunch date. Are you sure you're okay with this?"

"Max! Of course I am. Is there anything I can do to help?"

"No. But it's always nice to know that you're there if I need you."

"What about Joan? Is she with you?"

"Yes. As a matter of fact, you might want to call Randy. Maybe you, Randy and Courtney could get together for dinner or something. I'm sure they'd love to see Smokey and I think Joan and I would sleep better if we knew you guys weren't just sitting home alone."

With hesitation, she replied, "Max, that might be kind of awkward."

"Randy's a great guy and you'll love Courtney. She's too smart for her own good. Why do you think it would be awkward?"

"Because I can't drive at night, and if he suggests meeting somewhere, then . . . Do you think they'd mind coming to my house?"

"Not at all! To Randy, food is food and I'm sure Courtney couldn't care less. You know, pretty soon you're going to have to tell a few of your close friends about the RP."

"I know. And I will. Hopefully, I've got a long time before it impacts my life too drastically."

"Ah, the wonders of procrastination."

"You know, I just realized that I have a huge block of time open for lunch today, not to mention a feast fit for a king. I'll call them as soon as I finish my interview to see if they want to come over. And if it happens to fit in the conversation, I'll tell them about my RP. But don't hold your breath."

"That's a great idea. When life hands you lemons, make lemonade."

"I think mine will be pretty sour today, but I'll keep working on it. Is Cal nearby? Would he have time to talk to me for a second?"

"As a matter of fact, he wanted to talk to you, too. He's in the hangar. It'll just take a second for me to get him."

A few moments later, Cal snapped, "Hello."

"Hi, Cal. I'm very sorry to hear about your sister. I'm sure everything is going to work out fine. She has the best people in the world to help her."

His reply was blunt. "Thanks. I hope it does, too. Listen, Max would cut off his right arm if it would help a stranger. Should I shove him on the first flight home?"

"Of course not! Why do you ask?"

"People shouldn't take the ones they care about for granted. I'm glad to have him here to help, but only if it's okay with you."

"It's fine with me. You're sweet to ask. Listen, I'm worried about you, too."

"I've done this a million times."

"No, you haven't. This is personal. And we both know that when things get personal, it's hard to keep a professional distance."

He asked, "Are you worried about whether I should be flying?"

"No, silly, I'm worried about you. I know you're a great pilot, and I'm really glad that Max and Joan are there to help. I just want you to know that if you need someone to talk to, someone objective, you can call me any hour of the day or night."

Cal's voice was much more relaxed as he joked, "So, do I dial 1-800-RING-A-SHRINK?"

She laughed. "Just promise you'll call, even if it's only to vent about how frustrated you are. Use my unlisted home number or my cell, Max can give you both numbers. Seriously, Cal, anytime. I want to help."

"Thanks, Kaycee. You know, I have thought about you a couple of times since I found out that she was missing. She sent me a letter a few weeks ago. Is there any way you could take a quick look at the handwriting and tell me if she was okay?"

"I'd be happy to look at it. To save time, you could have Max scan it and e-mail it to me."

"You don't need to have the original?"

"Originals are great for determining pressure and depth, but those are only a small part of the big picture. If you've got an earlier sample of her writing, that would help the most. What I really need to do is compare two or more samples."

"I have a note she wrote me a couple of years back. Is that too long ago?"

"No. That would be fine. Have Max send both."

"Will do. Since Max is glaring at me like I'm trying to steal his girl, I guess I'd better get going."

"Take care!"

"You, too."

Max came back on the line and immediately protested, "I was *not* glaring."

"Whatever you say."

Lowering his voice, he asked, "Should I be concerned about him?"

"No. He needs you, though. Be strong."

"I'll do my best. Listen, this isn't going to be a normal search. I don't know when I'll get a chance to call. I have a feeling that we'll be hitting the trail even longer and harder than usual."

"That may not be humanly possible. You always work too hard."

Softer, as though he didn't want anyone else to hear, he replied, "Not like this. Because she's diabetic, we'll probably work all today and through the night, just stopping in the field long enough to let the dogs rest. Rescues are always on a short fuse, but this one's already lit."

"I understand. Don't worry about anything here. Just concentrate on finding her." Kaycee's doorbell rang, and she quickly added, "Max, my appointment must be early. I've got to go. Be careful!"

"Always. I'll call when I get a chance, but don't worry if you don't hear from me for awhile."

"Okay. Bye!" Kaycee hung up and went to the door. Opening it, she smiled and said, "You must be Tamara Conrad. I'm Kaycee Miller. It's nice to meet you."

"You too. Just so it won't be awkward later, my name is pronounced Ta-MAR-ah. I know it's a little different. My mother wanted to name me Tomorrow, but my dad freaked. So, the compromise was giving me a name that I'd have to explain twenty times a day."

"I know how you feel. Everyone thinks my first name is two initials, so I've had to do my fair share of clarifying."

As they shook hands, Kaycee noticed the tip of a tattoo peeking out from beneath Tamara's sleeve. Although she knew from her resume that she was in her mid-twenties, Kaycee was surprised at how young she seemed. On one ear, a row of small diamond studs climbed from the bottom of the lobe all the way around the upper ridge. The other ear was similar, but in place of the sparkling gems were tiny gold hoops. Her long blond hair was braided, and the tips of each braid were hot pink. Trying not to smile, Kaycee looked down. The girl's skintight shirt did little to conceal the outline of a navel ring, or anything else for that matter.

Curious, Kaycee wondered how many piercings and tattoos the girl had, but knew better than to ask. Apparently Tamara would fit right in with her more rebellious teenage clients, although she would probably make some of the middle aged women run away from the office screaming. Remembering her manners, Kaycee said, "I'm sorry, come in. The office is this way." Motioning to a chair, she added, "Please have a seat."

Tamara's green eyes darted about the office, finally coming to rest on an 8 x 10 photo on the credenza. Picking it up, she studied the picture that had been taken on the porch of Max's ranch house. Max, Stagga, Cal, Randy, Joan, Smokey, D.C. and Prince were proudly posed in full SAR gear.

Kaycee considered explaining the picture, but quickly realized that she needed to set an authoritative tone for the interview. Taking the framed photo, she handed Tamara a clipboard and an ink pen. "I'd like you to answer these questions. I'll check back with you in ten minutes, but if you need longer just let me know."

Looking slightly flustered, Tamara replied, "Oh. Okay."

Kaycee closed the door and sighed. After letting Smokey in, she made a pot of coffee and fixed a tray with a selection of light breakfast items to take back to the office. When the time was up, she carried it inside and placed it on the edge of the desk. Tamara grinned, obviously proud of herself as she handed over the clipboard. "All done."

"Great. Please help yourself to coffee, juice or fruits while I look this over, then we'll get down to business." Without being obvious, Kaycee scrutinized the girl's handwriting, paying more attention to it than the answers to the questions themselves. Her fluid, methodical strokes indicated a high degree of intelligence, but showed two problem areas: maturity and dwelling on the past. She couldn't help but smile at Tamara's answer to the one question on the form that Kaycee thought divulged the most about an individual: What are you most worried about being asked in this interview?

Tamara's response was as distinctive as the rest of her. *I've memorized impressive answers to all the interview classics, like 'What's your greatest weakness?' and 'If you were a tree, what kind of a tree would you be, and why?' . . . so fire away. The only question I'd prefer not to be asked is, 'What are you most worried about being asked in this interview?'*

Picking up Tamara's résumé, Kaycee bit her lip to keep from smiling. Sticking to her game plan, she commented, "I'm very impressed with your grades in high school and college. Why didn't you finish your degree?"

"Rent, groceries, you know. But once I find a really good job, I want to go to night school. Having a college degree is important, and now that I'm older I realize that I should have stayed in school when I had the chance."

Kaycee could tell from the hesitation in her voice that it hadn't been her idea to quit college. Curious, she probed, "So the decision was purely financial?"

"Not exactly." After a quick glance at the ceiling, she sighed. "I think it's safe to say that I listened to the wrong people. But I hope I've learned from my mistakes."

"The best part of getting older is being able to rely on the wisdom you gained when you were young."

With a sly smile, Tamara replied, "According to Oliver Wendell Holmes, 'What lies behind us and what lies before us are small matters compared to what lies within us.'" Reacting to Kaycee's silent admiration, she shrugged and explained, "I've always been into philosophy. When I was ten, I stumbled onto Kahlil Gibran's *The Prophet*, and I've been hooked ever since. For some reason, useless information sticks with me. Maybe someday I'll strike it rich on *Jeopardy!*"

"Let's hope so." Trying to get the interview back on track, Kaycee said, "Your supervisor at the bank gave you an excellent reference. Would you mind if I ask why you're leaving?"

She instantly looked away. "Mainly because they're not very flexible." One hot pink fingernail slowly flipped up each tiny gold hoop on her ear as she added, "I've been moved to a job in bookkeeping because they claim my attire is too distracting for a person in the public eye. Apparently, society still isn't quite ready to embrace complete freedom of expression. Most people tend to stare, a few laugh, some point." Leaning slightly forward, she cocked her head and grinned. "I'm surprised you haven't mentioned it, because I *know* you've noticed."

Suppressing the urge to psychoanalyze her, Kaycee consciously relaxed her posture as she asked, "Are your piercings new?"

With a nod, Tamara blushed and added, "Well, most of the obvious ones are."

Kaycee wondered exactly what that meant. Choosing to ignore it, she looked back at the résumé to help her stay focused. "Do you have much experience with computers?"

"You bet, but I don't type the old-fashioned way. I guess you could say that I get the job done but my style isn't perfect."

That's an understatement, Kaycee thought.

Tamara sat up straight, exuding a bright-eyed confidence. "The ad said that you need general office work, someone to run errands, and that the hours were flexible."

"That's right. As you can see, I'm a psychologist. I have both regular clients, and those who only call when they need to meet with me. In addition to my practice, I'm currently working on a computer program and will need someone to proofread the text and possibly make suggestions for improvement. In the future, the job might also entail acting as a sort of unofficial chauffeur."

With a brisk shrug, Tamara replied, "It's all good!"

"Great. I truly appreciate your enthusiasm. Do you have any questions you'd like to ask about the position?"

Openly scanning the office again, she shrugged and grinned. "I know it's a cliché, but where's the couch?"

Kaycee had been expecting her to ask about the job's pay or possibly the benefits. Her lack of concern about such things served to confirm the immaturity shown by her handwriting. "Well, I think stereotypes sometimes get in the way. I chose soft, comfortable chairs to make my clients feel more at home. I also have a state-of-the-art sound system that I can program to play calming music. I'm sure you'd agree that being a little different can often be a good thing."

"Awesome attitude." With an approving nod, she declared, "I like it here. Where will I be working?"

Caught completely off guard, Kaycee almost choked on a sip of coffee. Regaining her composure, she nodded toward the small room next door. "My new assistant will work in the adjacent office."

"Cool. When can I start?"

Finding Tamara's lack of pretense refreshing, she smiled and replied, "Honestly, I'm not quite ready to extend an offer yet. I have several more people to interview, so I'm afraid it will be a few days before I make a final decision." Kaycee stood and led Tamara to the front door. Shaking her hand, she smiled and said, "It was very nice to meet you. I'll be in touch."

Kaycee leaned against the doorframe and watched Tamara walk toward her car. The youthful bounce in her step and the vitality that she exuded brought home the fact that life was passing all too quickly. With a sigh, she smiled and thought of all the mistakes she'd made along the way.

As she was about to close the door, Smokey ran toward her carrying his leash in his mouth. Since the interview had taken a little less time than she'd allotted, she ruffled the fur on his head and declared, "Okay. But I'm wearing *real* shoes, so just one time around the block. Heel."

Smokey circled and obediently sat at her side, eager to go. After snapping on his leash, they headed down the street. The nip in the morning air was rapidly being swallowed by the sun, and Kaycee enjoyed the leisurely stroll. As they rounded the corner to head back home, she noticed a woman walking briskly toward them. To be polite, she led Smokey to the opposite side of the street, but the woman mirrored their movements.

Over the last eight weeks, she and Smokey had roamed the neighborhood at least once a day, rain or shine. They had encountered cats, kids, big dogs, little dogs, joggers, walkers, and dozens of rabbits. Never before had Smokey been anything but well-mannered, but the closer they got to the woman, the more he bristled and pulled at the leash. When she was within twenty yards, he started barking at her, then flatly refused to keep walking. Embarrassed, Kaycee smiled at the woman and said, "I'm sorry. I don't know what's gotten into him."

"Does he bite?" she asked anxiously, backing away.

"No." Stepping in front of the dog, Kaycee ordered, "Smokey, heel!" Once he reluctantly obeyed, she added, "Down!" As he lowered himself to the ground, his eyes never left the woman.

"Intense, isn't he?" the woman commented.

"Normally, he's as gentle as a lamb. I really am sorry."

"Don't worry about it. Do you live around here?" she asked.

Kaycee nodded, still keeping a wary eye on Smokey.

Pointing at Kaycee's house, the woman nervously asked, "Do you know the people who live there? I've been trying to reach them."

"Actually, I live there. Why do you ask?"

Fidgeting, the woman rattled, "Well, I'm new to the area and just wanted to meet all my neighbors. Your home phone number is unlisted, so I haven't been able to call to introduce myself. I left a note on the door a couple of weeks ago, but it probably blew away." Extending her hand, she declared, "I'm Pam Adams. Nice to meet you."

The woman's hand was cool and damp as it closed around hers. "Kaycee Miller."

"We've only lived here a couple of weeks, but it seems like a nice, quiet neighborhood."

"Most of the time it is," Kaycee agreed.

Rolling her eyes, the woman commented, "Except for last night. Someone's burglar alarm went off at one in the morning. Then there were sirens from the police cars. It was quite a scene. It scared my little Dakota so much that he insisted on sleeping the rest of the night in our bed."

Kaycee felt the blood rush to her cheeks, but kept quiet. She thought of saying she had a client on the way, but she hated the thought of being rude to a neighbor. Scolding herself for being so impatient, she tried to keep an open mind in spite of Smokey's odd behavior.

"Do you have kids?" Pam asked.

"Oh, no. I'm single."

With a glance toward Kaycee's house, she said, "Your place is gorgeous. You must have a great job, or a rich ex-husband."

"I'm a psychologist, and there's no ex-anything lurking in my past. I just believe that hard work pays off."

"I'm not trying to be nosy, but are you involved with anyone? I have this friend . . . "

Kaycee cut her off. "Actually, I do have a special man in my life." Even though Smokey was lying quietly, she could almost feel the tension pulsing through his body. Hoping to end his ordeal, she added, "I'm really sorry, but I've got to go. I have an appointment in ten minutes. Pam Adams, right?"

"Right. My house is the colonial around the corner. I'm having a get-acquainted brunch for the neighborhood ladies in a couple of weeks. If you'll give me your phone number, I'll put you on the list."

Holding up her free hand, Kaycee said, "Sorry, I don't have a pen."

"That's okay, I don't live far. I'll remember it."

Reluctantly, Kaycee replied, "555-2050."

"555-2050. Got it. It was nice to meet you."

"You, too. Smokey, heel."

As they walked toward her house, Smokey continued to watch the woman until she had turned the corner. Kaycee was relieved to be back home. Besides Smokey's odd behavior, there was something about Pam Adams that made her uncomfortable.

The moment they were inside, she closed the front door, twisted the deadbolt in place, then rushed to repeat the process on the back door. For several minutes, Smokey continued to act a little odd.

Pacing from the back door to the kitchen window, he would stop and look at her as if he had something vitally important to tell her.

Just watching him gave her goose bumps.

« « «   » » »

As Kaycee and Smokey walked toward their house, the woman who had called herself Pam Adams quickened her pace. As soon as she was out of sight, she reached into the pocket of her jacket. Her hands were shaking as she fumbled with the transmitter there and slipped on a small earphone. "Craig, she's coming! Are you there?"

"It's okay. I'm already out of the house."

Relieved, but still upset, she asked, "Did you hear everything?"

"Yes. We were right. She's definitely the one. I've got to circle around. I'll meet you as soon as I can. I'm going to go slow. There's no sense drawing attention to myself at this point."

"Okay." Practically jogging, the woman hopped into the passenger side of a pickup truck and waited. A few minutes later, Craig slid behind the wheel. Still agitated, she seethed, "That dog almost blew everything again! First last night, now this. Wouldn't it be easier if we just got rid of it?"

"No. We're sticking with our plan. The dog isn't part of this."

"Technically, neither is she."

He grunted. "Guilt by association. She made the choice to become involved with Max Masterson. Why did you introduce yourself as Pam Adams? I told you to make up a name."

"I haven't been Pam Adams since we got married. Besides, she's not going to remember me. She was practically itching to get away. Not a very neighborly person. Maybe she does deserve what she's going to get. When are we planning to snatch her?"

"If everything goes on schedule, we'll shoot for tomorrow. It might have to wait until the next day, depending on Masterson. Besides, there's no big hurry. Time is on our side."

"What are we going to do about the dog?"

He was silent for a few moments. "Don't worry. I'll come up with something. There are ways to work around everything."

As he started the car and pulled away, she asked, "Aren't you concerned about Evan Newsome? It's been almost three weeks."

"Why should I be?"

"There wasn't anything in the morning paper. By now, the others had all been found dead. At this point, the latest victim of the Natural Killer should be headline news."

"Newsome was in better shape than the others, plus the nights in Carlsbad weren't nearly as cold as we thought they were going to be. I'm sure his body will turn up soon."

"But what if he survives? He saw both of us."

Craig shrugged. "So? He doesn't know our names. To him, we're just two strangers. The multiple injections of psilocybe mushroom extract we gave him would've left him so confused and disoriented that he wouldn't have recognized his own mother at first. And once he does begin to remember, he won't be able to discern what was real from the hallucinations."

She was quiet for a few moments. "But he can't live. They all have to die, just like Dakota. That's what we agreed. It's the only true way to be certain that Dakota can move on."

He wrapped his hand around hers. "Pam, we both know that isn't entirely true. It's the suffering that counts, not the actual death. They need to learn that life isn't theirs to play with, that their actions, or *inactions,* have long-term ramifications. Retribution can take many forms. That's what will make up for what happened to Dakota."

A tear slid down her cheek. "He shouldn't have died. They could've found him in time if they hadn't been so arrogant."

"I know. I know. But he'll finally be at peace when all this is done."

Wiping away the tears, she took a deep breath. As if she had inhaled air so cold that it froze her heart, her demeanor completely changed. Her voice was callous, her gaze distant, as she whispered, "I could feel him at my side at the funerals of the first two. He whispered to me that they understood, and he smiled. Pretty soon, for the first time in their lives, the people who let Dakota die will know what it's like to be the one praying for a miracle."

Under different circumstances, flying through the Rocky Mountains would've been an awe-inspiring experience. The trees seemed to be floating on the thin, ivory mist, while the morning sunlight intensified the colors of the leaves and pine needles, encompassing every shade of green imaginable. But the sights were lost on Max, Cal, and Joan. They were focused on the task at hand, hoping that years of training and experience could help them save Aubrey's life.

Their flights were usually filled with friendly chatter, but that morning, the only sounds inside the helicopter's cabin were generated by the engines and rotors. On the rare occasion when Cal would check in with the closest airport, his voice was subdued, all business. Joan's eyes were closed, but Max doubted that she ever dozed off. He had worked with her long enough to know that she was always on edge, even when she appeared to be cool and collected. When Max noticed Cal leaning toward the bubble window so that he could see the ground, he keyed the intercom to ask, "Are we close to Aubrey's house?"

"Affirmative. Looking for a place to land."

Max scanned the stunning countryside. Although Cal's sister's address was within the city limits of Estes Park, it was actually in a small subdivision well off the main road, several miles west of town. Surrounded on the north, south and west by Rocky Mountain National Park, the rustic homes were nestled in native trees. No fences had been constructed, and minimal landscaping maintained the forest's natural beauty. If not for the paved road and driveways, from the air it would have been hard to tell that the small community even existed.

"How about near the main entry, the lot that's been partially cleared?" Max asked.

Cal replied, "Too close to the house next door. I think we'll have to settle for the turnaround on the road. It'll be a short hike, but we don't want the neighbors to panic."

"Looks good."

As soon as the skids hit the ground, Cal said, "You guys go ahead so the dogs can get some exercise. I'll catch up with you after I wait for the engines to cool down."

"Will do." Max helped Joan out and carried both backpacks until they were well away from the rotors. As Joan slipped her pack onto her shoulders, she asked, "You've been here before, right?"

Max nodded. "A few weeks after they got married. Since they eloped to Vegas, Cal flew his mother up to see them. I was still training Stagga, so we tagged along to attend a land cadaver workshop in Denver that weekend."

"So you didn't stay with Aubrey and her new husband?"

"No. We came here first and Aubrey fixed us a great dinner. Cal dropped off his mother, then we shared a room in town. Why?"

They crossed beneath the ornate wrought iron entry to the neighborhood as she replied, "I just wondered how well you know Aubrey. I know it's weird, but lately I've started to feel more connected to the person I'm searching for if I can learn a little more about their background. I get the feeling that she's not much like Cal. Are they alike, or as different as night and day?"

"I can definitely help you there. Aubrey is twelve years younger than Cal and they really don't have much in common. The family joke was that he got all the backbone and she got all the brains, although we both know that's not true. As far as I know, she was born a bookworm. She made straight A's her whole life, even through college. They're both type A personalities, but their methods of coping with the world are very distinct."

Joan absorbed the information. "Okay. Cal is pretty introverted unless he's around his close friends. I assume that means Aubrey is more outgoing?"

Max shrugged. "Yes and no. She always loved being alone, called it her 'quiet time.' In high school, she had two close girlfriends, but never really dated even though she was very pretty. In spite of her repeated claims that she was shy, she played varsity sports and was involved in every social activity you could think of. She went to college on a volleyball scholarship."

With raised eyebrows, Joan asked, "Volleyball?"

"She and her two best friends all ended up playing for the University of Tulsa. Cal and I used to go to most of their home games. Believe me, college volleyball is not a sport for the timid."

"What's she do now?"

"Last I heard she was the manager of a realty office that leases condos and houses to tourists."

"I wish Cal didn't feel so guilty about not calling her."

"Me, too, but I can see why it's getting to him. Aubrey idolized Cal, and I think he always felt as though he was supposed to protect her. Whenever I'd spend time with them, it made me wish I had a little sister." His eyes softened as the memories rushed back. Shaking his head he added, "It's really rather ironic that the one thing Cal loves most he can't share with her."

"Really? Why?"

"The first time Cal took her up in his helicopter, she got airsick. He wasn't doing anything daring, just flying low and level. By the time he realized she was having a problem, there wasn't a close place to land. She tossed her cookies in flight and was so embarrassed that she started to cry. We kept telling her that even experienced fliers have trouble with the vibration in helicopters, but she wouldn't listen. As far as I know, she hasn't ever flown with him again."

Joan shook her head. "And if I know Cal, he probably felt terrible about the whole thing, too."

"Of course. That was a long time ago. I'm pretty sure that he's never suggested she go up with him again, even though his new helicopter is larger and much more passenger friendly."

With a quick wink, Joan said, "Hopefully, he'll be flying her off that mountain in a couple of hours and she'll be well enough to realize that it's an amazing experience."

Since they could hear Cal jogging close behind, they stopped to wait. By the time he caught up, they were at the bottom of Aubrey's driveway. Even though both dogs were well-behaved, Max and Joan snapped on their leashes to be polite. Cal rushed ahead, his uneasiness apparent as he waited for someone to answer the doorbell. Max and Joan shrugged off their backpacks and leaned them against the house.

Aubrey's husband, Peter, opened the door, stiffly embraced Cal, then smiled and motioned them inside. Although Max had met Peter several years ago, he wouldn't have recognized him. Aside from the haunted look of sustained panic that was common in people who were searching for loved ones, his blond hair had thinned, and he had gained at least twenty pounds.

Peter vigorously shook their hands as he declared, "Good to see you again, Cal, Max . . . And you must be Joan. I'm Peter. Thank you so much for coming." Leading them into the den, he added, "I've always respected what you guys do, but I wish I didn't have to learn about it first hand. I can't tell you how much it means to me that you're all going to help find Aubrey. I don't know what I'd do without her."

"Hopefully you won't have to find out," Max replied.

A middle aged woman with short brown hair walked into the room carrying a tray laden with all the necessities for coffee. After exchanging a nervous look with Peter, she presented a broad smile and said, "I'm sorry, I didn't mean to interrupt. I'll just leave this on the table. Feel free to help yourselves."

Peter nodded and said, "Thanks, Phoebe." After a quick round of introductions, he added, "Phoebe lives next door. She's been a real godsend since this happened."

"If anyone needs anything, just ask!" she called, scurrying back into the kitchen.

Once she was gone, Max said, "We're all anxious to get started. As Cal has already explained, time is precious. As soon as you give us the things that would have Aubrey's scent, we'll hit the trail."

"Sure." Heading toward the master bedroom, he said, "Follow me, they're in here." Walking through the house, they came to a stop by the oversized bed. "Cal told me what kind of items would be best.

These were the most obvious, but if you want something else just tell me and I'll see what I can find."

Spread on the thick down comforter were an assortment of Aubrey's things — several sweaters, socks, t-shirts, a scarf, a pillow, a robe and two brushes. Tugging on a pair of surgical gloves, Max walked to the far side of the bed. He was about to place a pillow case into a zip-lock bag, when the toe of his hiking boot bumped against something that was barely tucked beneath the bed.

With his foot, he pushed back the bed skirt to reveal the edge of a book. A sick feeling overcame him as he used his shoe to nudge more of it into view. He had seen the ornately embossed cover of *Vis Medicatrix Naturae* far too many times not to recognize it immediately.

"Max, what's wrong?" Joan asked.

Looking first at her, then at Cal, he picked up the book by the outer binding, being careful not to disturb any fingerprints. Everyone in the room stared at it as though it were the Devil incarnate — except for Peter, who was obviously growing more frustrated by the second.

Peter cast each of them a questioning look. "What's the big deal? It's just a book. Cal didn't mention that you'd want to see some of her books. She's got tons of them. There's a whole box out in the garage that she's going to donate to the library."

"Have you actually *seen* Aubrey reading this particular one?" Max asked.

He shrugged. "Maybe. To tell you the truth, she's always got her nose in a book or a magazine, so I honestly don't pay much attention to the flavor of the day. Looks like something she'd like though. Anything about nature would be right up her alley."

Joan tried to reassure Cal by putting a positive spin on the situation. "You know, this could be a coincidence. That book's gotten a ton of publicity in the last few months and shot up all the bestseller lists. She could've been intrigued and bought it herself, especially since you've been working the related rescues, and she's into nature."

Peter shook his head. "It looks pretty expensive, and we've been seriously watching our budget. Every two weeks she gets a stack of books from the library. I doubt if she'd buy something like that when she could've just borrowed it from them."

Max gently opened the cover. "There aren't any library stamps or bar codes on it, and the jacket isn't laminated like those that are put into public circulation."

"She shares books with lots of friends. Maybe it belongs to a neighbor or someone at her office."

Looking at Cal, Max said, "I think we need to call Agent Collier. No matter where this came from, the FBI will need to have a look at it."

Cal slumped into the chair. "Jesus. This just keeps getting worse."

Staying confident, Joan declared, "Actually, this could be a break. With the FBI involved, we'll have more manpower and resources."

"And a hundred times the area to cover!" said Cal. "Before, we could've assumed she'd been on a trail within walking distance of here. Now, God only knows where she could be."

Peter interjected, "Would someone please tell me what's going on?"

Growing agitated, Cal asked, "Haven't you been watching the news or reading the paper?"

"No. I've been on the road for most of the last three months. If I'm lucky, I get to spend a day or two at home before leaving again. I eat, drink, and sleep my work while I'm gone. For all I know, California fell into the ocean last week."

Joan stepped between the two of them and led Peter into a corner of the room. After calming him down, she quickly explained the significance of the book. When she was finished, he turned to face the others. "So let me get this straight. You think Aubrey might have been taken into the park and *purposely* left there to die? Why? Who would want to hurt Aubrey? Everyone loves her."

Max replied, "We're just saying that it's a possibility. And it's also a possibility that she's not in this national park. Either way, at this point the reason she's missing isn't important. Finding her is all that matters." As he sealed the book in a plastic bag, Max added, "The house should be treated like a crime scene from this point on. Try not to disturb anything and keep everyone out."

Peter nodded, running his hands through his hair as he replied, "There have been a few people in and out of here already. Besides Phoebe, I asked one of Aubrey's friends from work to come see if she could tell what she might have been wearing. It never dawned on me that I shouldn't let people in here."

Cal patted him on the back. "It's not the end of the world. Don't worry about it."

Leading them back into the den, Peter asked,"So, what do we do now?"

As they entered the room, Max noticed Phoebe standing in the doorway of the kitchen. With interest, he watched her gaze lock onto the book and the color drain from her face. Looking away, she started twisting a button on her blouse. Placing the book on the table beside the coffee, he said, "Would you mind making certain that no one touches this while we're gone?"

She brusquely nodded, folding her arms across her chest.

Max turned to the others. "Since Aubrey's car is still here, I think we should stick to the plan of attack that we've already prepared. Once the FBI team arrives, we can regroup and reorganize back here. Until then, let's get busy. Joan, you'll follow whatever scent D.C. can pick up around the house, right?"

"Right. I should be able to let you know in fifteen minutes or so which trail you need to fly over," she replied.

"Everyone have their maps?" Cal asked.

Max and Joan both nodded.

Following them into the backyard, Peter called, "I want to help. Give me something to do. Anything."

Cal said, "You'll need to stay here and meet the FBI agents as they arrive. They'll want to know every detail, plus they'll be bringing a forensic team. Try not to disturb anything in the house or garage and keep everyone else out of there. Joan is going to work D.C. using Aubrey's scent. Once she picks up the freshest trail leading away from your house, we'll use the trail maps to narrow down which part of the mountain we're going to focus on. Meanwhile, Max and I will fly a grid looking for anything out of the ordinary." Handing Peter a radio, he added, "Keep this with you. Call me if anything comes up."

Looking dejected, Peter nodded and asked, "What about her diabetes? The doctor said that within twenty-four to forty-eight hours she could slip into a coma if she doesn't get her insulin."

Max declared, "We've got emergency medical supplies on the helicopter. The minute we find her we can test her blood sugar and administer insulin if needed. Plus, your brother-in-law will rush her to the nearest hospital in record time."

Looking as though he were on the verge of tears, Peter bit his lower lip and said, "Thanks, guys."

Max and Cal watched Joan and D.C. get started. As expected, the dog instantly began to scrutinize the area behind the house. Cal turned and said, "Let's go. The more area we cover, the better."

Stagga ran ahead with Max and Cal close behind. As Cal prepared for liftoff, Max buckled Stagga in and was about to do the same when he caught a glimpse of Joan. D.C. was hard on a trail, sniffing the air and brush along the side of the road. A few yards behind him, Joan followed. For a second their eyes met, and Joan shrugged as if to ask *now what do we do?*

The team had all assumed that Aubrey's trail would lead up the mountain, not down it.

They were wrong.

« « «   » » »

Kaycee carefully stepped onto the patio, balancing both plates of food on one arm while carrying a pitcher of raspberry tea with the other. Quickly coming to her aid, Randy took the beverage and asked, "Where did you learn to do that?"

"I was a waitress while I was in college. Every teenager should have to be a server for a while. It's a really good lesson in dealing with all kinds of people."

"No kidding. Maybe Courtney could give it a try."

"It's a shame she couldn't join us."

"These days, kids in high school have busier schedules than most working folks. Between the extra-curricular activities, volunteer work, and studying there's not much time to just enjoy life."

"I'm looking forward to meeting her. Joan told me she's done some modeling. Even a commercial."

He laughed. "That was a while ago. She didn't care for being in the spotlight, plus we always put school first. Modeling is a tough job — lots of rejection. We didn't encourage it."

"What was your first job?" Kaycee asked.

"I worked at the Circle N Stables — mainly cleaning the stalls. I didn't learn a thing about people, but I certainly discovered a few muscles that I never knew I had. By the way, thanks for inviting me to lunch."

"Thanks for coming on such short notice!"

They both took their seats at the small round table. After decorating the table with a white linen cloth and a bouquet of daisies, she fixed Reuben sandwiches with pasta salad, gourmet potato chips, and lemon meringue pie.

Although she had been out several times with Max and his friends, she sensed that Randy still felt a little uncomfortable being alone with her. To help break the ice, she asked, "Have you lived in Claremore all your life?"

He shook his head and took a bite.

"I see you're not on crutches anymore. How's your leg?"

"Better."

Remembering that Joan had always said that he was a man of few words, she tried again, making certain she phrased the question so it couldn't be answered with a simple yes or no reply. "I understand you're half Cherokee. Are you involved in any tribal politics?"

"Whenever I have the time."

As a psychologist, Kaycee was accustomed to having to draw people out of their shells. "Are tribal affairs as scandalous as some politics tend to be?"

With a soft chuckle, he said, "We've had our share."

Unwilling to give up, she tried a different subject. "I read a fascinating article last week about the Navajo Code Talkers who helped us win World War II. Do you speak Cherokee?"

Another nod. "But I really have to work to stay on top of it since I'm not exposed to the language much anymore. The tribe is working hard to preserve the tongue. My mother is a natural. We talk every day on the phone, mostly in Cherokee. She still lives in Tahlequah and volunteers at the Cherokee Nation Heritage Center. Since she's an actual Indian Princess, she's always popular at the historic events and presentations."

"Really? That's impressive." Looking down at Randy's new German Shepherd, she asked, "Is that why you named him Prince?"

"Not even close. We named him Prince because he has an arrogant attitude, like he knows he was born from a champion bloodline and expects to be treated like royalty."

"He doesn't look much like Stagga."

"His brown, tan, and black coloring is more true to the breed. Because white isn't an acceptable American Kennel Club color for a German Shepherd, dogs like Stagga are relatively rare. Even so, he and Prince share the distinctive Shepherd personality — they're direct, fearless, strong, agile, alert, and full of life. Did you notice when we first came in how he acted like he owned the place? One of the reasons I chose him was because he had such an air of self-confidence."

Leaning close, she whispered, "But he doesn't seem nearly as lovable as Smokey."

"Shepherds tend to be wary of people at first. But once he gets to know you a little better, I'm sure he'll warm right up. Judging from Max's version of how the two of you met, I wouldn't exactly say that you and Stagga found love at first sight."

"True! I thought he was going to bite my head off."

Motioning toward his half eaten lunch, he declared, "I had no idea you were such a great cook. This is delicious. Remind me to thank Max for standing you up."

Kaycee tilted her head to attain a perfect aristocratic air as she replied, "I prefer to think of it as a temporary postponement of our luncheon engagement."

Randy laughed and shook his head. "If you really talked like that, I wouldn't have let Smokey come stay with you."

Still arrogant, she replied, "Sir Smokey has a long, distinguished pedigree. He deserves all the finer things life has to offer."

"That he does. But he was raised by a country boy, so to him the finer things in life would be long hikes in the woods and big, chewy chunks of beef jerky."

Kaycee shook her head. "Apparently, he has a taste for the finer things in life. Until last night, he seemed pretty happy here. I guess I'll have to toss out the Milk Bones and spring for some beef jerky if I want to win his love and affection."

Randy abruptly placed his fork on his plate, giving her his full attention. "What happened last night?"

After filling in the details, she added, "And this morning he got very agitated when he met a stranger on the street. He's never acted this way before, and he's been around lots of people he's never met."

Leaning back, Randy said, "I wonder if he has PTSD."

Surprised, Kaycee asked, "Dogs can suffer from Post Traumatic Stress Disorder?"

"Afraid so. It's actually pretty common after working a particularly gruesome recovery effort. When we're doing searches in rubble and haven't found any survivors, we plant one so that the dog will have a successful find. It keeps them from getting depressed."

"*Plant one?* As in a live person? That sounds dangerous."

"Not at all. We have a volunteer hide under a safe area, then make sure the dog gets close enough to alert. The same thing goes for doing searches like Max and Joan are working on. Dogs gain confidence just like people do. Unfortunately, they can lose it, too. Stagga's successful find yesterday is the best positive reinforcement in the world."

"Do you think Smokey might be exhibiting depression from his forced retirement?"

"It's possible. Until he was hurt, we worked on search techniques at least every other day. As a team, we responded to eighty searches of various kinds. Maybe now that his hip is almost fully healed, he's starting to miss his old routine."

An image of her life before Smokey flashed through Kaycee's mind. She instantly realized how much she loved having him stay with her, and how lonely it would be without him. Trying to keep Randy's decision from being clouded by her emotions, Kaycee stared at her plate. While pushing around a snow pea with her fork, she asked, "Do you think he'd be happier if he went back to live with you? Maybe he misses the country even more than the rescue work."

Randy was quiet for so long that Kaycee was forced to look up. When she did, he was softly shaking his head. With a twinkle in his eye, he remarked, "He's a lovable mutt, isn't he?"

Embarrassed, she wiped a tear from the corner of her eye. "I'd certainly miss him."

"Then why don't I show you how to work with him? You have a fantastic neighborhood. Are there any friendly kids around here?"

"Plenty. They play outside every afternoon and evening."

"Perfect. Before I go we'll cover a few basic procedures. The main idea is to collect someone's scent, then ask them to run and hide. After they're gone, you give Smokey the scent and tell him to go find it. The kids will have a great time, and Smokey will feel useful again. If you just do that every other day, he'll probably be a happy camper. Unless . . . "

"Unless what?"

"It's possible that he's suffering from S.R.S."

"Which is?"

"Spoiled Rotten Syndrome. Maybe having so much attention is making him crave more. A vicious circle if I've ever seen one."

"Very funny. And yes, I'll admit it. I'm spoiling him."

"I knew you would. That's why I sleep like a baby every night. I know he's happy."

"I think working with him is a great idea. It will be fun to learn more about what Max does. Maybe then he won't be so averse to the idea of my tagging along on a search now and then."

Randy nodded. "That's how Joan got started. I'm warning you, though. Search and Rescue is highly contagious. Before you know it you'll be at Max's side, just like Joan's at mine."

"I'm pretty sure that's one bug I don't have to worry about catching."

"You might be surprised."

Laughing, she replied, "I can't imagine fitting another thing into my hectic schedule. Even Max thinks I try to do too much."

"Look who's talking!"

"No kidding. When can I start working with Smokey?"

"How about this afternoon?" Patting his belly, he added, "That is, if I can still walk after I polish off this piece of pie. It's incredible. And huge."

"Thanks. It's my mother's recipe. She thought that a meringue pie should be both delicious and impressive. If the meringue was less than 4 inches tall, it didn't deserve to be in her kitchen."

He pretended to measure the height of the pie, then declared, "You squeaked by with an eighth of an inch to spare. She'd be proud of you."

"Speaking of pride, is Prince living up to Smokey's high standards?"

Randy reached down to pat Prince on the neck. Spotting a tennis ball in a nearby chair, he grabbed it and hurled it across the yard. Both dogs took off as Randy replied, "Prince is a little high-strung, but coming along nicely. Smokey isn't the only one having a tough time with the change. It's always hard to start over, and I just wasn't expecting our time together to end for a long time. Even so, it's inevitable. Since a dog's life expectancy doesn't match a man's, we all know up front that the day will come when we'll have to train another canine partner."

"How many dogs has Max had?"

"Stagga is his second. His first was a adorable mutt named Oreo."

"A mutt? Really?"

"Sometimes mixed breeds make the best workers. Oreo was one of the finest SAR canines I've ever seen. She was a really hard worker."

"What happened to her?"

"Same thing that happens to all of us. She got old. It was really a tough time for Max. He loved that dog like she was his own kid. Even though we all know that it's coming, retiring a dog is never easy."

"Where is she now?"

"Last I heard she was living on Robin's farm."

"The woman who watches Max's place when he's out of town?"

Randy nodded. "She's a real sweetheart."

Sensing there was more, she probed, "Were she and Max ever involved?"

He hesitated, narrowing his eyes so that he seemed to be looking right through her. "That sounds like a great question for you to ask Max."

"But Max isn't here, and you know the answer."

After tapping his finger on the table and biting his lip for a few seconds, he said, "Let's just say that there are some things that are not meant to be. Max and Robin are a good example of two people whose lives are intertwined, but not as a couple."

"For a country guy, you certainly know how to dance around questions."

"That's the problem with city girls — they always ask too many questions." Leaning back, he winked and added, "As I constantly have to tell Courtney, there are some things best left alone."

"Okay, you win." For a few moments, they both watched Smokey and Prince playfully running the fence line. Kaycee said, "You know one of the things that I love most about Smokey?"

With a smile, he responded, "No, what?"

"How he knocks on the door when he wants back in. It's so handy. I don't have to worry about remembering to let him in because he makes so much noise that I always hear him. I know he's just pawing at it, but it really does sound like he's knocking. Are you going to teach Prince to do that?"

"Actually, I didn't teach that to Smokey. It came naturally. One day, he just started doing it."

She replied, "I knew he was brilliant. And I'll bet he passed all his certification tests on the first try."

"Of course."

"When do you think Prince will be ready to take his first test?"

"It's hard to tell. He's a natural at scent trailing, but he's got a long way to go on obeying commands. Once he's found the scent, he's off like a bullet. Even when I was in prime condition, I would've had a hard time keeping up with him." Patting his thigh, he added, "And with this gimp leg, it's next to impossible." He glanced at his watch, then jerked the cell phone out of his shirt pocket. "Speaking of keeping up, Joan said that if she could pick up a signal, she'd call when they rested for lunch." Nodding toward the phone, he added, "I have the hardest time with this contraption. Half the time the battery's dead, or I can't remember where I put it, or I don't hear it ring . . . Modern technology can be a real pain in the hindquarters sometimes."

"Which reminds me, I need to check my e-mail. Max was supposed to send me a sample of Aubrey's handwriting."

"I have the box from Cal's office in my car. I'll go get it and the SAR tools you'll need to work with Smokey."

"The box?"

"He said you needed to see some of his old letters from Aubrey. He called this morning and asked me to drop by R.R.M. on the way over so that I could leave them with you."

"While you get them, I'll check the computer." As Randy went out the front door, Kaycee scurried into the office. Although she had ten e-mails waiting, none of them were from Max. Disappointed, she met Randy in the entryway. In one hand he had a tattered shoe box that seemed to be held together by the ancient rubber bands wrapped around each end, in the other a mesh bag that contained Smokey's training aides.

Handing the box to her, he asked, "Did the e-mail arrive?"

She shook her head. "No. But I'm sure they're busy."

"Joan said they were going to hit the ground running. Let's just hope they find Aubrey soon."

"Are rescues always like this? Do they tend to come in clumps?"

Randy thought for a second. "As a matter of fact, it does seem like we'll have a couple in a row, then go for a few months without being called. But I can never remember anything like this. If I didn't know better, I'd think someone put a curse on every SAR team between here and the Pacific Coast."

"At this point, that seems to be as good an explanation as any other."

"Joan told me that you ruled out the possibility that they were suicides."

"Not one of the victims was emotionally unstable. I'm glad Cal sent Aubrey's old letters. They'll give me a good idea of her personality. Do you know her?"

"No. But Max does. Ready to give the dogs a workout?"

Kaycee said, "I guess it's time to teach this old dog new tricks."

"Actually, Smokey's not that old."

Nudging him, she shook her head as they walked outside. "I was talking about me, silly."

By the time Randy finished giving his crash course on wind direction, voice commands, and techniques for maintaining agility and confidence, Kaycee had a much better appreciation of the dedication such work required. He had just promised to drop by with some manuals on SAR training when his cell phone rang.

Kaycee waited anxiously as he carried on a brief conversation with Joan. In response to her eager stare, the moment he hung up he explained, "She said that they had to revise their anticipated search pattern shortly after they arrived. D.C. has been working all morning and needed a break, so she's letting him rest for a few minutes. Max is further down the mountain . . . "

"And? I could tell from your tone of voice that something unexpected happened. Why did they have to revise the search pattern?"

Reluctantly, he said, "The trail led down the mountain, not up one of the trails as they had anticipated. Plus, the FBI has been called in to handle the case. They found a copy of the book under her bed."

Kaycee's hand flew to her mouth. "Oh, my God! Is Cal doing all right?"

"Joan said he seems fine." Heading to the door with Prince at his side, he added, "Listen, I need to get going. Courtney is leaving on a school trip for DECA in about an hour and I want to see her off. If

Smokey starts acting squirrelly again, give me a call."

Following them outside, Kaycee replied, "Thanks for coming, Randy. It was nice to have the chance to get to know you and Prince a little better."

"It was our pleasure." Climbing into his pickup, he added, "When Joan gets home, we'll have everyone out for a goat roast."

Kaycee resisted the urge to ask if he was kidding. Instead she called, "Sounds great! Drive carefully!"

After collecting the mail from the box at the curb, Kaycee turned to go back inside. If she hadn't dropped a letter on the sidewalk by the front steps, she probably wouldn't have noticed a large gray rock nestled among the hyacinths and pansies in the flower bed near the door. Squatting, she pushed aside the purple flowers and greenery to read the beautifully engraved message:

A Cherokee Blessing
May the warm winds of heaven blow softly on your home
And the Great Spirit bless all who enter there.
May your moccasins make happy tracks in many snows,
And may the rainbow always touch your shoulder.

Picking it up, she carefully placed it closer to the front of the bed where everyone who came to her front door could see it. With a smile, she realized that Max had been right — Randy really was a big softy at heart.

As she stood, she noticed a woman strolling down the street, and realized it was Pam Adams. In the time it took for her to wonder why she was still walking, Kaycee instinctively rushed inside and locked the door. It was rare for her to instantly dislike someone, yet the feeling in the pit of her stomach was undeniable.

There were four colonials in the neighborhood, and Kaycee found herself wondering which one belonged to Pam Adams. It would be easy enough to find out, but she knew she would never try. In fact, she hoped she never saw the woman again.

"This is Rescue Two. Come in."

Max called for Stagga as he carefully placed his flashlight on the ground so that his hands were free to retrieve his radio. "Go ahead, Joan."

"We're at a standstill. The trail led south again, then circled back east. D.C. lost the scent at a dirt road about five miles from where we started. I let him rest for fifteen minutes, then re-scented him. Still nothing. There's a strong possibility that she got into a car."

Pushing the button on the side of his watch, Max looked at the glowing numbers. "It's one in the morning. At this point, I think it would be best if you got some rest. Are you listening, Cal?"

Cal's voice crackled with static. "Ten four. I'll be there in less than five minutes, Joan. Max, how's Stagga holding up?"

"Getting a little sluggish. I think he needs to call it a night, too."

"Will do. Be there as fast as I can."

Max tucked his radio into his pocket and began massaging Stagga to decrease the dog's stress. It seemed like ages before Cal arrived, but less than ten minutes had actually passed. The ride to Aubrey's house was short and silent. When they touched down, Max noticed that Cal didn't start his usual cool down procedure. Turning to Joan, he asked, "Would you take care of Stagga?"

With a glance at Cal, she sighed and nodded. After giving Max a hug, she whispered, "Take care. Make sure he gets some sleep tonight."

As Joan led the two dogs toward the house, Max climbed into the front passenger seat, buckled up and put on his headphones. "No rest for the wicked, right?"

"Something like that. We can make much better time with you operating the FLIR."

With a thumbs up, Max replied, "Then let's go."

Without wasting a second, Cal lifted off. "We'll be going too fast for a few minutes to use the FLIR. I've been working a grid all night. When we get close to the next sector, I'll let you know."

"Okay." Max noticed they climbed higher than normal. Leaning his head back, he searched the night sky. The combination of altitude and complete darkness made the stars unusually brilliant and bright — a stark contrast to the falling temperature outside. Shifting his gaze to the starlit forest, he thought of Aubrey lost and alone.

Closing his eyes, he remembered the last time she accompanied them on a rescue. To his surprise, he realized it had been over six years ago. As if it were yesterday, he remembered quizzing her about what to do if she ever got lost. In typical Aubrey form, she had replied, "It doesn't matter because I'll never get lost."

"How can you be so sure?" he had asked.

With a broad smile, she had nodded toward her brother. "Because Cal won't let me out of his sight."

At the time, it had been true. Opening his eyes, Max looked at Cal. Since he was wearing a flight helmet, only part of his profile was visible. Even so, Max could see the toll of the last few hours.

As if he sensed that he was being watched, Cal eased back on the stick and announced, "We're almost there."

"I'm ready." Max positioned the FLIR's control panel on his lap as Cal maneuvered the helicopter above the tree line. He quickly became accustomed to analyzing the thermal images on the small digital screen, and directing Cal's flight pattern to the hot spots. For an hour they checked every large object on the ground that was warmer than its surroundings, which included eight mule deer, four elk, three coyotes, a wolf, and a bear.

Max yawned, fighting hard to stay awake. A slight glow on the FLIR screen caught his attention, mainly because it was unlike anything he'd seen. Instead of a relatively sharp outline, the warmth was diffused. "Cal, take us down and slightly to the left."

"Can't get too close. We're pushing against a pretty steep grade. I'll have to back up and turn the nose in."

As Cal repositioned the helicopter and maneuvered them closer, Max watched the size of the lighter image increase, but it still lacked the sharp distinctive shape that the other animals had produced. Pointing, he said, "Let's light up that area."

Flipping on the spotlight, Cal flooded the ground with light. After a few seconds he said, "The canopy of trees is pretty thick. What are we looking for?"

Max admitted, "I'm not sure." Tilting the screen to where Cal could see it, he added, "Have you ever seen anything like this?"

Cal leaned close to scrutinize the image. "You know, I've had police buddies tell me that when a suspect tries to hide inside a building, if he leans against an exterior wall, the FLIR will pick up the change in the wall's temperature from absorbing the body heat."

Nodding, Max said, "Well, there aren't any buildings, but it might be a cave. God only knows what's inside. Could be another bear."

"Could be Aubrey. The only way to know for sure would be for you to long-line down and check. As much as I'd like to do that now, considering the trees and the grade, we'll have to come back when it's light so I can find a place to lower you. Besides, it's almost two in the morning. I think we should get some rest and start here early before the winds kick up."

With relief, Max agreed. "Great idea."

The nose of the helicopter dipped as they zoomed back toward the base. When they were almost there, Max asked, "How are you holding up?"

"As well as can be expected. Mainly, I'm just tired."

"No matter how this turns out, you have to know that you've done everything you could."

He shook his head. "Let's just hope it's enough."

« « «   » » »

It was a few minutes before seven a.m. when the phone rang. Kaycee grabbed the receiver and muttered, "Hello."

Max spoke softly. "I'm sorry to wake you, but we're headed out soon and I wanted to hear your voice."

Stretching, she replied, "It's okay. I should've been up an hour ago."

"Another long night?" he asked.

"Uh huh."

"Smokey acting up again?"

"No. I stayed up to work on the box of Aubrey's letters that Cal had Randy bring for me to analyze."

"Find anything interesting?"

"I think so, but I really need to see the more recent one to be sure. Have you e-mailed it to me yet?"

"Sorry, I haven't had a chance. I'll try to send it before we leave."

Kaycee was rapidly coming to her senses. "Where are you staying?"

"Since there aren't any hotels close by, we're using Aubrey's house as the base."

"Didn't the FBI seal it off as a crime scene?"

"No. They collected a zillion fingerprints, but too many people had contaminated the area for it to do them much good. Besides Peter, Aubrey's husband, several neighbors had been through it, plus a co-worker. Agent Collier was not a happy camper."

"I'm sure a person's first inclination would be to assume that everything is going to be okay. Most people would prefer to believe their loved one is going to miraculously reappear."

"Which can delay getting a search party organized in time."

"True. Why were so many people inside the house?"

"It's a close-knit neighborhood. From the moment Peter mentioned that Aubrey was missing, they've been bringing food non-stop. Several have even offered to let SAR teams and FBI agents sleep and shower at their houses. Her next door neighbor, Phoebe, has bent over backward to help. She's here 24/7."

"I'm glad they're taking good care of you. But you sound exhausted. Did you work through the night?"

"A lot of it. We got back here around two in the morning."

"So you only got five hours of sleep?"

"Four. We're on Mountain Time, which means it's only six a.m. here."

"Are you sure you're okay?"

"Considering everything, I actually feel pretty good. If I hadn't been so tired last night, using the FLIR would've been a treat. Thermal imaging is an amazing technology. We spotted a few deer, some elk and woke up one really grumpy brown bear."

"If it was dark, how do you know it was brown, or grumpy, for that matter?"

"The spotlight on the helicopter lit him up like a Christmas tree. He wasn't very happy with us."

"Can't say as I blame him. How's the search going?"

"It's not looking good. D.C. was hot on a trail that ended at a dirt road. Stagga and I have tried five different sectors without luck."

"Does the scent ending at a road mean she got into a car?"

"Probably, but that doesn't make a lot of sense. If someone picked her up, she would've called."

"Maybe she was hurt. Have you checked the hospitals?"

"Yes, but no luck so far. The FBI will be notified if any unidentified person shows up matching her description."

"Max, I know both you and Cal can be pretty intense. Are you sure you aren't pushing too hard? Neither of you has had a good night's sleep in days."

"It's his only sister. I know if I were in his position, I'd be doing the same thing."

"But it's dangerous, Max. When the teams are fatigued, they can't think clearly."

"True. We're doing T-Touch therapy on the dogs every six hours to make certain they don't get too stressed."

"T-Touch?"

"That's short for the Tellington Touch method. It mixes circular massage, sliding pressure, and ear rubs to help the dog relax. I've been using it on my dogs for years. It seems to work really well."

"So who massages the handler?" she asked seductively.

Max sighed. "I wish. Supposedly, the human half of the team has higher intellectual capacity and is trained to avoid becoming overly stressed and depressed."

"If I were there, I'm pretty sure I could figure out a way to cheer you up."

"Unfortunately, right now I'll have to settle for a coffee buzz. Cal said he'd be refueled and ready to go in ten minutes." He sighed. "Kaycee, do you remember our first official date?"

"Dinner at O'Malley's Landing? Somehow, I don't think that's a night I'll ever forget!"

"Unfortunately, for all the wrong reasons. I mean the early part of the evening — in the restaurant when we discussed why we were still single."

Leaning back onto the pillows, Kaycee smiled. "Well, there's my career and your inclination to run off at the drop of a hat to help total strangers . . . " She paused, pushing aside the flood of horrible images that accompanied memories of what happened later that night.

As if moving would help her stay focused, she rolled out of bed and ran a hand through her bed-head hair. Pacing, she declared, "Max, of course I remember our first date. I even remember the smell of your cologne and the way you swept me into your arms in the parking lot. Why do you ask?"

After a brief hesitation, he replied, "I was . . . well . . . I was wondering if you wanted out of this relationship. I've been gone so much lately, and it just isn't fair . . . " With a sigh, he added, "I know how hard it is . . . and I feel guilty leaving you, knowing you're alone."

Stunned, Kaycee countered, "Max, I was alone before I met you, and I somehow managed to survive."

"That was different. Everything has changed since we met."

Her breath caught. Slumping onto the bed, she wondered if Max was really trying to break up with her. After all, eventually her RP would impact both their lives, and he probably preferred a long distance good-bye over an awkward *this isn't working* speech. Even though neither had said the words *I love you* in the three months since they'd met, she had never felt so completely in love in her life. It broke her heart to think that he didn't feel the same way.

"Kaycee? Are you there?"

A lump rose in her throat and tightened. "Yes."

"It's hard, isn't it?"

Tears threatened. Trying not to let her voice crack, she quickly said, "Almost everything worthwhile in life is hard."

"Exactly. And that's what we need to remember. I just don't want you to give up on us. I really need you."

"Me? You're worried about me giving up on you?" A nervous laugh escaped as she added, "I thought you were trying to break up with me."

"No way! Listen, I know I'm tired and I'm probably not expressing myself as well as I should. I just wanted to be sure we're okay. We are okay, aren't we?"

"Max, we're better than okay. We're great. You have a lot of things to worry about right now, but I'm not one of them. I've never been happier in my life. I swear."

"Thank goodness . . . And, me, too."

"Don't forget to e-mail Cal's letter from Aubrey."

"I'll do it right now."

Kaycee cradled the phone and closed her eyes. With three interviews and six clients scheduled, she knew that it was going to be a crazy day. Even so, the minute that e-mail arrived she wanted to see it. If it confirmed what she suspected, Aubrey had a lot more problems than anyone realized.

« « «   » » »

After Max hung up, he dressed quickly and took Stagga outside. Since they were facing another long day, he was relieved to see that his partner was alert and playful. Rolling his shoulders, he tried to stretch away the stiffness in his arms and neck.

When he stepped into the kitchen a few minutes later, Special Agent Collier was already seated at the table. Her auburn hair still seemed to be in the same tight, unflattering pony tail, and she was once again wearing an FBI raid jacket and navy slacks. The only difference in her appearance was the look of exhaustion clouding her eyes.

Glancing up, she smiled and said, "No offense, but I was hoping not to see you again so soon."

"Yeah. Me, too. How's Evan Newsome doing?"

"Still unconscious, but his vital signs are strong. The doctors have upgraded his condition to stable."

Max nodded as Peter came in. He, too, appeared stretched to the breaking point. After exchanging greetings, he asked, "Any new leads?"

She shook her head. "This case is a lot like the others, but there are a couple of significant points that are way out of line."

Pouring himself a cup of coffee, Max asked, "Such as?"

"Well, for starters this book has fingerprints on it. Lots of them. We're not sure what to make of that yet."

"Any of them Aubrey's?" Max asked as Peter began pacing.

"Actually, yes. And not just on the jacket. We're working on trying to ID more of them, but it could take awhile."

Biting his lip, Max thought for a few moments. "And you don't think it's possible that our killer is just getting sloppy?"

Agent Collier replied, "That would be highly unlikely. Serial killers tend to be intelligent and follow a set routine. The other books were pristine, the only fingerprints on them were from the victims, and even those prints were abnormally clear — as if they were purposely put there one by one. Aubrey's book has smudges on the outside, the spine has actually been creased, and Aubrey appears to have read the first few chapters."

Max nodded. "Her car being left in the garage is another change. Then again, have any of the other victims lived near a national park?"

"No. But if our killer came inside this house, then we might get a break. Forensics went over this place with a fine tooth comb yesterday. They lifted hundreds of fingerprints and collected hair and fiber samples. In spite of the level of contamination, I'm still hoping something will turn up."

"But what good will that do? It won't help us find her in time, will it?" Peter asked.

She shrugged. "It could. The FBI maintains an extensive database of evidence. If we were lucky enough to get a match, then we might be able to find the killer. There's always a chance we could get a break from analyzing his prior crimes. It's definitely a longshot, but we aren't ruling out anything at this point."

Cal came in, looking only slightly better than he had at two a.m. Max knew from the hard set of his jaw that Cal wasn't happy. "More bad news?" Max asked.

"The high pressure system has pushed off, so we're going to be fighting strong winds today." Virtually ignoring everyone else, he glanced at Max and asked, "Are you ready?"

"I will be in a second." Max motioned toward Agent Collier's laptop computer. "Would you mind if I sent an e-mail?"

"Not at all." She quickly opened the appropriate program and moved so that he could take her seat.

Max slipped the diskette with the digital image of Aubrey's letter into the machine and quickly uploaded it. In a matter of minutes, the file was on its way to Kaycee. Standing, he and Cal each shook Agent Collier's hand and thanked her.

The moment they were outside, Max asked, "Where's Joan?"

"Down by the helicopter. I think we need to rethink today's plan of attack." He broke into a slow jog.

Running to keep up, Max asked, "Because of the weather?"

Cal nodded and quickened his pace.

They greeted Joan as they slipped the tie-downs off the rotors. As they worked, Cal said, "This is not going to be easy. By mid-morning we're going to be fighting twenty to thirty mile per hour west winds. I just checked the topo maps of the place we found last night. If the wind really does kick up, long-lining on that side of the crest will be next to impossible. There's a hiking path near the top of the peak where I could drop you off before the winds hit, but it looks like the area we found with the FLIR will be difficult to get to, and even more difficult to get out of."

After exchanging a wary look with Joan, Max said, "Define difficult."

"The dogs wouldn't be able to handle it." Cal shook his head. "At this point, I'm not even sure I can handle it. The combination of wind, altitude, and mountaintops are a pilot's worst nightmare. One minute you can be flying fine, the next you've dropped hundreds of feet. Plus, if the map is accurate, it's going to take some serious rappelling to reach the area. I'm just not sure it's worth the risk."

She patted Cal on the back. "Of course it is. Stop worrying. You're a great pilot and we've got everything we need to tackle any terrain onboard the helicopter."

Still wary, Cal climbed into the pilot's seat as Max buckled Stagga in the back. Moving to the front passenger seat, he leaned so that he was eye to eye with his friend. "Never lose hope."

With a tight smile, Cal replied, "I know. Let's go."

In a matter of minutes Cal announced that they were approaching the spot. It didn't surprise Max that the area seemed totally unfamiliar in the daylight. When Cal pointed at a tract of dense pine trees, Max picked up the FLIR controls and keyed his intercom. "I think we should double-check for our heat source before we try this."

"Good point."

Swinging wide and dropping altitude, Cal repositioned the helicopter so that the nose was pointed toward the side of the mountain. Max adjusted the controls and held the screen up so that Cal could see it, too. "It's still there. Doesn't seem to have moved."

Joan's voice came through his headset. "Hey, I want to see!" After Max showed the image to her, she added, "Impressive. And it looks like Cal was right. That's a pretty sheer rock face above the tree line. We could . . . "

Her words were cut off as the helicopter abruptly dropped. The skids barely buzzed the tops of the trees as Cal veered away in the nick of time. Max had instinctively grabbed the hand grip above the door to stabilize himself, but his heart was pounding wildly.

Once they were flying level again, he glanced back to be sure Stagga was okay.

Joan gave him an affirming nod while stroking both dogs to keep them calm.

"As I said, it's going to be a little rough today," Cal declared.

Max asked, "What the hell was that?"

"That was what it feels like to fall two hundred feet."

"I could've figured that out by myself. Why did we fall?" Max asked.

"As the air begins to heat up, it causes what are called mountain waves. That was a particularly nasty downdraft, caused when the air is forced to rise up the windward side of the mountain, then sink down the other side. It causes a bounce, forming a series of standing waves of air. If there was smoke in the air so you could see the wind currents, they'd be swirling over the top of the mountain and crashing down the side like waves onto a beach. It actually sucks the performance from the rotors. Countless crashes have been caused by the phenomenon."

Joan asked, "So how are we going to do this?"

"I should be able to get a good approach angle at the top of the peak, heading into the wind. We'll check it out. The secret to flying in dicey conditions is to always have an escape route planned."

Max shot him a glance that was both curious and guarded.

"The real danger is overcorrecting. After you've flown a long time, you get to where you can feel the way the wind is pushing the aircraft. When something unexpected crops up, you veer into the wind and crank up the power. It's like driving on ice — you always turn into the skid and accelerate."

Shaking his head, Max admitted, "You never cease to amaze me."

« « «   » » »

By eleven Kaycee had interviewed three more people — two women in their fifties and a single man in his thirties. Although they had all seemed amply qualified on paper, she never felt a real connection with any of them. In fact, by the time she escorted the last one out, she was beginning to wonder if she might be the pickiest person alive.

Closing the door behind her, she rushed back into the office and pulled up the e-mail from Max. After downloading the attached file, she read the letter on the monitor, then printed it. Grabbing her magnifying glass, she was beginning to scrutinize the handwriting when the doorbell rang. Knowing her next appointment wasn't scheduled for thirty minutes, she considered not answering it. Smokey stretched as he left his bed in the corner, then stopped in the doorway. When the chime sounded again, he cocked his head and gave her a look that said, *Come on! Can't you hear that? There's someone waiting!*

Kaycee reluctantly answered the door. At first she didn't recognize the young woman standing on her porch. "May I help you?" she asked.

The girl playfully cocked her head. "Remember me? I'm Tamara Conrad. I interviewed with you yesterday." Grinning, she added, "I know. I look a little different."

Trying not to be rude, Kaycee studied her short bob haircut and the lack of obvious body piercings. Nodding, she said, "Yes, I'd say that's an understatement. I really like what you've done with your hair, and that's a very attractive outfit."

Tamara blushed. "After I left yesterday I met some of my friends for lunch. I guess you could say that they talked some sense into me." She motioned to her businesslike white silk shirt, black skirt, and modest white sandals. "Ashley and Katherine gave me a makeover." She laughed, her green eyes sparkling as she leaned forward. "I told them how awesome you were and they convinced me that I should come back. I'd really like to work for you, and I promise to dress very conservatively so that I don't freak out your older clients."

Opening the door, Kaycee said, "Come in."

Tamara practically danced across the threshold. "I know what you're thinking."

"You do?"

"Sure. People don't just change overnight. She'll dress like this for a few days, then be all punked out again before I know it."

"Well, not exactly. I was wondering why you were willing to undergo such a complete transformation. I find it hard to believe that one interview could sway a person's fashion choices very far."

Tamara bit her lip. "Well . . . It's always best to tell the truth, right?"

"Most of the time."

"When I left here yesterday I decided to drop by my boyfriend's place. I knew he was there because his truck was parked in its usual spot, but he didn't answer the door. I thought I'd surprise him, so I used the spare key he keeps on top of the doorframe. At any rate, it turned out he wasn't alone. So . . . we broke up."

Kaycee watched her carefully, waiting for some sign of emotional turmoil. Sensing none, she replied, "You certainly seem to be handling it well."

Squaring her shoulders, Tamara replied, "Ashley and Katherine have been right about him all along. He was a jerk. A pothead. I can do better."

"I'm sure you can," Kaycee agreed.

"You know what's funny? I really like this look. People have actually been polite to me today. I never realized how much anger and resentment I brought on myself just by being defensive all the time. Respect is much easier to deal with than disgust."

"Very true. And your new look suits you well. Do you regret the tattoo on your arm?"

"That's the best part! I absolutely hate needles, and I'm even more afraid of getting some disgusting disease. But Nate was always bugging me about getting a tattoo and I got tired of him calling me a chicken. So . . . Ashley made me a fake one! Every few days she'd ink it back in for me. He never knew it wasn't real!" Rolling up her sleeve, she proudly showed the faint outline that still remained on her upper arm. "We got most of it off last night with fingernail polish remover and baby oil."

Kaycee smiled. Although she wasn't one to rush into decisions, she couldn't deny that she had instantly liked Tamara the first time she met her. Plus, the combination of self-improvement and confidence pushed her way ahead of the others. Surprising even herself, Kaycee asked, "Would you like to start your new job in the morning?"

Ecstatic, Tamara jumped up, ran around the desk and hugged Kaycee. "I can start right now if you like!"

"No need. It'll take me a little while to arrange what I'd like you to do first. Why don't you plan on being here around eight tomorrow morning?"

"I will! Thank you so much! I promise I won't disappoint you!"

As she led her to the door, Kaycee replied, "I'm sure you won't. See you soon."

After closing the door, Kaycee leaned against it and smiled. Hiring Tamara was definitely a risk, but everything about the decision felt right. Excited, she rushed back to her desk to work on Aubrey's letter.

« « «   » » »

Cal had found a small spot to land on the opposite side of the mountain, nestled in a hollow that blocked the strongest gusts of wind. After ten minutes of arguing, he had conceded that it would be best for him to stay with the helicopter and the dogs while Max and Joan hiked to the location pinpointed on the GPS.

Since the rock formations at the top of the mountain had appeared to be unstable, they decided it would be faster and safer to walk downhill to the hiking trail, then follow it uphill to the proper place. Once they were above the area indicated on the FLIR, they could rappel down and see what was there.

Although both Max and Joan had ample experience in the field, neither had been rock climbing in years. They made excellent time hiking, but found that the altitude made the exercise a much bigger challenge than normal. Since Joan was struggling more than Max, he successfully argued that she should stay on the trail while he rappelled. Even though they were calling it a trail, the spot where they had to work was hardly more than a ledge — a shelf that was barely twenty-four inches at its widest.

After the rappelling gear had been rigged and was ready to go, Max dug through his pack, took out his gun, and loaded it.

Surprised, Joan asked, "What's that for?"

With a sly grin, he said, "Name something that likes to sleep in caves."

"Oh. Good point. Well, in that case, I'm glad you convinced me that you should go alone. Be careful."

"It's good to know I can always count on you for moral support," he replied, then took the rope in his gloved hands and eased over the edge. He easily slid down the first thirty yards, but had to fight to get through the heavy tree limbs that blocked the lowest part of the descent. When he was finally on the ground, he called to Joan, "Piece of cake!"

"Great! Try to hurry! The wind is really picking up."

Now that Max was back on solid ground, he wished Stagga were at his side. The terrain was just like what they'd been trudging through all morning — crowded trees, smooth rocks, and thick undergrowth. Using his GPS, he moved toward the exact spot, but didn't see anything that resembled a cave.

He was about to give up when he noticed a place on a pine tree where a branch had been torn off. Touching the sticky sap, he knew that the wound was relatively fresh. As he looked around, he discovered several more trees were missing branches. What struck him as odd was that the broken limbs weren't lying on the ground beneath the trees. Walking several feet each way, he finally spotted a pile of them in the dirt by the rock wall. Squatting, he realized they had been carefully, purposely stacked in a neat pile.

Although he doubted any animal could be responsible for what he had found, he stepped back, took out his gun and made sure it was ready to fire. Keeping the weapon pointed at the ground, he kicked the largest limb with his boot.

It barely moved. Max dropped to his knees, his heart pounding in his chest.

A woman's hand was clutching the branch.

CHAPTER 7

"Rescue One! I found her! Pulse is weak, but she's alive! Cal, she's at the GPS coordinates we marked last night. I'll be out of radio contact for a few minutes while I crawl into the cave to check her for injuries."

Max had been able to take her pulse from outside, but the entrance was too small for him to do anything else. After clearing the area, he slipped off his backpack and dug out a flashlight and a blanket. Lying on the ground, his shoulders were almost too wide for him to wiggle through the narrow opening.

Aubrey was unconscious, sprawled with her back against the rock wall. Dried blood was caked on one side of her face, and she had used her socks and several tree limbs to make a splint for her lower left leg. Max carefully checked her other limbs, then pulled up an eyelid and tested the pupil's reaction to light.

As he gently wrapped her in the blanket, he said, "Aubrey, it's Cal's buddy Max Masterson. You're going to be okay. Your brother is close by. We'll have you to a hospital in a few minutes. Hang in there. I'll be right back."

Pushing himself outside, he grabbed the radio. "Rescue One to Air Support One. Aubrey is unconscious. She has a head injury and a broken leg. Her pupils are responsive. Cal, we'll need the blood sugar test kit, and more ropes lowered in the stretcher."

"Already got them ready. I'll be right there," Cal responded.

Joan asked, "Max, do you need me to come down?"

"No. Once I've got her stabilized, we'll have to pull her up there and carry her down the trail. Between the wind and the thick trees, I don't see any other way to get her out of here."

"I'll start working on another safety line."

"Any openings for the stretcher in the area?" Cal asked.

"None down here. Rescue Two?"

Joan declared, "This shelf is too narrow to try to work with the basket. There was a break in the trees about a quarter mile east of here. Cal, I'll meet you there."

"Ten-four."

Riffling through his backpack, Max gathered the supplies he would need before crawling back inside to check on Aubrey. Checking her vital signs one more time, he was encouraged that they still remained strong. With the help of the flashlight, he took a few seconds to scan the inside of the cave. Although it was roughly fifteen feet deep, at the tallest point the ceiling was only about four feet high.

It was obvious that Aubrey had been conscious for quite some time after she found the cave. Inside were the empty wrappers from several packages of peanut butter crackers and a couple of candy bars. Judging from the scorched area near the entrance, she had apparently succeeded in starting a small fire at some point. In a pile next to her were various leaves and roots, plus strips of bark from an arctic willow shrub. Max was impressed that she remembered that the tender young shoots and roots were edible and a rich source of vitamin C. Cal would be proud of her.

She had also taken a stick and lightly scratched a message in the dirt. Cocking his head so that he could see it better, he realized that he had wiped out two main parts of it with his knees when he crawled inside the cave the first time. He tried to softly blow away the smeared dirt, but the impressions had been too shallow. The rest of the words were lost, leaving only:

> My   is Aubrey Dol
> P   pushed me off   trail
> Left me to die

Cursing himself for not noticing it sooner, Max wondered what it might have said. Was *P* the first letter of the person's name? Could it have been the word *Please?* Or maybe it wasn't a *P* at all, maybe it was a *B* or an *R* and his knee had erased part of it.

With a frustrated sigh, he resumed his work, knowing that the only sure way to ever find out was to make certain that Aubrey survived. After preparing her to be transported, he avoided what remained of the message and moved back outside.

The whisper of Cal's helicopter blended with the sound of the wind blowing through the tall pines. As it grew closer, Max caught a glimpse of the stretcher on the long-line. Although the trees were thick, off to the east he could see enough of the helicopter to tell it was hovering about five hundred feet off the ground.

Over the radio, he heard Joan say, "Almost there. Another twenty feet. Oh, my God!"

Joan's exclamation had accompanied another sudden loss of altitude. Max dove onto the ground behind a tree as the helicopter came racing right at him. At the last moment, Cal veered off, dropping both the cable and the stretcher attached to it. Like a giant metal kite with its fierce tail whipping erratically, the basket crashed through several trees, scattering twigs and leaves before coming to a stop in the middle of one. Looking up, he saw the cable balanced across the treetops, the limbs still bouncing up and down beneath the added weight.

Regaining his composure, Max brushed the dirt off his chest and took a deep breath. The dogs were barking in the background as he heard Cal ask, "Rescue One and Two, everyone okay down there?"

Joan replied, "I'm good. Max?"

"Shaken, but fine. Cal, give Stagga and D.C. the command to settle."

"Will do." After a few seconds, it was quiet as Cal came back on the radio to add, "Don't worry, the dogs are okay now."

"Leave it to Cal to keep things exciting. Looks like he hasn't lost his pitching arm, either. The stretcher stopped about thirty feet above my head, and the package you strapped in is still there."

Cal said, "Sorry about that. If I hadn't hit the disconnect button, that cable could've easily brought this bird down. That's some of the nastiest turbulence I've ever run into. I lost over 350 feet in a heartbeat. There's no way we can risk a long-line rescue in these conditions."

"Then Joan and I will carry Aubrey out the same way we came in."

"Negative. That'll take too long. There's got to be a better way!" Cal protested.

As he climbed the tree to get to the stretcher, Max paused to say, "We don't have a choice. Listen to me, Cal — we need you to be the calm, cool professional you've always been. This isn't the time or the place to let emotions cloud our decisions. Aubrey is only going to be all right if we *all* make it out of here in one piece. You'll be very proud of how she handled herself so far, and at this point, we both know that hurrying is the last thing we should do. Come on, buddy, we've got to be a solid team, right?"

"Ten-four. I'll set down on the windward side and install the spare cable onto the winch."

"Great idea. And see if you can get word to the FBI. They're going to need to come out here. Aubrey tried to tell us who did this to her."

"Tried?" Cal asked.

Max sighed, then radioed, "It's my fault. I didn't notice that she had scratched a note in the dirt when I first went inside, so my knees smudged the most important part of it. I'm keeping away from it now, so there might still be a way for the FBI to figure out what the rest of it says."

"Are you telling me that you're certain this wasn't an accident?" Cal asked.

"Absolutely. Someone pushed her off the trail where Joan is waiting. According to the note, they left her to die."

Anger dripped from Cal's voice as he replied, "I'll contact the FBI right now."

« « «   » » »

Pam Adams Sanderson tossed the morning edition of the Tulsa World in front of her husband. "I knew something like this was going to happen. We should've just killed them. Now what are we going to do?"

Craig saw the headline, **LATEST "NATURAL" VICTIM RES-CUED,** and grunted. After scanning the article, which included a picture of the beaming SAR teams from Oklahoma, he softly shook his head. "Don't worry. Once we snatch Kaycee Miller and take care of her, we'll slip out of the country and into our new lives. The two of us will be the only people in the world who truly understand."

"No! We can't let this happen again. This time we have to be certain that she dies."

"Simply killing her defeats our purpose. I could've easily done that yesterday if that's all we wanted. No, Masterson has to feel the growing sense of panic. He has to know that he should have been there, that he could have found her in time if he'd only tried."

"Fine. Then let's have a backup plan. We need to be certain that if he does manage to get there in time again, that they'll both die."

Leaning back, he thought for a few seconds. "The only way to do that is to keep track of her after we drop her off."

"Why not? You've got all sorts of high tech listening devices. Why not put one on her? That way we'll know if she's found."

"I don't think that will be necessary. Besides, we wouldn't be able to tell where she was just by listening." With a growing smile, he added, "But I know just how to finish them off. A true form of poetic justice."

Wrapping her arms around him, she replied, "I knew you would. You always know how to make everything better."

He shook his head. "Everything except Dakota."

« « «   » » »

The moment Tamara left, Kaycee rushed back to her desk. Long before reading the words Aubrey had written, the handwriting itself had sent chills down Kaycee's spine. The single sheet of paper that Max had scanned had virtually no space that wasn't used. Filling every void, as though she were trying to command a longer, fuller life, was a classic sign that she was afraid of dying in the near future.

Continuing, Kaycee studied the zones and noted the falling baselines. Comparing the letter to one of the older letters, she realized that Aubrey's writing had changed drastically. The letter she had sent to Cal just a few days ago showed a lack of harmony in her life and strong feelings of tension. The pressure was so light that there were places that the pen skipped, a sign of nervous anxiety coupled with feelings of being out of control. Aubrey was agitated, frustrated, and overly concerned about the future, but she still didn't exhibit any of the classic characteristics of depression that would be associated with someone on the verge of suicide.

Like arranging a big puzzle, Kaycee retrieved the various samples from the box Cal had saved over the years and began placing them in chronological order. By the time she was finished, her entire desk was covered. Starting with those from when Aubrey was a teenager, she worked forward, noticing the gradual maturing process. The writing revealed the expected progression through life, up until last November. Although the sample from that time was still relatively normal, it showed the beginning of the crisis. Comparing it to the most recent writing made it clear that Aubrey's life had been in a downhill spiral for almost six months.

With a sigh, she realized that she had been so focused on Aubrey's handwriting, page placement, and pressure that she had ignored an important factor — the words themselves. Feeling that the older letters would probably yield little relevant information, Kaycee began reading the most recent ones first. Although they were generally about her work, she frequently wrote about the deer and other animals that came to her house. Twice she mentioned a woman named Phoebe, the first time in the letter that had initially exhibited signs of stress.

Speaking the words aloud, she fought to read between the lines. "I met our new next door neighbor this morning. Her name is Phoebe Stewart and her husband travels a lot, too. Since they don't have any children, I'm afraid she might be the clinging type. Even though she seems nice enough, I doubt that we'll be friends. You know how stingy I am with my time, especially when I'm in the middle of a project. Remember when I got grounded because I refused to go to the family reunion? Well, some things never change . . . "

Kaycee was working so intensely that she practically jumped out of her chair when Smokey bounded off of his bed and started barking. Tearing through the entryway, he slid across the tile floor and almost ran into the patio door. Acting the same way he had in the wee hours of the morning, he began running from door to door, barking like crazy except when he would stop long enough to cast a pleading look her way.

Since it was a few minutes past noon, Kaycee walked to the French doors and looked outside. Seeing nothing out of the ordinary, she unlocked the deadbolt and allowed Smokey to dash past. At top speed, he raced up and down the fence line, stopping at one point to sniff the ground.

She was about to call Smokey back inside when the doorbell rang. Looking at her watch, she realized that her appointment had arrived. Since it was a beautiful spring day, she left the French doors open, certain that once Smokey had satisfied his curiosity he would come back inside at his leisure.

As she walked to answer the door, a rush of adrenaline made the skin on the back of her neck crawl. Stopping, she turned back one more time to check on Smokey. He was slowly walking toward the back fence, apparently no longer agitated. Taking a deep breath, she shook off the feeling of impending doom and greeted her client.

« « «   » » »

Once he managed to recover the stretcher from the trees, Max quickly utilized the emergency medical supplies that Cal had secured to it. When he was sure that Aubrey's blood sugar was back within the normal range and that her spine was immobilized, he gently moved her onto the stretcher. Wrapped in three blankets, she resembled an oversized papoose as he folded up the sides of the basket and cinched the straps tightly across her chest, hips, thighs, and feet.

Crawling out of the cave, he had to lie on his stomach to wiggle the stretcher back and forth through the narrow opening. Although only her face showed, seeing Aubrey in broad daylight made him cringe. She was far too pale and seemed so fragile that he worried she wouldn't survive being transported. Even so, he knew there was no choice. The clock on the golden hour was ticking, and every second could mean the difference between life and death.

Max strapped on his backpack, grabbed the basket's front hand-grip, and started dragging it through the trees. The heavy underbrush slowed his progress, but within a few minutes he had positioned Aubrey beneath the part of the trail where Joan was waiting. "Everything okay up there?" he shouted.

"Ready when you are!" she called back.

Joan had rigged two ropes with pulleys around a tree limb about fifteen yards away from the rappelling line. The limb hung far enough over the edge to keep the stretcher from catching on rocks as they hauled it upward. After Max secured a line to each end of the basket, he slipped on his gloves and started the steep climb alone. As they had anticipated, his feet dislodged numerous small rocks, but they bounced off the ground well away from Aubrey.

When he was finally at Joan's side, she handed him a bottle of water and said, "You really should take a few minutes to rest before we try to haul her up."

Max took a long drink, then shook his head as he wiped the sweat out of his eyes. "No time to spare. Let's get her moving."

After each of them had wrapped a rope around their gloved hand, Joan said, "On three. One, two, three . . . "

As they continued to rest and pull, the rescue stretcher slowly ascended with Aubrey tucked safely inside. The wind batted it to and fro, bumping it occasionally against the rock wall, but never hard enough to do any harm. When it was finally within reach, Joan tied off her rope and reached out to turn the basket parallel with the trail. Max took the other end and they lowered Aubrey to the ground.

Leaving the ropes in place, they each grabbed one end of the stretcher and started the long hike back to the helicopter.

« « «   » » »

Kaycee's appointment was with a woman in her mid-forties who suffered from anxiety attacks and depression. She was what Kaycee considered a high maintenance client — one who constantly seemed to invite trouble into her life. By the time she left over an hour and a half after she arrived, Kaycee felt completely exhausted.

As she had done since her assistant had moved, Kaycee had transferred her phone to an answering service at the beginning of the session. She quickly checked for messages, jotted down the names of the three people who had called, and hung up. Although she was relieved that no other emergencies had arisen, she was still disappointed that Max hadn't called.

Aubrey's file was on the corner of her desk, and she picked it up again. The more she looked at the writing, the more she realized that Aubrey had been in serious trouble. *Was she being stalked? Had she known her attacker? Why else would her fear have increased steadily over the last six months? Why didn't she want to become friends with Phoebe?*

None of the other victims had exhibited any significant change in their behavior, yet Kaycee was certain that the people closest to Aubrey would have noticed her altered mental state. Quickly deciding that she had nothing to lose, she dialed Max's cell phone, hoping to be able to talk to Cal. After four rings, his voice announced, "You've reached Max. Leave me a message and I'll get back to you as soon as possible."

Preferring to speak to someone in person, she simply hung up. Digging through the file, she found Aubrey's home phone number and dialed it.

A woman answered with a brisk, "Dolenz Residence."

"Hi. My name is Kaycee Miller. I'm a friend of Max Masterson. Would either he or Cal Stevens happen to be there?"

"No, but I expect to see them soon. They found Aubrey a little while ago."

"That's fantastic! Is she all right?"

"We're waiting to hear more information about how she's doing. Last time they checked in, they were still trying to evacuate her from the top of the mountain." Sounding impatient and agitated, she added, "Peter has already left for the hospital and I'm getting ready to lock up the house and leave. I'd really like to be there when they arrive."

"Do they think she's going to make it?"

"It's too soon to tell. I've got to go."

"This will just take a second . . . I'm sorry, I didn't catch your name."

With an impatient sigh, she replied, "Phoebe Stewart. I live next door. What do you need to know?"

"Is there anyone there who was close to Aubrey in the last few months? I just need to ask a couple of quick questions."

"I am. We've become the best of friends since I moved in six months ago."

Kaycee took a deep breath, clearly visualizing the letter where Aubrey had mentioned Phoebe. "As I said, I'm helping Max try to determine the cause of her disappearance. Would you mind telling me if Aubrey acted differently in the last two or three months? Was she nervous about something?"

Phoebe hesitated. "Not that I know of. She seemed fine. To tell you the truth, I've been rather busy myself lately. I'm sorry to say that I haven't been able to spend much time with her. But everything will be different now. That is, if she makes it."

"I'm sure she'll be fine. Max and Cal will take good care of her."

She hesitated, then asked, "Is that all you wanted?"

"Yes. I'm sorry for keeping you. Thanks for the help."

Kaycee hung up and instantly wished she'd left a message for Max. Picking up the letters scattered on her desk, she realized that since Aubrey had been found, her work was probably unnecessary. Even so, she still thought it was important for Cal to understand the implications of his sister's recent handwriting.

If nothing else, he needed to find out what she was so afraid of and convince her to get help.

« « «   » » »

Shortly after they started downhill, it became obvious that Max needed to be on the leading edge of the basket so that he could bear the largest part of Aubrey's weight. It was particularly important at the steep points in the path, where the person in front had to fight gravity while keeping his footing on the loose rocks.

As they struggled to creep down a particularly narrow, craggy ledge, Max called, "How are you holding up back there?"

Joan replied, "Not too bad. This altitude is a killer. So hard . . .

to breathe. How about you?"

"Pretty good. If I remember right, it's only another hundred yards before the path flattens out and we start heading uphill again. Next time there's a wide place in the path, we need to switch ends."

"You won't get any complaints from me. When we do, we really should take a couple of seconds to radio Cal. It must be hell just sitting there waiting."

"Good idea."

When they came to a good stopping point, Max slowed and lowered the stretcher to the ground. Joan checked Aubrey's vital signs as he called Cal. "Rescue One to Air Support One. Cal, we're at the lowest point on the trail. We're heading back uphill and should be at your location in less than fifteen minutes."

Cal replied, "Thanks for checking in. The trauma unit is on standby at the hospital in Boulder. The FBI is lining up a forensic team to scour the area. They expect to arrive within the hour, and they've requested that one of you to stay behind to lead them back to the place where you found Aubrey."

"Not a problem. Aubrey's vitals are strong. We'll be there soon."

"Thanks for checking in. If you can give me a heads up when you're a couple of minutes out, I'll start the pre-flight warm-up."

"You got it." Max tucked his radio back in his pocket and switched ends with Joan. They picked up the basket as he said, "When we get there, I'll hang around and lead the FBI agents back to the site. I think you'd be better at babysitting Cal while he waits at the hospital."

"Stagga's not going to like leaving you here."

"He may sulk a little, but I'm sure you won't have any trouble handling him," he replied — then almost plowed through Joan with the rescue stretcher when she abruptly stopped in her tracks. Max muttered, "What the . . . "

Motioning with her head, she remained still as she whispered, "Trouble . . . "

Max followed the direction of her gaze. Behind a bush a few feet off the path, a mother wolf was crouched, ready to spring. The hair from her neck down the length of her back was standing on end, and her muzzle quivered over bared teeth. Two cowering pups flanked her, one was still, while the other seemed ready to pounce. Under different circumstances, seeing such beautiful creatures would have been a rare treat.

Very softly, Joan asked, "What should we do?"

"Let's take a few steps backward so she won't feel threatened. Nice and slow, okay?"

"Okay."

Stooping, they each took five small steps. The mother's eyes never left them, although she did appear to relax a little. Continuing backward for another ten yards, Max thought they were in the clear. Breathing a little easier, he said, "If we can get out of her sight, she'll probably move on."

"And if she doesn't?"

"I'll scare them off with the gun."

"Can you get to it now?"

"Not without putting down the stretcher. It's in my pack."

Suddenly, one of the pups decided it was time to have some fun. Romping over his mother, he nipped his sibling on the hindquarter and ran onto the trail. Apparently in a playful mood, he headed directly toward Joan. The other cub followed, bowling over his playmate and nipping at his ears.

Instinctively protecting her young, the mother wolf growled a warning, leaped over both pups, then lunged viciously at Joan. Screaming, she turned her back and dropped her end of the stretcher. By the time the wolf landed on her, she was tightly tucked in a defensive ball, her backpack blocking the initial blow.

Max released his end of the stretcher as well, which slapped the ground hard. Knowing it would take too long to get to his gun, he grabbed a rock the size of his fist as the wolf intensified her attack. Joan's screams filled the air as the animal's teeth ripped into the back of her neck.

Shouting, Max rushed forward and pummeled the wolf with the rock. When that didn't seem to phase her, he landed a solid kick with his hiking boot to the side of her head. Startled, she let go long enough for him to place another hard kick to her ribs, which sent her tumbling down the path.

Temporarily stunned, the wolf slowly turned to assess the situation. Max carefully watched her golden eyes as he stooped to grab a three-foot-long broken tree branch. Wielding it like a baseball bat, he aggressively stomped toward her and bellowed, "Back off! Now! Go!"

Realizing her pups had already fled to safety, the mother wolf dashed into the woods. Joan was still frozen in a tight ball as Max rushed back to say, "It's okay, they're gone." His heart was pounding as he dropped the stick and dug his gun out of his backpack. Shoving it in his pocket, he took out the first aid kit.

Joan still hadn't moved or said a word as he hurried to her side. Kneeling, he gently slipped off her backpack and pressed a gauze bandage against the line of jagged puncture wounds that made a semicircle along the tender flesh on the sides and back of her neck. Blood had already soaked through the top of her shirt and jacket, and she was shaking. Folding her in his arms, he softly said, "It's over."

She nodded.

"Hang in there. I need to keep some pressure on it to stop the bleeding."

Another nod.

After a few moments, he barely lifted the bandage to be certain the blood had stopped flowing freely. Relieved that the worst had passed, he asked, "Can you press this down for a second?"

Joan's hand was trembling as she reached back to maintain the pressure.

Tearing open a fresh pack of gauze, Max placed several thick pads over the deepest cuts. He wrapped them tightly, securing the bandages with a generous amount of surgical tape. Trying to lighten the mood, he softly said, "Come on, Joan. It isn't like you to be so quiet. Cuss, yell, say something."

From her trembling lower lip, he knew she was fighting back tears. Touching the damp cloth of her shirt, she took a deep breath and replied, "I've lost . . . a lot of . . . blood. How . . . bad . . . is it?"

Max debated telling her the truth, opting for, "The cuts are mostly superficial. You're gonna be fine. Stay put. I'll be right back."

Taking out his radio, he moved a few steps down the path and chose his words carefully in case she was listening. "Rescue One to Air Support One. We need to change our plan. Rescue Two was attacked by a wolf and is injured. Situation is serious but not critical. You need to lock up the dogs, arm yourself, and start this way on foot."

Cal must have sensed the need for discretion. His voice was equally soft and controlled as he replied, "Be right there. Need any other medical supplies?"

"No."

"Is Joan mobile?"

"Yes. Just hurry."

When he turned back around, Joan had wiped the tears from her eyes and was trying to stand. "I'm okay," she claimed, taking a deep breath. "Let's go." Her hand was still trembling as she reached for the stretcher.

Shaking his head, he tilted her chin so that they were eye to eye. "No, you're not okay, but I intend to make sure you will be. Those wounds aren't a major problem right now, but they might have nicked an artery or a vein. We both know that any strenuous activity on your part could be dangerous. Cal's on his way. He and I will carry Aubrey and you'll walk."

"There isn't time for that! We won't make it in the golden hour!"

"Nonsense." Reaching down, he picked up her backpack and laid it on top of the lower part of Aubrey's legs. Grabbing the handles on the opposite end of the stretcher he said, "Lead the way."

Hesitating, Joan must have realized that arguing with him was a hopeless cause. She turned and started walking. Max followed, dragging Aubrey in the stretcher. A few minutes later Cal came running toward them, completely out of breath.

Seeing her blood-soaked clothes, he carefully hugged Joan and asked, "Are you okay?"

"I've been better."

"We'll have you both to the hospital in no time."

Glaring at Max, she snapped, "I'm okay. Really!"

With a quick nod, Cal said, "Great. Then let's get going." Winking at Max, he added, "We've got to hurry. God only knows what those dogs are doing in my helicopter."

Max saw Cal's first glimpse of Aubrey. He swallowed hard and bit his lip, then leaned over and kissed her forehead. "Hang in there, baby sister." Slipping Joan's backpack on, he picked up the other end of the stretcher and said, "Let's roll."

No doubt intent on showing them how tough she was, Joan stepped up the pace. In a matter of minutes they arrived back at the helicopter. As Cal and Max positioned the stretcher, Max leaned close to whisper, "I think I'd better ride along, just in case there's trouble. Joan's in no shape to handle the evacuation alone."

"I agree. Once everyone is being treated at the hospital, I'll fly you back to meet with the FBI team."

"Sounds like a good plan."

« « «   » » »

By mid afternoon when her last patient left, Kaycee realized that she'd never had a chance to break for lunch. Walking toward the kitchen, she noticed the French door to the backyard was still cracked open, and that Smokey was stretched out in the grass, apparently sunning himself. Whistling, she called, "Chow time! Come here, boy!"

Smokey didn't move.

At first, Kaycee thought he was just sleeping soundly, so she raised her voice to call, "Smokey, come! Quit playing hard to get." When he still didn't move, she rushed to him, dropping to her knees at his side. Placing her hand on his chest, she was thankful he was breathing, but realized that he was far too hot. Running a hand over his face and ears, she checked him for wounds, but found none. Although she considered picking him up, she knew that he was too heavy for her to carry. Patting him softly, she said, "I'll be right back."

Rushing back to the house, she grabbed a portable phone and a beach towel. After dialing Randy's cell phone number, she ran back to

Smokey. He answered on the second ring, and Kaycee said, "Randy, something's wrong with Smokey! I just found him outside. He doesn't appear to have any injuries, but he's unconscious."

"I'm about five miles from your house. I'll be right there and we'll get him to the vet."

"Thank you so much. The front door isn't locked. We're in the backyard." Hanging up, she tossed the phone on the ground and stretched out the beach towel next to Smokey. Lifting each end of his body, she centered him on the fabric, then pulled him into the shade. Softly stroking his neck, she started to cry.

Only a few minutes passed before Randy was at her side. Taking one look at Kaycee, he said, "I'm sure he's going to be all right."

"It's my fault. I left him outside."

Working his hands under the towel, he scooped Smokey into his arms as he replied, "He's spent most of his life outside. No matter what happened, this isn't your fault."

"I should've checked on him. I'm so sorry."

"He'll be fine."

Kaycee heard the words, but didn't believe them for a second.

In spite of the high winds, the flight to the hospital was relatively smooth. Having learned from prior experience, Max knew that the best thing for him to do was stay out of the way so the doctors and nurses could do their jobs. By the time he took the dogs for a long overdue walk, Aubrey and Joan were both under the professional care of the hospital's trauma team.

As usual, when he walked into the waiting room with two dogs in tow, he got a mixture of stares. Some were curious, others nervous, a few made him feel as though he were breaking every rule in the book. Since Cal was nowhere in sight, he crossed to a vacant corner and ordered both the dogs to lie down.

Deciding it was a good time to call Randy, he dug out his phone and dialed the number. When there was no answer at Randy and Joan's house, Max tried Randy's cell phone. Surprised to hear Kaycee answer, he said, "Hi! I must be more tired than I thought. I could've sworn that I called Randy."

"You did. He asked me to answer his cell phone for him. Max, I found Smokey unconscious in the backyard a few minutes ago. We're on our way to the vet's."

Slumping into one of the nearby chairs, Max replied, "I'm sorry, Kaycee. I hope he's okay. Any idea what happened?"

"No. He tore through the house barking again, so I let him outside. After making a beeline up and down the fence line, he calmed right down. It was such a beautiful day that I left the door open thinking he'd just wander in at his leisure. One minute he was fine, the next ..."

Max thought that the same thing applied to both Aubrey and Joan. "Listen, we found Aubrey and she's still alive, but we ran into a little trouble during the evacuation. Nothing serious, so keep your cool. I don't want Randy to think that things are worse than they are, and I really don't want anyone to upset Courtney."

Her voice was soft as she asked, "What kind of problem?"

"We stumbled onto a mother wolf and her pups, and she attacked. Joan's going to need some stitches but she'll be fine." He listened as Kaycee relayed the message to Randy.

Back on the line, she said, "We just pulled into the vet's parking lot. Randy's carrying Smokey inside, but he wants you to tell me exactly what happened."

Max quickly relayed the story, finishing with, "Be sure he knows that Joan walked out on her own and has been as stubborn as a mule about getting treatment. That way he'll know that she really is okay."

"I will. How are you? It sounds like it's been a pretty tough day."

Sighing, he rubbed his forehead. "Tired. I can't wait to get home. I feel like I could sleep for a week."

"When do you think you'll be able to come back?"

"Honestly, I haven't got a clue. In a few minutes Cal's going to fly me to the mountain again. The FBI needs to process the scene where Aubrey was found, plus we'll retrieve all the equipment we left behind. To tell you the truth, that's as far ahead as I've planned. I suppose we'll stay at the hospital until Aubrey's out of danger. Cal's going to want to be with his sister, and all of us need a good rest. My best guess is that Joan and I will find another way back to Tulsa in the morning. We could easily catch a commercial flight out of Denver."

"You're not planning to stay there until the situation with Aubrey is resolved?"

"If Cal really wants me here, I'll stay. But I'd rather be with you. Plus, Joan will need to recover at home and I don't want her trying to fly by herself. These days it's hard enough to manage being in an airport alone, and she'll have D.C. to handle, too. She's been joking about being the guinea pig for the North Face's new wolf-repellant backpack, but it was still a pretty harrowing experience. In fact, if she hadn't been wearing that backpack, I'm afraid it would've been much, much worse."

"Did you say you're going to lead the FBI back to that same area in a few minutes?"

He smiled, warmed by her concern. "Yes. And I'll have both my backpack and a gun. Besides, that wolf was just protecting her pups. It was purely a case of being in the wrong place at the wrong time. Wolves rarely attack people."

Kaycee laughed. "Tell Joan that. You'll be seeing Cal soon, right?"

"Any minute now."

"Could you give him a message for me?"

"Sure."

"Tell him that I found something that really concerned me when I analyzed Aubrey's handwriting." She hesitated, then added, "Max, she was afraid she was going to die. In fact, I'd go so far as to say that Aubrey was terrified of something or someone."

Max closed his eyes, trying to force the information through his weary mind. "Wasn't that letter written a long time before she actually disappeared?"

"Not quite two weeks. But what's important is the trend. A year ago, everything about her samples was normal, then last November something changed. Her writing began showing definite signs of anxiety and concern for the future. The last letter was practically screaming for help. Not in words, of course, but in the extreme way her emotions translated onto the paper. Since she was the type to write longhand letters when most people would've either called or sent an e-mail, it's very possible she has a journal or a diary stashed somewhere. If she had one, it probably would give us a better idea of what was going on in her life."

"Excellent point. I'll ask her husband if she had anything of that kind. I know this is a dumb question, but would she have necessarily known what she was afraid of, or could it have just been a gut feeling?"

"Either is possible. Handwriting is an expression of both the subconscious and the conscious. The fear could've been on either level, or both levels, for that matter. Why?"

"Because we used to tease Aubrey about worrying too much. Could her handwriting just be exhibiting her tendency to fret about things?"

"I don't think so. The key is in the changes. If she always tended to be stressed, then over the years that trait would've manifested itself in a consistent pattern in her handwriting. Whatever happened six months ago was caused by a different factor, some recent change in her life or surroundings."

Max stood and started pacing. "Okay. Listen, Cal has had even less sleep than I've had, which isn't much. When I tell him his sister was scared to death, he's going to want to kick some ass."

She laughed. "You're probably right, but I have no clue whose ass we're talking about, or if it's even something that has an ass. Her fear may have had nothing to do with what happened on the mountain."

"Or it could be the answer to all the natural killings. Either way, Cal's going to need an outlet for his anger. He's already feeling guilty for not being there when she needed him, especially since he didn't get hold of her as soon as he got that last letter."

"Help him focus on what he can do to help her. He should talk to her — calmly, reassuringly, but not pressure her in any way."

"Kaycee, she hasn't regained consciousness yet."

"Then he should stay by her. The moment she's aware of her surroundings he should make absolutely certain that she feels safe. I realize that after what she's been through, that's a tough assignment, but he needs to take her fears seriously. If she asks for an armed guard, then he should get one. If having her best friend in the room makes her nervous, Cal should make her leave. Which, by the way, brings up another interesting question. When Phoebe Stewart moved in six months ago, Aubrey wrote that she didn't intend to become friends with her. Yet when I talked to Phoebe a few minutes ago, she implied that they were very close. I doubt if it's relevant, but it struck me as odd."

"Aubrey's always been a loner. Phoebe seemed to have set up camp at their house. You should've seen the look on her face when she saw the book."

"Was she shocked?"

"Horrified would be a better description. I'll tell Cal to check her out."

"Good idea. Aubrey doesn't need to be around anyone who will upset her. He should do everything he can to reduce her stress, even if her requests don't seem logical. Understand?"

"Totally. And thank you for the help. If I were there, I'd kiss you."

"Which will be soon, right?"

"Let's hope so. Listen, the FBI agent in charge of the case just came into the waiting room. I'll try to call you back in a couple of hours. Tell Randy not to worry, I'll make sure Joan behaves and I'll personally deliver her to his doorstep."

"I will. Take care!"

"Bye." Max hung up. He stretched and yawned, then crossed the room to greet Agent Collier.

She smiled and shook his hand. "Great job. You and Cal are batting a thousand."

"Sometimes we get lucky."

"From what I understand, luck has nothing to do with it. Listen, I just got some more great news. Evan Newsome regained consciousness this morning. He remembers a few things already, and the doctors are optimistic that he'll recover more memories as his condition improves."

"That's fantastic! Has he recalled anything that can shed some light on what happened to him?"

"He was in the underground parking garage of his office when someone called for help. He got a good look at the man before getting knocked out. Evan knows the guy gave him some sort of injection, but after that his memories aren't very clear. He's agreed to work with one of our artists to develop a sketch of the suspect later today. Unfortunately, he admits that he can't distinguish the hallucinations from what actually happened."

"Were the hallucinations caused by the injection?"

"Looks that way. Whatever drug they used didn't show up on normal toxicology screens, so they're going to run more sophisticated tests. Of course, we'll have the blood of the other victims re-tested as well."

"What makes Evan so sure that his memories aren't real?"

"Some things he described were pretty bizarre. For instance, he thinks he was moved from his car to the top of the mountain in a casket filled with sewage, but that seems highly unlikely."

"From the way the victims have all smelled, that may not be so outrageous."

"There's one thing that Evan is sure about. He specifically asked his attacker why he had been kidnapped. Evan says that he'll never get the words out of his head."

"What words?"

"He says he was left there to die as retribution for someone else's ineptitude. He remembers those two words because they struck him as particularly odd: retribution and ineptitude."

"I agree with him. That is odd."

After starting to turn away, she whirled back around. "Oh, and does the word Dakota mean anything to you?"

Max shook his head. "Other than the obvious, nothing special. Why?"

"Evan's sure he heard them say something about Dakota. In fact, he thought that's where they'd left him to die — somewhere in one of the Dakotas. He was really surprised to find he'd been wandering around Carlsbad Caverns National Park in New Mexico."

"Did you say they? I thought serial killers were typically loners."

"They are. Evan claims it was a man in the parking garage, but later he heard a woman's voice, too, so he assumed that the man wasn't working alone. Once again, we have to remember that the voices Evan heard weren't necessarily real. Even so, someone leaked the information to the press. They've already named them the Natural Killers."

"Was the man who attacked him definitely a stranger? Someone he'd never seen before?"

"Yes. Why?"

"I just talked to Kaycee Miller, the psychologist who's been analyzing the victims' handwriting. She says that Aubrey was afraid of something or someone. Apparently it started about six months ago. It's possible that the victims are stalked before they're kidnapped."

Flipping open her cell phone, she replied, "I'll have the agent ask Evan if he noticed any unusual activity before this happened.

Anything in particular she thinks we should look for?"

"Unfortunately, no." Cal appeared in the waiting room's doorway long enough to signal that he was ready to go. Max extended his hand once again and said, "Looks like I'm off to meet some of your fellow agents. Thanks for everything."

"Let me know if you think of anything else that might help."

"I will."

Max led the dogs to the helicopter and climbed into the back passenger area. While they were in flight, Max brought Cal up to date with the information about Evan Newsome, then carefully conveyed Kaycee's message about Aubrey's state of mind.

By the time they landed, Cal seemed very distant, which Max attributed to a mixture of exhaustion and worry. As they tied down the rotors, Cal suddenly stopped, looked at Max, and asked, "What would you do?"

Caught off guard, Max asked, "About what?"

"If it were your sister. How would you make her feel safe?"

Max sighed. "I'd make sure someone was always there, 'round the clock."

"Mom is arriving late tonight, and there's Peter. We could take eight hour shifts." He shrugged. "Then again, I haven't got anything else to do. I could just stay with her the whole time."

"Whatever it takes, but if you're physically and emotionally exhausted you won't be of much use to her. Once she can tell you what's going on, things will be easier."

Shaking his head, he sighed. "At least she's alive."

Cal climbed back into the helicopter and confirmed that the FBI agents were still a few minutes from landing. As he worked, Max let the dogs out to play. Max was tossing a Frisbee when Cal patted him on the back and said, "Tell Kaycee I said thanks, okay?"

"You bet. She was happy to help."

"I swear, if anyone tries to hurt Aubrey again, they'll answer to me."

With a confident smile, Max replied, "And me."

« « «   » » »

Kaycee watched Randy pace across the veterinarian's waiting room for the thousandth time. "You know, you're going to wear a path in the carpet."

With a grimace, he sat in the chair next to hers. "I hate this."

"Me, too. Maybe we should just barge back there and demand to know what's going on." When Randy started to stand, she grabbed his arm. "I was just kidding! They're doing all they can. We have to be patient."

Dropping his head, he rubbed his eyes. "What a lousy day. First Smokey, then Joan. I still can't believe she was attacked by a *tsv-s-gi-no wa ya*. My mother used to tell us a story about one when we were kids."

"Cherokee legend?"

He shrugged. "Knowing my mother, it was probably more a figment of her imagination than an actual legend. A couple of years ago I found out that she made up stories to keep us from roaming around in the woods at night when we were kids. I remember the one about *tsv-s-gi-no wa ya* like it was yesterday. It means *devil wolf*. We were all terrified of it." With a laugh, he added, "She even admitted that she had made a plaster mold of a huge paw print and put it on a stick. After a good rain when the ground was soft, she'd go for a hike and sprinkle a few fake tracks near the paths where we liked to play. I remember when I was four I spotted one and ran all the way home. I locked myself in my room and didn't go back in the woods for weeks. Nowadays they'd probably claim she was being mentally abusive, but I know she was just protecting us the only way she knew how."

"Sounds like it worked. I can't wait to meet her."

"Any time. She loves company."

"You know, not everything about today has been bad. A few good things happened. Aubrey was alive when they found her. Joan's backpack probably saved her life. And I hired a new assistant . . . "

"Even so, the bad has outweighed the good." His eyes met hers. *Sv-no-yi-e-hi-nv-do a-de-lv-di-yi. A-gi-s-di a-ga-se-s-do-di.*" Grinning, he explained, "That's a very rough translation of what Max always says about several things going wrong at once."

"Really? What's that?"

"Our moons are wobbling. We should be careful."

Grinning, Kaycee remembered Max telling her the same thing shortly after they met in New Mexico. "Then let's hope they straighten up and fly right soon."

The vet opened the door and motioned for them to follow him inside. Tall and lean, Dr. Adin's easygoing manner seemed perfect for his choice of profession. He led them past the normal consultation area to a sterile recovery room.

Kaycee had to fight back tears when she saw Smokey lying on a table with a monitor tracking his vital signs. Although he was strapped down, his eyes were alert and his tail flipped up and down when he saw them. Randy carefully stroked Smokey's back and whispered something Kaycee suspected was a Cherokee prayer in his ear.

Dr. Adin declared, "He's doing pretty well right now, but he's not out of the woods just yet. Until all the tests come back, I won't know for sure, but I think he either ingested something toxic or had an allergic reaction to an insect bite."

"By ingested something toxic, do you mean someone might have intentionally poisoned him?"

"Not necessarily. At this time of year, there are a few indigenous weeds that are quite poisonous, although it's too soon to rule out foul play."

"I don't see how it could be a poisonous weed. My yard is fenced, and I have a lawn service that regularly sprays my yard for weeds. I haven't noticed anything unusual."

"If the toxicology comes back negative, we may never know what caused it. The important thing is that Smokey should be fine. He'll need to stay here overnight so that we can monitor him, but as long as he keeps steadily improving, he can go home in the morning."

Kaycee sighed. "Thank you so much."

"My pleasure."

As Randy drove her back to her house, Kaycee tried to ease the tension with light conversation. After a few of his classic yes or no answers, she felt certain that he blamed her for Smokey's condition. When they pulled into her neighborhood, he said, "As soon as the vet releases Smokey in the morning, I'll pick him up and bring him to your house."

Surprised, Kaycee said, "But . . . You heard the doctor, my yard might not be safe."

"I'll check it when I drop him off. Besides, if your backyard isn't safe, then there's no place in Oklahoma where he'll be safe. His only choice would be to come back to Claremore with me. We live in the country. Besides the fact that weeds are ninety percent of our yard, he'd probably be jealous of Prince. He's much better off with you."

Climbing out of the truck, Kaycee smiled and said, "Thanks, Randy. Not just for this afternoon, but for trusting me with Smokey. I know how much he means to you."

Embarrassed, he looked away and muttered, "He likes it here. That's what's important."

"Max and Joan will be home soon. Why don't we plan a celebration dinner this weekend?" Remembering his earlier suggestion, she added, "A nice goat roast, right?"

Winking, he nodded. "Sounds great. I'll see you in the morning."

Kaycee watched him drive away, still wondering if he were serious about roasting a goat. As she stepped inside, she quickly realized that without Smokey to greet her, the house seemed cold and empty. Since it would be dark soon, she bolted the deadlock and began her evening ritual. Walking from room to room, she flipped on every light as she went upstairs to change into something more comfortable.

In spite of the warm spring weather, she felt a slight chill as she hung up her business clothes. Grabbing her favorite pair of faded jeans, she wiggled into them. Next, she slipped on a soft T-shirt and topped it with a grey hooded sweatshirt that had a pocket across the front.

Momentarily forgetting that she wouldn't be taking Smokey for a pre-sunset walk, she tugged on a thick pair of socks and her running shoes. To relax the tight muscles across her back and shoulders, she reached each arm slowly above her head as she plodded down the stairs. The stretch felt wonderful and she began considering what to whip up for dinner.

Passing the den, she crossed the room to look across the backyard. The lawn appeared to be perfectly manicured, making her wonder what could possibly have happened to Smokey. She was about to turn away when something caught her eye. It was hard for her to see much in the fading light, but it was clear that there was a black oblong object in the middle of the yard, near the place where she had found Smokey earlier.

As she reached to unlock the French doors, her hand froze on the bolt. A wave of anxiety pulsed through her veins, even though logic dictated that there was nothing to fear. *It's not dark yet. Everything will be all right. Just go see what it is.*

Forcing herself, she slowly walked across the patio and stepped into the grass. When she was close to the object, she had to smile. In all the commotion, she had left her portable phone lying in the middle of the back yard. Stepping forward, she started to reach for it, then stopped. As her weight shifted, the edge of her tennis shoe pressed into the soft grass, revealing the tip of something shiny.

Kaycee stepped back, crouched, then carefully patted the ground. Picking up the thin, metal object, she placed it in the palm of her hand and stared at it. A small orange cap topped what looked like a three inch long needle to a hypodermic syringe.

The darkness seemed to close around her as Kaycee grabbed her phone and ran back into the house. She slammed the door, locked it, and dialed Randy's number. In her trembling hand was a dart: the kind used in blowguns to poison people. And animals like Smokey.

« « «   » » »

When Max and Cal slowly pushed open the door to Aubrey's hospital room, Joan was sitting in a chair at the side of the bed with her eyes closed. Peter was near the window, seemingly staring at the passing clouds.

As his eyes swept the room, Max noticed that Joan was wearing a cervical collar and that the machines monitoring Aubrey's condition showed a strong, steady heart rhythm. They had barely managed to slip inside when Joan commented, "The two of you are back faster than I expected. D.C., come!"

Peter snapped around, throwing them a weary smile as D.C. ran to her master.

All too aware of his surroundings, Max kept Stagga at his side as he quietly explained, "The winds are finally being cooperative. After I showed the FBI agents where we found her, Cal dropped me a line and we left them to do their work. Apparently, they'll scour both the upper path and the area where she was found for evidence." Squeezing Joan's hand, Max added, "Besides, we were so worried about the two of you that we wouldn't have been much help."

"Somehow I doubt that," Joan remarked. "Do they think they can make out the message she left in the dirt?"

"Unfortunately, no. She must have been really weak when she wrote it. The impressions were very shallow." Touching her shoulder, he asked, "What did the doctor say about your injuries?"

"That it's a good thing my skin is like leather from spending too much time in the sun."

Max smiled. "Seriously. Why did they put you in a neck brace?"

"Promise not to gloat?"

"Do I have to?"

"Only if you want me to answer."

Grinning, he conceded. "In that case, I promise."

"Apparently one of the puncture wounds barely nicked my jugular, which explains why I bled so much at the time. I've got forty-two stitches and I'm on some heavy-duty antibiotics. They want me to wear this thing for a few days to restrict my movement and give it time to heal." With a warning glare toward Max she added, "And when the doctor interviews you, you'd better corroborate my story. If he thinks there's any way that wolf might have attacked because it was rabid, then I'm going to have to take a series of rabies shots. He swears they aren't that bad these days, but I have no intention of finding out for myself."

Lowering his brows, Max cocked his head. "You mean you don't want me to tell him about the savage gleam in her eyes and the way she was foaming at the mouth?"

"Very funny," she snapped.

Cal was at the side of the bed, holding his sister's limp hand. "Any better information on Aubrey's condition?"

Peter shook his head. "They're waiting on a lot of test results. For now, they say she's holding her own."

"Why isn't she in the ICU?" Cal asked.

"Believe it or not, it's full. But actually, this will work better. In ICU they don't allow visitors to spend the night. This way I can be here when she regains consciousness."

Pulling up a chair, Cal said, "Well, then I guess that'll make two of us."

"There's no use both of us being here. You've been up most of the night. Why don't you go back to the house and get some sleep? I'll call you as soon as anything happens."

Slowly shaking his head, Cal said, "Thanks. I really appreciate the offer, but I'm not going anywhere until I get a chance to talk to Aubrey."

Peter took a deep breath, then smiled and said, "She's lucky to have you."

"No, I'm lucky to have her." Shifting his gaze to Max and Joan, he ordered, "Now that we've got that settled, you guys really do need to get back to the house and get some rest. I'll call if anything happens. Otherwise, I don't want to see your smiling faces until you've each logged a good night's sleep."

Suppressing a yawn, Max said, "Agreed." He gave Joan a hand and they started toward the door as Max added, "I almost forgot. Kaycee wanted me to tell you that we should try to find either a journal or a diary that Aubrey might have been keeping." Turning toward Peter, he asked, "Any idea where we should look?"

Peter's eyes darted across the room as he shrugged. "I don't think I've ever seen her writing anything down." After a brief hesitation, he asked, "How are you guys going to get back to the house?"

"I guess we'll take a cab," Max replied.

"Since Cal is going to stay here, why don't I run you home? That way, I can pack a few things that I know Aubrey will want when she wakes up."

With a wide grin, Max added, "SAR teams always accept free rides. Right, Cal?"

"Truer words have never been spoken. Take as long as you need, Peter. As you said, there's no need for both of us to lose another night's sleep."

Joan stopped to hug Cal and said, "She's going to be fine."

Dropping to one knee, he embraced each dog. "I know. Now get some rest. Just looking at you makes me tired, and these poor dogs need a break."

With a wide grin, she replied, "Thanks. We love you, too."

« « «   » » »

Kaycee paced across the living room as she waited to hear Randy's cell phone ring. After a few seconds of dead air, she realized the battery on her portable phone must have gone dead while it was lying in the backyard. Tossing it on the sofa, she rushed toward the kitchen and grabbed a different phone. For several moments she listened, slowly coming to grasp that the battery wasn't the problem — there was no dial tone.

As usual, her cell phone was in her purse, which she'd left on the table in the entryway. After placing the dart on the kitchen counter, she ran toward the front door to get it, but stopped in her tracks when the doorbell rang. Praying that Randy had forgotten something, she peeked outside.

Through the window she could see that it was Pam Adams, the neighbor she'd met on the street. Her skin crawled as she remembered the way Smokey had acted. Wishing she had completely closed the blinds so that she could've ignored the doorbell without seeming rude, she sighed and hoped to get rid of the woman as quickly as possible.

Without being invited in, the woman pushed past Kaycee so that she was standing inside the threshold. Practically beaming, she declared, "Hi, Kaycee! Remember me? Pam Adams from around the corner. Sorry to drop by unexpectedly. It's such a beautiful evening that I thought you might want to join my husband and me for a walk. He really wants to get to know you."

When a man suddenly appeared next to Pam, Kaycee wasn't sure if her failing night vision had played a trick on her, or if he really had been intentionally lurking in the shadows. He boldly stepped forward, pushing his wife further into the entryway as he said, "Hi, I'm Craig. Pam has told me all about you."

Feeling ill at ease, Kaycee wondered how that could be possible, but politely shook his hand and replied, "Really?"

"Yes." Nonchalantly moving toward the kitchen, he commented, "And what a beautiful house you have!"

Kaycee turned to watch him as she replied, "I'm sorry, but I'm very busy right now. I'm afraid I don't have time for a walk, or anything else for that matter." Motioning to her casual clothes, she added, "My boyfriend will be here any minute. And as you can see, I really need to get ready for our date."

Hearing the unmistakable *click!* of the deadbolt sliding into place, Kaycee whirled around. Pam had brought in a package, then closed the front door. As Kaycee watched in stunned silence, Pam began cranking the blinds so that they were fully closed.

A rush of adrenaline washed through Kaycee's body. Trying to appear calm, she asked, "What are you doing?"

The sick smile on Pam's face made Kaycee cringe as she replied, "Well, to tell you the truth we don't want any nosy neighbors wondering what's going on for the next few minutes."

She could practically hear Max saying, *Always trust your instincts,* and she knew that she had made a huge mistake. Even Smokey had tried to warn her. Knowing she had to act fast, she tried not to be obvious as she backed toward the keypad to the burglar alarm. Since it was near the corner of the wall across from the front door, she kept her eyes fixed on Craig as she stepped backward and asked, "What exactly is going on?"

"You're taking a little trip with us."

As if to steady herself, she reached back. "Why? Why would I go anywhere with you?"

Craig laughed. "Because you don't have a choice."

Whirling, Kaycee hit the panic button on the alarm's control panel, expecting the sirens to immediately blare. When nothing happened, she frantically began searching for something else to use as a weapon, but there was nothing within reach.

With that same repulsive grin, Pam explained, "Craig disconnected the sirens on your alarm the other day when we were talking out on the street. By the way, how's dear old Smokey doing? I'll bet he's still feeling a little bit under the weather, isn't he?"

"That was you? You poisoned him?"

"More like drugged. We couldn't have him alerting the neighbors. Don't worry, the effects of Craig's concoction are short-term. Not that you'll be around to play with him anymore."

"Why don't you two just take what you want and leave? I don't have much in cash or jewelry, but you're welcome to take what little I have."

Opening a plastic bag, Pam tugged on a pair of surgical gloves, then carefully pulled out a copy of *Vis Medicatrix Naturae*. Stepping forward, she tried to hand it to Kaycee as she explained, "We're not here to rob you. We already told you — you're going on a trip with us. Now take the book and hold it firmly."

Since it was large and heavy, Kaycee considered using the book as a weapon. Just as her fingers closed around it, Craig pulled a gun from beneath his jacket and warned, "Don't even think about it. We want everything left just the way it is. There can't be any sign of a struggle. Now, I want you to turn to Chapter 3, *The Extreme Alternative-Suicide by Nature*."

"This isn't going to work. The police already know that the people aren't committing suicide. They know they're being kidnapped and left to die."

"Good for them. If that's true, then they should easily be able to solve the mystery of your disappearance. Now do as you're told."

Shaking her head, she asked, "Why should I help you set up my own murder? It's obvious that you two are the Natural Killers. The question is, why are you doing this?"

"Retribution. You've been chosen to pay for the ineptitude of others. The innocent must suffer. Now, we can do this the easy way, or the hard way."

"Meaning?"

"I can easily place the fingerprints inside the book after you're unconscious — or dead, for that matter. Or you can simply do as we ask. Either way, the result will be the same."

"As I said, the FBI knows that your victims haven't committed suicide. Why continue the charade?"

Craig seethed, "Because I said so!"

The psychologist in Kaycee instantly realized the depth of their psychoses and that it must be linked to an event they shared. Cradling the book with her left arm, she flipped through the pages looking for the right chapter. Her first conversation with Pam raced across her mind, and she paused to ask, "Where's your son? His name is Dakota, right?"

Fire practically jumped from Craig's eyes as he glared at his wife for a moment, then turned his anger back at Kaycee. "Shut up! Is your car in the garage?"

Certain she was on the right track, she persisted. "Where's Dakota? Why isn't he here with you?"

"Stop asking questions! You're going to place the book on the table, then slowly turn around and put your hands on the back of your neck."

Trying a different approach, Kaycee asked, "Don't you think the police will wonder why I had *two* copies of the same book in the house?"

Craig took a step forward, threatening her with the gun. "Where's the other one?"

Hoping to split them up, she motioned with her head and replied, "Under the coffee table in the den." As he left, she knew her window of opportunity would be short-lived, and that if they managed to restrain her, her chances of ever escaping would be slim. Quickly deciding that it would be better to risk everything than to simply do as they asked, she made certain he was in the other room before making her move.

With all her strength, she hurled the book at Pam and bolted toward the staircase. As she passed the table in the entryway, she grabbed her purse off of it and gave the table a shove. The vase of silk flowers crashed along with the wood and glass as they hit the ceramic tile floor and broke into a million pieces.

Bolting up the stairs, Kaycee ducked low as gunshots echoed in the entryway. As she slammed her bedroom door and wedged the chair from her makeup table under the doorknob, she heard them barreling up the steps. Without wasting a second, she dumped everything in her purse on her bedspread. Stuffing as much as she could into the front pocket of her sweatshirt, she shoved her cell phone into the back of her jeans.

One of them was kicking the bedroom door as she headed toward the nightstand to get her gun. She was almost there when the lights went out. Looking toward the French doors that led to her balcony, she realized the yard lights outside had gone off, too.

They threw the circuit breaker. Stay calm. Find your gun.

Her hand was shaking as she dug through the drawer in the darkness. Behind her, the unrelenting kicking was splintering the door frame, and she knew she was almost out of time. Giving up on the gun, she crawled to the French doors, quietly unlocked them, and slipped outside onto the balcony. After pulling them closed, she stood in the darkness, her heart racing as she tried to decide what to do. The sound of the bedroom door flying open made her decision easy.

Running to the balcony's smooth white railing, Kaycee climbed over it and jumped.

CHAPTER **9**

The moment they stepped into the house, Peter insisted that Max and Joan relax in the living room while he prepared a simple meal. Max led Joan to an easy chair and made her promise to stay put while he fed and cared for Stagga and D.C. When he was alone in the kitchen with Peter, he explained what Kaycee had discovered about Aubrey's handwriting.

After listening intently, Peter nodded and said, "So that's why she suspects there's a diary or a journal." In a more contemplative tone, he added, "She may be right. Ever since we got married, I've traveled extensively. Aubrey could easily have hidden something like that from me, or only done it while I was away. I'm afraid she's had a lot of long, lonely nights."

Max replied, "It's important for us to find it right away."

Staring into space, Peter said, "No wonder Cal won't leave her side."

"That's right. He's there to protect her. Had she been acting odd lately?"

"Not any more than usual. Don't get me wrong, Aubrey's a great woman, but she's always had a pretty vivid imagination."

"Such as?"

He shrugged. "Well, she's never liked staying here alone at night."

"Really? Why?"

"She says we're too far from help, and that by the time the police or fire department could get here, it would be too late."

Max watched Peter, noticing that he was gripping the knife so tightly that his knuckles were white as he sliced a loaf of French bread. "Do you think that's true?" Max asked.

Peter replied, "Of course not. If I did, I would never have left her here alone. And you've seen for yourself what great neighbors we have. If she called, any of them would be happy to help."

Thinking of what Kaycee had told him about Phoebe, Max asked, "Was she particularly close to any of them?"

"Not really." He glanced around to be certain she was nowhere in sight. "Phoebe has tried to be her friend, but Aubrey wants nothing to do with her."

"Why not?"

"One of Aubrey's co-workers convinced her that Phoebe is nuts. I tried to persuade Aubrey to be open minded, but she said that Phoebe was always watching her. It creeped her out so much that she got new curtains for that side of the house and insisted that we keep them closed."

"Do you think Phoebe could've been involved in Aubrey's disappearance?"

Peter took a long, deep breath. "I honestly don't think so."

"Have you told Agent Collier about her?"

"Of course not! Think about it — Phoebe hardly ever leaves her house. How could she be one of the Natural Killers?"

"Good point. Was Phoebe the only thing she was worried about?"

"Ever since we met, Aubrey has been pretty insecure. And they weren't necessarily logical fears, either. For instance, she hated driving the road that runs from the entrance down to the highway in the snow. You've seen that road. It's narrow, but there isn't anything particularly dangerous about it. No steep drops or sharp turns, plus there's the wide turnaround where Cal has been landing the helicopter. That road is snow packed from late fall through early spring. Since nothing bad has happened in all these years, you'd think she'd get over it."

"Yet she wasn't afraid to hike in the mountains alone?"

Peter hesitated, searching through the bottled spices neatly stacked on a turntable in the cabinet. "Not at all. It wasn't unusual for her to pack a lunch and be gone all day."

"You're right. That's not exactly rational behavior," Max agreed.

Stopping, Peter turned to him. "Why not? Most of the people

who live here hike in the national park."

"I could understand taking long hikes before she was diagnosed as diabetic, but I'd think she'd want to have someone with her until she was more comfortable treating the condition. I understand it wasn't completely under control."

"But her doctor made it very clear that being diabetic wouldn't require her to change her lifestyle. In fact, he encouraged her to keep exercising."

"I'm sure he did. It's a good thing she always planned ahead. The food she had with her probably saved her life."

Obviously surprised, Peter asked, "She had food with her?"

"There were several candy bar and cracker wrappers in the cave."

"Did she have water, too?"

"Nothing obvious, but it was clear she had put her wilderness survival training to good use."

Peter smiled and shook his head. "It never dawned on me that Cal had probably trained her. Thank God for small miracles."

The spaghetti sauce on the stove had started bubbling like hot lava, releasing an aroma that made Max realize how hungry he was. Motioning toward the food, he asked, "Anything I can do to help?"

"No. It just takes awhile for the water to boil at this altitude. All I have to do is pop the garlic bread in the oven, boil the pasta, and set the table. Go relax. I insist."

Heading into the living room, Max replied, "You don't have to twist my arm."

Joan was still in the recliner as promised, talking on her cell phone. When he came in, she smiled and tossed the phone to him. "Randy wants to talk to you."

Catching it, Max sat on the sofa. "Hey, old buddy. How's Smokey?"

"He's going to be okay. Listen, I wanted to thank you for watching Joan's back for me. I appreciate it."

"Any time. Is Kaycee okay? I know she was really worried about Smokey."

"She's fine. The vet says he can go home in the morning."

"That's great. I hate the idea of her being there alone."

"It's just one night."

Rubbing his temple, Max tried to suppress a yawn, but failed. "True. I think I'll give her a call, then hit the rack right after dinner."

"Take care, buddy."

Max grinned. "I will. And I'll make sure Joan doesn't try to wrestle any other wild animals before I get her home. See you soon."

"You, too."

Tossing the phone back to Joan, Max stood and walked down the hall toward the bedroom. Pulling out his own cell phone, he dialed Kaycee's home number. After ten rings, he hung up, wondering what was wrong. If she wasn't available, the answering service should have picked up, even if she were on the phone.

Trying not to overreact, he dialed her cell phone.

« « «   » » »

Fiery pain shot up her shins as Kaycee hit the ground and rolled. Practically blind in the dark, she began crawling toward the east, staying as close as she could to the small shrubs that lined the flower bed beyond her porch. She knew that if she could get to the fence, she could follow it to the south gate. From there, she might be able to see better in the light from the street lamp on the corner. Above, the French doors banged open, and the balcony's boards creaked under the weight of angry footsteps.

As usual, Kaycee had her cell phone set to vibrate for five seconds before ringing. At first she was startled by the sensation in her back pocket, then she realized that its high-pitched ring would lead them straight to her. Freezing, she reached back to grab it, trying to hide the glowing screen as she punched the button to keep it silent.

Kaycee was about to answer when the lights in the house started returning in blocks. Certain she was out of time, she softly said, "I need help. Call the police. I have to be quiet or they'll find me. Please send help!" Leaving the connection open, she tucked the small phone into the front pocket of her sweatshirt and bolted toward the fence.

Just as the yard lights snapped back on, her fingers wrapped around the cool metal handle of the gate. Twisting it, she pushed hard, wincing at the hinge's loud creaking noise. Slipping through, she started to run forward but stopped.

From the shadows, his voice was low and clear. "Take another step and I'll kill you right here, right now."

« « «   » » »

Max ran down the hall, holding the phone away from his mouth as he called, "Joan, tell Randy to send the police to Kaycee's house and make it clear that it's an emergency. She's in trouble."

Joan cast him a questioning look, but immediately responded the moment she saw his face. While she did as he asked, he paced and listened to the muffled conversation:

"*Okay. You win. The least you could do is tell me is what you mean by retribution and ineptitude. Come on, Craig, be fair. I deserve to know.*"

"*Keep your voice down. You don't deserve anything.*"

"*Exactly! If this is about paying back someone, why not go about it directly?*"

"*Be quiet. Are you trying to get your neighbors killed, too? This gun is loaded and I will use it.*"

"*Is this Pam's idea? Are you just going along with her because she couldn't cope with whatever happened?*"

"*Actually, it was my idea. Now get in there.*"

Max heard shuffling and a door being slammed closed, then struggling.

"*What are you doing? You don't have to give me a shot! Please stop! I'll do whatever you ask!*"

Hearing a muffled scream made Max's entire body shake. More scuffling was followed by the sound of car doors slamming. A few seconds later, he could barely hear Kaycee's voice as she weakly asked, "*Where are you taking me?*"

A woman replied, "*To Dakota.*"

« « «   » » »

Max's heart threatened to leap out of his chest as he realized the connection was lost. Turning to Joan he asked, "Did Randy send the police?"

"Yes, and he's on his way to her house. What's going on?"

Pacing, he replied, "I think I might know who the Natural Killers are, and I'm pretty sure they've just kidnapped Kaycee. If you'll contact Agent Collier, I'll call to see if Cal can fly me back."

Max raced into the kitchen looking for Peter, but he wasn't there. Assuming he was changing clothes, he darted to the master bedroom and swiftly knocked before barging in. Peter wasn't there. Phoebe was standing in the closet, pulling what looked like a leather-bound journal out from under a shoe box on the top shelf. The moment their eyes met, she casually put it back where it had been.

"Where's Peter?"

"He left a couple of minutes ago to pick up some Parmesan cheese for dinner."

"Is that Aubrey's diary?" Max asked.

"Unfortunately, no. It was her mother's. Peter asked me to check. He thought that if she was keeping one of her own, she might stash it in the same place. What's wrong? You look like you've just seen a ghost."

"A good friend of mine is in trouble. I know Cal turned off his cell phone because of the hospital's rules, but I need to talk to him right away. Can you get me the number?"

"Sure." Rushing out of the closet, she closed the door and led the way to the kitchen. Pulling a phone book out of a drawer near the phone, she found the number, dialed it, and handed the phone to Max.

Cal answered on the first ring and Max blurted, "Buddy, I know you're already pushed to the limit, but Kaycee's in serious trouble. Is there any way you could fly me to Tulsa tonight?"

Without hesitation, Cal replied, "My mother arrived about fifteen minutes ago, so she can stay with Aubrey. It'll take me about thirty minutes to fuel up and get back there. I'll pick you up on the road just south of the house. What's the problem?"

"It looks like she's the next victim of the Natural Killers. I'll explain on the way."

Hanging up, he went to pack. Passing the room Joan was in, he realized she was doing the same. Casting him an intimidating look, she remarked, "You really don't think you're leaving me here, do you?"

"You're in no shape to go on a rescue."

"Fine. Then I'll man the base station. But I am going."

Knowing better than to argue, Max sternly replied, "Cal's picking us up in thirty minutes on the road. Leave your gear right there. You are not going to carry it yourself. I'll take it down with mine. Understand?"

She started to nod, but winced. "I'll be ready in a couple of minutes." Embracing him, she added, "Max, she'll be okay."

"If not, I'll never forgive myself. They're from my past, Joan. I can't believe they're doing this. Why didn't they just come after me? Or Cal, for that matter?"

"Apparently, they prefer a more direct route to your heart."

« « «   » » »

Kaycee slipped in and out of consciousness, occasionally aware that she was in a moving vehicle. The powerful hallucinogenic drug had immediately taken control, creating terrifying images that bounced inside her mind and chased her to the corners of her sanity. Although she was tightly rolled in a heavy blanket, in her mind she was soaring through a void of darkness, clinging precariously to life as the entire universe spiraled toward the heart of a black hole. Fear was like a tide, rising and falling in regular waves.

Screams quickly turned to whimpers, all muted by a tightly bound gag. Even though her arms and legs weren't tied, the constricting wool cocoon insured they remained useless. Any effort expended to work herself free resulted in near suffocation, and her breathing became as labored as though she were on the summit of Mt. Everest. Lapsing in and out of a lucid state, time and miles passed.

Although it seemed like days, it was really only a few hours before she was aware of the world again, roused by sweat stinging her eyes.

Woozy, but briefly clearheaded, she listened to her captor's voices and struggled with the hopelessness of her situation.

Pam said, "It's almost over. Dakota will rest in peace soon. Solomon, Roegiers, and Newsome have all paid. Now it's Masterson's turn."

"And then we can move on. Start another life, a fresh new beginning."

"According to the news, Evan Newsome can definitely identify you."

"Maybe so. He may live long enough to give the authorities a good description, but he will never testify against us in court. Once we're done here, the sins of his father will be visited upon him again. After that, we'll be out of the country in a matter of hours. We're prepared. The wheels of justice don't turn fast enough to stop us now."

"What about this one? Judging from the fight she put up at her house, she might survive for weeks. It's too risky now. We can't let that happen."

Craig's laughter made Kaycee cringe. "Don't worry. I'm not leaving anything to chance this time. If Masterson doesn't find her in less than twenty-four hours, he'll be doing a cadaver search."

"Are you sure?"

"Positive. In fact, if things go as planned, they'll burn in hell together."

Only the engine noise filled the Bell 427 passenger compartment as it soared through the dark sky toward Tulsa. Max rode shotgun beside Cal, and the back cabin was occupied by Joan, Agent Collier, D.C., and Smokey. Everyone except Cal tried to catch up on some much-needed sleep, certain that finding Kaycee would require all their strength and patience.

When they were within a couple of miles of Kaycee's South Tulsa neighborhood, Cal nudged Max to wake him. After shaking his head to clear his mind, Max asked, "Where are you planning to land?"

"Having the FBI onboard came in handy. The police have closed the main crossroads to accommodate us. I'll set down long enough for all of you to unload, then go refuel at R.R.M. I'll wait there until you call."

"You're not going to fly back to Colorado?"

He shook his head. "Mother will take care of Aubrey. Right now, Kaycee needs all of our support. A wise man recently reminded me that friends are always there when you need them."

Max nodded. "Thanks, buddy."

In a matter of moments, Kaycee's house was visible, easily identified by the line of police cars parked in the street. Cal must have sensed Max's emotional low, because he said, "Listen. The next few hours are going to be the hardest. Feeling helpless is hell, so try to stay focused on the ultimate goal. We'll find her as soon as we can, but first we have to establish a search zone."

"I know, and thanks. Collier has already alerted the officials at all the national forests in a five-state area. They're doing everything they can."

After climbing out of the helicopter, Max helped unload the gear and the dogs as Agent Collier greeted the two detectives with the Tulsa Police Department who were waiting nearby. Randy rushed to meet them, wrapping Joan in a tender embrace. In a matter of minutes they had walked to Kaycee's front yard and were being introduced to the people in charge of her case.

Max stared in disbelief at the line of CRIME SCENE-DO NOT CROSS tape that skirted the perimeter. During the entire flight he found himself unable to accept what had happened. Like so many other times in his life, he yearned to turn back time, to see the pieces of the puzzle come together just a few moments sooner.

Agent Collier's voice made him focus on the task at hand. "Max Masterson is Kaycee's close friend. He was on the phone with her at the time of the kidnapping. He and his canine are nationally certified in search and rescue. I think it would be a good idea for him to bring everyone up to speed on his theory about the kidnappers and their motive."

All eyes turned to Max as he explained, "One of my first rescues was in the Ouachita National Forest in southeast Oklahoma. It was late fall, and the Sanderson family had gone on a camping trip. Since Craig Sanderson is a botanist, they frequently went on long hikes and camped out regularly. We were told that their five-year-old son, Dakota, wandered off sometime during the night. About five a.m. the next morning, a cold front pushed through, but they didn't discover that Dakota was missing until a little after eight in the morning. By then, the temperature had fallen from the mid-fifties to almost freezing. To complicate matters, the child was barefoot and only wearing his pajamas."

"I hitched a helicopter ride with Cal Stevens, who was on his way to Dallas on business. By the time I arrived at the base station, three other SAR teams were already at work. It quickly became apparent that the boy had fallen in a creek. Since he was swept away by the current, it took some time for the dogs to pick up the scent again. We located him two miles downstream the next day. He had survived the water long enough to wander back into the woods. When we found him his body was still warm. Even so, we were too late to save him."

Max sucked in a long breath, then continued. "Agent Collier has confirmed that the first victim of the Natural Killers was the daughter of Benjamin Solomon, who was the Incident Commander at the scene. Ben retired shortly after that rescue. The second fatality was the stepson of Will Roegiers, who still does SAR work in California, and Evan Newsome was the son of Richard Newsome, also retired. We recently located our helicopter pilot's sister, who went missing a couple of days ago. Now Kaycee, my girlfriend, has been abducted. As you can see, all five abductions can be directly tied to the search for Dakota Sanderson."

Ken Smith, the lead TPD detective, asked, "You think they're targeting the loved ones of the SAR teams?"

Agent Collier replied, "It certainly looks that way. If Cal and Max had children, they probably would've targeted them. Since they're both single, they snatched a person close to each."

Detective Smith asked, "How many SAR teams worked Dakota's rescue?"

Max replied, "Just the four of us and Cal. Technically, Cal didn't provide air support as he has done in the recent cases. Back then, he was still working full time. He just happened to be going the same direction at the time I needed a ride."

"Is there some valid reason why this couple might blame the SAR teams for the death of their son?" a different detective asked.

With a shrug, Max shook his head. "As far as I know, everything was done by the book. Looking back, I can see that telling them that we had almost found Dakota in time probably gave them a reason to second-guess the tactics that had been used, but we really did the best we could. In a situation like that, every SAR team questions whether they could've done anything differently. I know I did. But in the end, the weather played the biggest factor in his death. If it had been a few degrees warmer, or if he'd been more appropriately dressed, he probably would've survived."

Agent Collier stated, "At this point, we have to assume that the Natural Killers are Craig and Pam Sanderson, the parents of the boy. They're apparently seeking some sort of twisted revenge for Dakota's death by making the SAR team members suffer a loss similar to their own. If that's the case, then Kaycee should be the last victim. Photos and detailed information on the two of them will be available in the next few hours. We've issued watches for their last known vehicles, as well as for Kaycee Miller's missing car. A Federal Search Warrant on their residence will be executed in approximately three hours, which will hopefully turn up some valuable clues."

She shot Max a look of concern, glanced at her watch, then continued, "It's almost two a.m. A special FBI team will assemble here at seven in the morning. Our plan is to target several areas relevant to the case. The first critical step is to determine where they have taken her. As most of you already know, the choice of locations where the victims have been dropped don't seem to adhere to a logical pattern."

Taking a map out of her briefcase, she pointed at each red circle as she explained, "Victim number one was abandoned over five hundred miles from her home. Number two was approximately two hundred miles, Evan Newsome was within eighty miles, then Aubrey Dolenz was found within five miles of her residence. It is possible that the Sandersons may have abandoned the last two victims in the national forests by their houses because it was more convenient. Since there aren't any national forests near Tulsa, we have to assume that Kaycee will be transported to one of those that are reasonably close. We can rule out Kansas, since there aren't any there. Texas has four national forests, there are six in New Mexico, two in Arkansas, one in Missouri, and one in Southeast Oklahoma. That's a lot of ground to cover."

Detective Smith asked, "Other than what we've been reading in the newspapers, is there anything we need to know about how the other victims were located?"

She shook her head. "Their vehicles were all found abandoned at the parks where they were eventually discovered. The minute Kaycee's car is spotted, we'll focus most of our energy on that location." Shifting gears, Collier added, "But our second concern is that the Sandersons may no longer be following the same method of abduction and abandonment. There are some differences in these cases that indicate they aren't sticking to their established procedure." Turning to Detective Smith she asked, "I understand there are obvious signs of foul play in the residence. Is that right?"

He replied, "Definitely. There was a struggle in the entryway, and two broken doors — one leading to the master bedroom, the other opening onto the second-floor balcony. The phone lines were disconnected at the junction box on the back wall of the house and the burglar alarm has been tampered with. The book was found on the floor of the entryway. It was open and crumpled as if it had been thrown across the room. The only fingerprints on the cover belonged to Ms. Miller. What's really odd is that we found a second copy of *Vis Medicatrix Naturae* halfway up the staircase. Again, it was open and appeared to have been dropped there. Unlike the one on the ground floor, it has multiple fingerprints."

Max nodded. "That was probably the copy Kaycee finished reading the other day. Since it was connected to the rescues I've been working on, she thought it might give her some insight into the disappearances."

"We noted another strange thing, too. Almost every light in the house was left on, so it's possible they were looking for something. We'll know more once the fingerprints are all processed."

Before Max had a chance to say anything, Agent Collier quickly replied, "They're getting very sloppy. Except for Aubrey, the book was always left in the victim's car, and there have never been any indications of resistance in the homes. Judging from the conversation Max overheard, they may not be aware that Kaycee successfully alerted the authorities, so we might have a slight advantage this time." Turning to Detective Smith, she asked, "Has the forensic team wrapped up the initial evidence collection?"

"We've completed the digital photos and videos. Now we're in the process of collecting trace evidence. Last, we'll spray for latent fingerprints. Since the fumes are toxic, once the house is sprayed it'll be sealed and guarded for twelve hours."

Randy, Joan, and Max all started to speak at the same time. Since Max was the most animated, the others fell quiet as he said, "We really need to retrieve several scent articles before the place is sprayed."

"Not a problem. Because you've given us such a strong lead on the suspects, there isn't any hurry." Reaching into his pocket, he pulled out a sealed evidence bag and added, "We recovered this dart near the phone in the kitchen. Any idea why she might have had something like this in her possession?"

Randy's eyes lit up, and he shook his head as he muttered, "Smokey." Raising his voice, he explained, "I'll bet that's how the kidnappers made certain that Smokey wouldn't be in their way."

"Smokey?"

"My former SAR dog has been staying with Kaycee. He's a black Lab. Very well trained and loyal." Rubbing his forehead, Randy added, "It's all starting to make sense. Kaycee said that Smokey has been agitated several times in the last couple of days — running from door to door and barking. I'll bet those people were snooping around her house."

Detective Smith asked, "Where's Smokey now?"

"Kaycee found him unconscious in the backyard this afternoon. He's still recovering at the vet's."

Holding up the dart, he asked, "Do you think they intended for whatever was in this to kill him?"

"Doesn't seem likely. There are a lot easier ways to kill a dog than to use a dart. I think they just needed to be sure he didn't spoil their plans."

"But does that make any sense? It's okay for them to kill people, but not dogs?" Joan asked.

Detective Smith shook his head. "I've seen stranger things."

Agent Collier nodded, then looked at Max. "Is there anything you can tell us about Kaycee that might help the investigation?"

A million irrelevant details crossed Max's mind, from the way her smile lit her eyes, to the tiny mole beneath her left ear. "You're right about her fighting. Kaycee wouldn't have let them just waltz in and take her. She'll be aggressive at every opportunity." He hesitated. "There is one other thing about Kaycee you should all know. A few months ago she discovered that she is going blind from an inherited disorder called *retinitis pigmentosa*."

Max glanced at Joan and Randy, who both reacted with shock, before he continued. "She didn't want the world to know yet. The disease usually progresses very slowly. Her night vision is the only thing that is seriously impaired at this point." Looking at Detective Smith, he explained, "I have a feeling the fingerprints will show that Kaycee turned all the lights on herself. It's become a nightly ritual. She hates being in the dark."

Detective Smith nodded. "I can certainly understand why. Do you think her condition will impact your search?"

"The first three victims wandered aimlessly, both night and day. Kaycee may look for food and water in the daylight, but by nightfall she'll establish a camp."

Collier shook her head. "According to Evan Newsome, the drug they administered left him extremely disoriented for quite some time. The preliminary report on his blood work indicates that they're administering some sort of homemade mushroom extract that has hallucinogenic effects. If they give the same thing to Kaycee, she may not act in a rational manner."

Max sighed. "True. In fact, I heard her beg them not to give her the shot. Has anyone contacted her sister in New Mexico yet? She's the closest relative."

Detective Smith replied, "The sheriff in Taos stopped by her house, but no one was home. This isn't exactly the kind of news that you leave in a note or on an answering machine. He's going to try again first thing in the morning."

"I'd appreciate it if you'd ask him to have her call me. I want her to know that we're going to find Kaycee as soon as humanly possible," Max replied.

"Not a problem," Detective Smith replied.

Agent Collier shrugged and added, "If no one else has any suggestions, then I think we need to regroup in a couple of hours. By then, we should have a more complete profile of the Sandersons. For now, I'd suggest you all go get some rest." Touching Joan on the shoulder, she added, "Especially you."

Randy nodded. "I've got us a suite at the Doubletree. It's only a couple of miles down the road. We can be back within a few minutes, ready to go on a moment's notice."

Max agreed, "Great idea. Joan definitely needs to rest."

"You do, too," Randy replied. "There's plenty of room."

Shaking his head, Max said, "I'm staying here, but if you could take Stagga it would really help. Did you clear taking the dogs to such a ritzy place?"

"A friend of mine from high school manages the hotel. He gave me his personal guarantee that the dogs would be welcome. If you change your mind, give me a call and I'll come pick you up."

Walking away from the others with them, Max stopped near Randy's pickup and asked, "Where's Courtney?"

Randy answered, "She's on a school trip. If we're not back by the time she gets home, my mother is going to stay at our house with her."

Lowering his voice, Max said, "I'm sorry I couldn't tell you guys about Kaycee sooner. She made me promise not to say anything. She thinks that people will start treating her differently once they know."

Joan touched the padded cervical collar and said, "She's probably right. I never realized how curious people were until I had to wear this thing. I feel like everyone is staring at me. It's only been a day and I'm already tired of explaining what happened. I can see why she'd want to postpone the impact as long as possible."

Opening the truck's door, Randy settled Stagga and D.C. in the backseat of the extended cab. Turning to face Max, he said, "If it's going to make her uncomfortable, Kaycee doesn't need to be told that we know. I doubt that it will come up, and once she feels that we should know, she'll tell us herself."

Max smiled. "You guys are the greatest. Thanks for being here."

"Any time."

« « «   » » »

Kaycee had no idea if it was night or day when they stopped moving. She listened intently, but heard only a few odd noises — metal scraping against metal, something heavy being pushed slowly on the ground, and what could have been chains rattling. After a few minutes, the door near her head was opened and she overheard Craig say, "Remember, this isn't going to be like the others. Just do what we planned and everything will be okay. Do you have the next shot ready?"

Pam's reply was so faint that Kaycee strained to catch her words. "Yes . . . still don't . . . a good idea . . . first . . . hasn't completely worn off yet. Today's paper . . . another survivor. Can't . . . let them . . . away with it! We . . . just kill her . . . dump the body . . . until they find it. A double dose . . . easily . . . do the job. What if you . . . trapped . . . too?"

Craig seethed, "No! We're not going to get off track now. For all we know, that story in the paper is nothing more than a ploy to rattle us." After a brief hesitation, his voice was more like a man trying to talk patiently to a child. "Pam, I'll be fine. Just monitor the radio and let me know if anyone gets close to the area sooner than we expected."

Pam must have moved closer, since Kaycee could hear her more clearly. "I will." She paused, then added, "Dakota is here. I can feel him all around us, stronger than ever. He's anxious. He knows we're going to free his soul soon."

"Let's get on with this. Once you abandon her car at the recreation area, you'll be on your own for a few hours. If you need help, radio me."

"I will. Just don't stay up there too long."

"We already discussed this. It's going to take a lot more time than the others, so don't panic if I'm not there right on time. Leave the rest to me. See you soon." He hesitated, then shouted, "Don't forget to wipe down her car!"

Through the blanket, Kaycee felt arms wrap around her midsection. As if she were nothing more than a roll of old carpet, she was suddenly pulled outside. The end with her feet slammed the ground and she was dragged along a bumpy surface that felt like gravel. Finally, her upper body was lifted and haphazardly folded over the edge of something she guessed was a metal box.

Hanging with her head down, she quickly became dizzy and con-fused. Groping hands pushed against the rough wool, edging slowly down her spine. She felt kneading fingers and slowly came to realize that he was searching for the right spot to give her another injection through the thick material.

Even so, the sharp sting of the second hypodermic being thrust through her flesh still caught her off guard, and she instinctively jumped. Pain shot through the top of her hip bone, but as the tears began to roll down her face she felt a gush of warm fluid being absorbed by her jeans. Realizing her movement must have made the needle angle so sharp that it had gone in the flesh on one side of her hip and out the other side, she sighed. Tears ran down her cheeks, not from the pain but from the knowledge that she had narrowly escaped another dose of that horrible drug.

With brutal force her ankles were seized and lifted to one side, pivoting her weight on the upper edge of the metal container. With another push, she tumbled inside, landing with her head face down in a corner. Squirming did little to ease her into a more comfortable position, although she managed to shift her hips until she fell to one side. Hoping to get an idea of where she was, she wiggled and tried to move, but the container's narrow walls stopped her. As though a cold hand had clutched her heart, she came to realize that she was not only helpless, she was trapped in a long and narrow box. *A casket?*

As she struggled to figure out what to do, she heard footsteps and the sound of something heavy being dragged. Craig groaned as he hefted whatever it was that suddenly came tumbling down on her. From the weight and the way it conformed to her body, she initially thought that it was just dirt, but it had an odor unlike anything she'd ever experienced. Growing in intensity by the second, it reeked of cof-fee grounds, kerosene, cow manure, and urine. The stench made her eyes burn as more loads were dumped, each adding a layer of pressure until the agony was almost unbearable.

Rapidly succumbing to both the remnants of the powerful drug and the suffocating force, Kaycee's heart raced as she struggled to breathe.

He's burying me alive! was her last terrifying thought before she slipped into a welcome, peaceful darkness.

« « «   » » »

Max spent the rest of the night in the back seat of one of the police cars, falling in and out of a fitful sleep. At seven a.m., the forensic team finished their preliminary work and the FBI special team began assembling to organize their efforts. While they worked, Detective Smith allowed Max to walk through Kaycee's house, gathering items the SAR teams could use for scent.

As they slowly moved from room to room, Max connected the scene with the last cryptic words he had heard her speak. He easily pictured what must have happened, envisioning all too clearly both Kaycee's struggle and her muted cries for help. As Cal had predicted, the waiting was sheer hell.

Trying to occupy himself, Max began calling in every favor in the SAR community that he'd ever earned. After notifying friends across Oklahoma, he asked Agent Collier to contact the St. Tammany Parish Sheriff's office to formally request the Louisiana Search and Rescue Dog Team, or LaSAR, be put on alert. Over the years, he had become close to several of the team's members, and he knew that if Kaycee's car was found in Texas, Oklahoma, Arkansas, or Louisiana, they would be happy to help in any way possible.

After digging his laptop out of his gear, Max began looking through his database of SAR associates. In half an hour he had compiled a list of over fifty people he could ask for assistance, depending on which national forest the Sandersons picked. Tapping his fingers on the keyboard, he looked out the window and tried to think of anything else he could do.

For a few seconds, he closed his eyes and thought of Kaycee, but fond memories quickly gave way to the thought of her current peril. Abruptly folding down the screen of his computer, he stuffed it back in his pack and climbed out of the car. The looks of pity thrown his way only increased his anger.

Taking a deep breath he turned away, running his fingers through his hair as he leaned against the patrol car. With clenched fists, he wanted to scream, to run, to do *something*. For once, he allowed himself to mentally rail against all the injustice in the world and it actually felt good.

Max was beginning to regain his composure when he noticed a car turn onto Kaycee's street. He watched as a girl driving a red Pathfinder pulled up and parked in front of a neighbor's house. From the look in her eyes, it was obvious that she was either nervous or upset. She stared at the front of Kaycee's house as though she were too stunned to move, her hands gripping the steering wheel so tightly that her knuckles were white.

Trying not to gawk, Max found it impossible not to watch her. There was something about the fear in her eyes that made him certain she was there to see Kaycee. Practically running across the street to her car, Max waited as she nervously fumbled to roll down the window. With a friendly smile, he asked, "Can I help you?"

Staring past him at the yellow crime scene tape, the young woman's blond hair hardly moved in the stiff wind. "What . . . What happened here? Is Ms. Miller all right?"

Without Max realizing it, Agent Collier had stopped right behind him. Before he had a chance to answer, she snapped, "Who are you?"

The girl's bright green eyes darted between the two of them as she replied, "I'm . . . I'm Tamara Conrad."

Scrutinizing her, Collier demanded, "Why are you here?"

"I was . . . supposed to start work this morning. Yesterday, Ms. Miller hired me to be her new assistant." Turning her watch where they could see it, she added, "I was going to start at eight."

Max could see the girl's uncertainty and fear had been elevated by Collier's intensity. Trying to be reassuring, he extended his hand and said, "I'm Max Masterson, and this is Special Agent Collier with the FBI." Motioning toward Collier with his head, he added, "Don't mind her, she hasn't had much sleep lately. Would you mind answering a few questions for us?"

"Not at all."

Nodding toward Kaycee's open garage, Max said, "How about in there where the wind is blocked?"

Tamara quickly climbed out of her car and followed them into the garage. Max was impressed that Kaycee had hired such a professional looking young woman. Her black slacks and turquoise sweater set complimented her youthful figure, yet were subdued enough to keep from being suggestive. From her precisely manicured nails to her trendy short hair, it was apparent that she was trying hard to make a good impression on her first day on the job.

Max noticed her shivering as Agent Collier led the way into the garage. Once they were out of the cool morning breeze, he asked, "When did you last speak to Kaycee?"

"Yesterday."

"What time?"

With a shrug, she replied, "Late morning, noon-ish, I think."

"Here?"

"Well, not in the garage, of course. We talked in her office." Her eyes gleamed. "I had interviewed with her the day before, and when I came back to ask her about the job, she hired me!" Shifting her gaze to Max, she pleaded, "I really liked her and I need this job. Please tell me what's wrong. Is she okay?"

Max replied, "She will be. There was some trouble here last night, and we have reason to believe that she was kidnapped. But don't worry, we'll find her."

Tamara cocked her head and stared at him. Recognition slowly lit her eyes. "I know you! You're one of the rescue guys in the picture on her credenza."

"You're very perceptive," Agent Collier commented.

Eagerly looking around, Tamara asked, "Where's your dog?"

"His name is Stagga, and he's resting with a friend right now. He'll be at my side as soon as we have some idea where Kaycee might be."

"He looks very intense in that picture."

"I'm pretty sure he could find her blindfolded in a hurricane if necessary."

"How will you know where to look?" Tamara asked.

Agent Collier replied, "Once we locate her car, we'll have a better idea of where she might be."

"Is there any way I can help?"

Max replied, "Not unless you saw or heard something unusual while you were here. Was there anyone hanging around the neighborhood? Did you notice anything unusual?"

Closing her eyes, Tamara appeared deep in thought for several seconds. Suddenly, a smile lit her face and her eyes flew open as she declared, "There was a truck parked around the corner at the top of the street on both days! I thought it was odd because there was a woman sitting inside it the first day, then a man in it the next."

"Can you give us a description of it?"

"An old model, green pickup truck. There was a trailer hitched to the back with a camouflage tarp stretched over the top of some stuff. Inside the trailer was a blue four-wheeler and something long and black, like a horse trough. I remember the ATV because I could see its muddy tires and I thought that it must not have been driven around here lately."

"Why not?"

"My boyfriend used to take me four-wheeling on some land between Tulsa and Oklahoma City. A lot of the dirt in this part of the country is that nasty red clay that ruins whatever you get it on. The dirt on the tires was dark, almost black. Like the potting soil you can buy for houseplants, but without those weird white specks in it. Besides, it's been ages since it rained anywhere around here. No rain, no mud."

Agent Collier was excited, her attitude completely changed as she asked, "Tamara, do you think you could identify the people you saw in the car from either sketches or photos?"

"Sure. She was a cross between Mrs. Knoll, my Calculus teacher, and my dad's old girlfriend." With her right hand, she motioned about two inches above her shoulder as she added, "Her hair was frosted, a blunt cut about this long. Not very flattering for her facial structure."

"What about the man? Do you remember him?"

Tamara shivered and her eyes narrowed as she replied, "He glared right at me."

Max asked, "Glared? In what way?"

"You know, that condescending 'If you were my kid, I'd kick your ass' kind of look." As if she had remembered something embarrassing, she moved away slightly. "Oh yeah, I almost forgot. That was the first day I came to talk to Ms. Miller, so everyone would've still been staring at me."

Max waited for her to explain, but when she didn't continue, he asked, "Why?"

Digging through her purse, she pulled out a photo and handed it to him. "They say a picture is worth a thousand words. Up until a couple of days ago, that's the way I looked."

Max and Agent Collier glanced at the photo, back at Tamara, then at each other. It was a picture of three young women sporting black lipstick, punk haircuts, and very little clothing. Collier asked, "Why the drastic change?"

"I dumped my boyfriend and decided that it was time to get my life back on track. Working for Ms. Miller was going to be my new beginning." She sighed. "But that might not happen now. Someone wants to hurt her, don't they?"

Max firmly stated, "Not if we can help it."

"There must be something I can do to help."

Collier replied, "We're doing everything that's humanly possible."

Looking around the empty garage, Tamara walked along the side wall, seemingly studying the spotless gardening tools hanging in neat rows on the pegboard. Step by step, she seemed to consider each item. After a few seconds, Max asked, "What are you doing?"

"Looking for clues."

Max noticed that Collier had to bite her lip to keep from saying something more condescending than, "This is a crime scene, so don't touch anything and don't go inside."

Stepping in front of her, Max suggested, "I'll stay with Tamara for awhile in case she remembers something else that might be useful. Looks like your team is getting a little antsy waiting for you."

Nodding, Collier said, "Great idea. I'll check back in a few minutes."

Step by step Tamara worked her way toward the door that went into the house. She stopped in front of a dry erase board that Kaycee had divided into three sections using red marking pen. At the top were the titles: *Oil, Tires, Tag,* and *Misc.* The first three categories contained the date or mileage when the next action was required, and beneath the last was written *OE #1558824.* Staring at the board, Tamara cocked her head and asked, "What kind of car does Ms. Miller drive?"

"A charcoal gray Lexus."

Still studying the board, she asked, "Why did they take her car?"

"It's part of how they work. They abandon the victim's car to make it appear that he or she committed suicide."

Whirling around, Tamara declared, "Oh my God! She was taken by the Natural Killers!"

"It appears that way," he sighed.

"I was just reading about their latest victim being found in the Rocky Mountain National Forest. Was that you? Did you find her?"

Max nodded.

Turning back to face the board, Tamara softly said, "I think I know how you can find Ms. Miller, too."

C H A P T E R **11**

Kaycee heard birds. Lots of birds. Squinting, she fought to focus. Slowly, fuzzy greens and greys took shape, forming tree limbs that gently swayed overhead in the morning breeze. Waves of nausea passed as rhythmic bursts of sunlight touched her cheeks. In time, she came to realize that she was lying on the ground in a thickly wooded area.

Something was crawling on her hand, but she didn't move. It wasn't real. None of this was real. She was trapped in another nightmare. Closing her eyes, she stayed perfectly still for what seemed like an eternity, certain she would awake safe and warm in her own bed. But when she opened her eyes again, nothing had changed. She was still cold, still filthy, and still scared.

She tried to swallow, and found that her throat was raw and swollen. A large black bird shrieked as it swooped low, spread its wings as if it were going to land on her face, then whooshed away at the last second. Panicked, she rolled onto her side, smashed the spider crawling on her hand, and scrambled to the base of the closest tree.

Moving had ignited every raw nerve, and for a long time she huddled in a ball, rocking back and forth as bizarre fears slithered in and out of her mind. The drug seemed to seize her in short bursts, then ease its grip. She thought that the dirt had turned to quicksand, and that she was being sucked into the ground. After a few moments of lucidity, the earth became a sea of brown and yellow snakes so genuine that she repeatedly tried to climb the tree to escape from them. Exhausted, she turned to see the sky slowly rip open, then begin to bleed.

It's not real! It's not real! It's not real! She silently chanted, holding her head in her shaking palms. Crawling on hands and knees, she spotted a perfectly square piece of marble on a small pedestal beneath a tree. Stopping in front of it, she brushed the dirt from its surface to reveal a beautifully engraved stone. Beside an etched image of a young boy, was the inscription:

In loving memory of Dakota Sanderson
Lost at the hand of man
Found in the hands of time

Rubbing her arms to quiet the goose flesh, Kaycee realized that the Sandersons had been sick for many years. For a few minutes Kaycee stared at the marker, wishing there was a way to bring the child back. Tears slid down her face, first for him, then for herself.

Except for Aubrey, the other victims of the Natural Killers had all been found in the wilderness several weeks after they had disappeared. Remembering some of the things Max had told her, she thought about finding shelter, following animal trails toward water, and a few of the roots he had claimed were edible. She wished she had paid closer attention.

Soon after she began to assess the full weight of the situation, reality started slipping into the drug's twisted world again. She was sure the dirt beneath the marble marker was shaking, because the devil was pushing Dakota back into the world. Struggling to her feet, she thought he was hunting her down so that he could rip her to shreds and throw the pieces into the wind.

Unlike the other fears, this one slapped all her senses. She heard the ground breaking open, smelled the creature's horrid breath, and felt the touch of his hot breath on the back of her neck as she fled. Twigs and branches tore her flesh as she raced through the forest. Although she never saw exactly what the resurrected boy looked like, each time she glanced over her shoulder, she was positive that he was just inches away and closing fast.

Eventually, Kaycee fell, tumbling head over heels down a steep embankment. Exhausted and terrified, she tried to go on, but knew it was hopeless.

Shaking violently, she curled into a ball and waited for the child's ghost to put an end to her misery.

« « «   » » »

Max rushed to Tamara's side. A mixture of hope and doubt filled his eyes as he asked, "Why do you think you can help us find Kaycee?"

Pointing at the handwriting on the board, she replied, "This is obviously where she kept the information about her car." Moving her finger to the bottom of the last column, she added, "A friend of mine's dad bought her a new car for her college graduation. It has *OneEarth*, that new satellite tracking system. If you get lost or scared, you can just push a button and the operator will tell you where you are, or call the police for you. They can even unlock the car from the satellite, or tell you where it is if it's been stolen."

She tapped her finger beneath the red numbers. "I helped my friend set up her system, and the security number looked a lot like this." Turning to face Max, she offered a weak smile. "I only talked to Ms. Miller for a few minutes, but I could tell that she's really well organized. She probably wrote the code here with the rest of the information about her car, so that if she ever needed it quickly, she'd know right where to find it."

Sweeping her into his arms, Max whirled around as he said, "Tamara, you're brilliant! Come on!"

Practically dragging her, Max rushed to Agent Collier. Within five minutes, *OneEarth* had pinpointed the location of Kaycee's Lexus. Max spread a map across the hood of the patrol car as Collier announced the exact coordinates. "It's in the Ouachita National Forest in Arkansas. According to the satellite, the car is in a region known as the Caney Creek Wilderness. The closest town is Mena, Arkansas." He looked at his watch. "With Cal's help, we could be in the park and searching by noon."

Tamara waited patiently next to Max as he alerted all his friends. By the time he confirmed that the teams from LaSAR were responding as well, Randy and Joan had arrived with Stagga, D.C., and Smokey. Dropping to one knee, Max warmly greeted Stagga, then stood to ask, "What are you going to do with Smokey while we're gone?"

"The vet said that he checked out fine," Randy replied.

"Whatever drug they gave him seems to have completely worn off. He's good to go."

Max stood and called Smokey to his side. After giving him a quick rub, he looked at Randy and said, "Cal's going to be here any minute. You can't just leave Smokey here. They're going to spray Kaycee's entire house for prints."

"He's coming with us," Randy stated as though it were a matter of fact.

Eyeing his friend, Max shook his head. "Not a good idea."

"Last time I checked, Smokey and I still had our SAR Tech III certification. Prince isn't ready for this, but Smokey can handle it."

Max bit his lip, then said, "Don't take this wrong, buddy, but you're the one who isn't ready."

"Smokey and I are going. If we prove to be a burden, we'll withdraw. I know LaSAR is sending a whole crew, but it'll take them eight to ten hours to respond. We may not be the fastest team in the hunt, but we'll hold our own weight." Grasping his shoulder, he added, "Kaycee needs all the help she can get right now."

"Wouldn't it be better for you to work with D.C.? Smokey's been out of the field for months."

"I'll be working with D.C., as usual," Joan declared.

Glaring at her, Max snapped, "You're manning the base station and assisting the Incident Commander, which leaves D.C. free to work with Randy." Turning to Randy, he added, "Surely you're not going to support her on this."

"Actually, I am. We called her personal physician this morning and met him at his office a little while ago. He's not exactly thrilled with the idea, but he said that Joan could help if needed. We've talked it over and we agreed that we should all be ready to work if necessary. If the conditions are such that one or both of us need to step down, then we'll cross that bridge when we get to it. Otherwise, we're going to do whatever we can to bring Kaycee safely home."

Joan added, "If we needed help, Kaycee would be there for us without giving it a second thought. Please let us do the same for her."

"But . . . "

Taking his shoulder, she lowered her voice. "There's only one thing more frightening than being alone in the dark in the wilderness."

Eyeing her, he asked, "What's that?"

"Being blind in the dark in the middle of nowhere. You have to let us help her."

The whisper of Cal's helicopter broke the silence. Max nodded as he fought the wave of emotions that had knotted his stomach. He gave each of them a quick hug before rushing to gather his gear. Chasing him, Tamara asked, "Can I come, too? Please? I want to help."

Max shook his head as he pulled his backpack onto his shoulders. "Listen, I'm eternally grateful for what you've done, but I can't let you come along. If I remember correctly, there are over 65,000 acres of wilderness in that forest. We'll have to work quickly and efficiently." Taking a pad of paper out of his pocket, he asked, "Do you have a cell phone?"

She nodded.

"If you give me the number, I'll call you as soon as I know anything."

A smile lit her eyes. "Promise?"

"I promise."

« « «   » » »

Craig pulled onto the grassy shoulder of the dirt road, and slammed the truck into park. Keying the radio, he muttered, "Pam, are you there?"

Yawning, Pam fumbled in the leaves until she found her own radio and replied, "Yes."

"I'm at the pick up point. Where are you?"

Jumping to her feet, she replied, "Sorry, I must have nodded off. I'm in the woods, just a few hundred feet from the road. I'll be right there. Did everything go okay?"

"Exactly as planned."

Running as fast as she could, she made her way through the thick underbrush. When she could see the pickup and trailer, she slowed to catch her breath. Climbing in the passenger side, she asked, "Can we leave now?"

Craig shook his head. "Not yet. What's the hurry?"

"Dakota says we should go soon. He says they're coming."

Biting his lip, he muttered, "That's impossible. There's no way they could know yet."

"He told me we were in danger."

As if he could no longer contain his anger, he turned and shouted, "Dakota's dead! He can't talk to you or anybody else! He's gone." Taking a deep breath, he leaned his head back and declared, "By now, Max Masterson is getting a small taste of the kind of hell he put us through. In a few hours we'll have avenged Dakota's death. You have to promise me to let him go now. That was our deal."

Pam nodded. Looking at her own reflection in the window, she was quiet as the miles rolled by. When they stopped to fill up with gas in the small town of Poteau, she stayed in the pickup. Once Craig was out of sight, she turned to the back seat and smiled. Although to the outside world the seat appeared to be empty, she nodded and said, "I know, son. He doesn't understand. But it's okay now. Everything you asked us to do has been done."

« « «   » » »

With Cal's help, Max's prediction that they would be at the scene by noon came true. Since most SAR teams aren't fortunate enough to have a helicopter at their disposal, they were the first to arrive at the public parking lot where Kaycee's car had been abandoned. Based on *OneEarth's* directions, the local sheriff's department had located the vehicle and sealed off the vicinity. As soon as they landed, Agent Collier assumed command of the investigation.

Because it was a weekday and school was still in session, the recreation area was deserted. The Lexus had been parked in the far corner of a gravel lot, backed into a slot beneath a tree so that the license plate wasn't visible from either the road or the playground on the opposite side. Agent Collier insisted that the car remain untouched, so that the FBI's forensic team would be able to collect as much evidence from it as possible.

Although no one expected Kaycee to be in the near vicinity, Max gave Stagga her scent and commanded him to search. Within a few minutes, he returned to the site, confirming their suspicions that her abduction was following the same course as the others. The car was nothing more than a carrot dangling on a stick, a way to lure the rescuers to the general area.

Agent Collier, Randy, Joan, Cal, and the Polk County Sheriff were all gathered around the squad car scrutinizing a map of the Ouachita National Forest. As soon as Max walked up, Agent Collier introduced him. "Max Masterson, this is Sheriff Redman."

Shaking hands, the sheriff said, "Just call me Red."

Max instantly liked the soft-spoken older gentleman. Tall and dark, he had a friendly smile and seemed genuinely eager to help. "And I prefer Max and this is Stagga. Thank you for your help."

"Anything you need, all you have to do is ask. Mena is a quiet retirement community, and there isn't a soul in this area who wouldn't be glad to help in any way they can." Returning to his map, he ran a finger along the shaded green area that designated the national forest lands as he asked, "Are you all familiar with this part of the country?"

Everyone except Max shook their heads.

"This is the only national forest in the United States where the mountain ranges run from east to west instead of north and south. People who are used to hiking in other parks frequently get turned around out here, so be careful and check your compasses. There are also bears in this area. We haven't had any trouble recently, but it's still a good idea to be alert, especially since they may have cubs this time of year."

Reacting to the looks Randy and Max both gave her, Joan shot them a scowl. "Don't even think it."

Max grinned as Randy added, "Seriously, keep the gun where you can get to it. There's no use taking chances."

"Yes, sir," Joan snapped before giving him a playful hug.

Red continued, "We're also dealing with an extreme drought, so many of the creeks and streams that are noted on your maps will be dry right now. If a heavy rain should come in, there could easily be flash floods in the low lying acres."

Turning to Cal, Max asked, "What kind of weather will we be facing?"

Cal replied, "This afternoon is going to be warm and calm, but a front is supposed to come through around midnight. The wind will kick up quite a bit, but the chance of rain is still slim."

"How windy?"

"Overnight the gusts could be between twenty and thirty, then tomorrow it'll drop back to ten to fifteen."

Red shook his head. "This has been an unusual spring — it already feels like June or July. Maybe that global warming stuff isn't such nonsense after all."

Max replied, "Right now, the warm air will help the scent rise. A little wind is good, but too much is bad. How well do cell phones pick up in these mountains?"

"They're sporadic at best, and that's from the top of the peaks. This isn't a very populated area, so there aren't a lot of microwave towers." With a curious look, he asked, "Don't you communicate with each other by radio?"

"Yes, but there's a slight possibility that our victim has a cell phone with her. Once she regains her senses, she might try to call for help. If she succeeded, the cell phone people could narrow down her position by triangulating the signal from the towers."

Agent Collier added, "We've already alerted them to watch for any action on her account."

Red asked, "Why don't you try to call her?"

"If she's managed to hide the phone and the Sandersons are still with her, its ring could put her in jeopardy," Max replied.

"I thought they always dumped their victims and ran."

Agent Collier stated, "We have no way of knowing how long they stay with them before they're found. The only survivor says that the drug they gave him made him lose all sense of time. We just can't take the chance."

"Do they usually leave their victims in a particular type of forest land?" Red asked.

Agent Collier asked, "What do you mean by type?"

"Do they choose the highest mountain? The point farthest from any trails? Somewhere away from a source of water? Areas designated as wilderness preserves?"

"I can't technically answer your question," Max said, "but I know that the first three were definitely left in sections that had virtually no exposure to trails and roads. They were also densely forested. The last woman was near a trail, but in an area that had no direct access to it without rock climbing gear."

The sheriff tapped his finger on the map over two tracts of land marked as the Poteau Mountain Wilderness. "There are no trails in either portion of these sections, and not much water because of the drought. Would they be within the right distance from here?"

Agent Collier replied, "There's no way to tell. The first abandoned car was located a few miles from where the victim was found, but there hasn't been any obvious pattern established from the recovery of the other vehicles. In the last case, the vehicle was never moved — it was left in the garage. That victim was found within a few miles of her home, so it's probably not relevant to Kaycee's case."

Red shrugged. "Then what's the farthest point a vehicle was discovered from the victim?"

"Around twenty miles."

The sheriff took a pencil and drew a circle that encompassed a large part of the national forest, extending west into Arkansas and east across the Oklahoma border. Shaking his head, he admitted, "Guess that's too big an area to be of much help."

Max stared at the circle, his eyes focused on the Oklahoma side of the map. Slowly an idea formed in his mind, until he finally declared, "I think I know where we should start."

All eyes turned to him.

Pointing at the Winding Stairs National Recreational Area on the Oklahoma side of the national forest, he stated, "The Sandersons were camped somewhere in this area when Dakota wandered away.

Seeing that circle on the map made me realize that it's possible that they've come full circle as well."

Joan's eyes lit up. "You think they left Kaycee in the same place that Dakota disappeared?"

"Or possibly where his body was found. Whether we can see the patterns or not, I think we would all agree that the Sandersons have done extensive planning to carry this off, and that they've methodically moved from victim to victim. From the book to the injection of hallucinogens to keep their victims too confused to find help in time, they knew exactly what they were doing. It's logical that they would want to end their killing spree in the same place it all started."

Agent Collier said, "At this point, it's your call, Max. You tell me where you want to search and that's where I'll have the teams report."

Taking a deep breath, Max knew that Kaycee's life rested on his shoulders. Looking at Randy, Joan, and Cal he stated something they'd all heard many times. "Always trust your instincts. My gut tells me that the Sandersons' need for revenge will pull them back to where Dakota died. Unfortunately, I was in a different sector when he was found. Although I heard the reports, I was never actually at the exact location."

"Then what are we waiting for? You know the general area, right?" Cal asked.

Max nodded and replied, "I can get us close enough for the dogs to take over." Jogging with the others toward the helicopter, he added, "It was a long time ago. I'm sure the terrain has changed a lot in the last ten years. We need to request a copy of the official report on the search and recovery of Dakota."

Agent Collier called, "Already done. One of my coworkers will have it with him when he arrives in a few minutes."

Once they were in the air, Max keyed the intercom to announce, "I think we should establish the base at the mountaintop camp site adjacent to the Talimena Scenic Byway. It has ample room for Cal to land, full facilities, and it's near a hiking loop with access to the Ouachita National Recreation Trail. Since Randy and Joan have no business long-lining right now, Cal can drop me near the east edge of the search zone, then I'll work my way back toward the base. Randy can work north of the base, Joan can take the south sector. Once the LaSAR teams arrive later today, they can begin working the more mountainous east/west grids that will connect with my area."

"You're planning on staying in the field, aren't you?" Randy asked.

"I don't see any reason not to at this point. Stagga is rested and ready. Even if Cal flew me in and out of the base, I'd be too worried to get any rest. I've got ample supplies in my pack, I'll be fine."

Agent Collier keyed in. "As the Incident Commander, I can't let you do anything that might risk your life."

Everyone tried to stifle their laughter as Max asked, "Who's going to stop me?"

« « «   » » »

Kaycee slowly came back to reality, awakened by the noise of her stomach growling. Since she had been tucked in a tight ball for several hours, her feet had gone to sleep and she had little sensation in her right arm. Still muddled from the drug, she had no recollection of her panicked flight through the forest, much less of where she was or why she was there.

Feeling completely helpless, she sat up and looked around. In response to her stomach grumbling again, she rubbed it and wondered how long she had been stranded. Judging from the fact that her hunger was only surpassed by an all-consuming thirst, she guessed that it could have been days. The smell of something foul had been growing since she'd awakened, and she slowly came to realize that she was the one who reeked.

Scanning her surroundings, she saw that she was three-quarters of the way down a steep embankment densely packed with trees of every size. The canopy was so thick that there was little besides dead leaves and twigs littering the forest floor. The opposite side of the hill appeared to be a mirror image, divided from its twin by a narrow dried creek bed at their base. The cracked ground where water once flowed made Kaycee realize the critical nature of her situation once again. Already thirsty, she swallowed hard.

Stiff and achy, she tried to stretch and flinched when a sharp pain shot through her right hip. Pushing down the top of her jeans, she saw two puncture wounds sealed with dried blood. From the amber stain beneath the lower of the two, it was clear that she had been right — the hypodermic had gone in one side then out the other, sparing her another full dose of the drug.

The uncomfortable sensation of pins and needles spread through her feet and legs, announcing the return of full circulation. Knowing better than to try to move until the irritating feeling passed, she closed her eyes and fought to remember what had happened. Bits and pieces returned in jumbled flashes, although she couldn't discern the real events from those that had to have been her imagination. Was she really dumped in a coffin and buried alive? If so, how did she get out? Did she jump into a black void to escape a ghost, or were both the flight and the ghost figments of her imagination? Although she knew the sky couldn't bleed, she shivered and recalled a woman's haunting voice declaring her impending death.

Rattled by the memories, she shook her head and realized that a new noise was overpowering the quiet rhythm of the forest. With mechanical precision, the steady *chirp chirp chirp* grew closer and stronger. Listening with detached fascination, the helicopter was almost overhead before Kaycee understood the significance of its presence.

She leaped up, but her tingling feet refused to cooperate. Realizing the creek bed was the only place with even a small opening in the canopy of trees, she fell several times making her way to the bottom of the hill. The helicopter was flying high and fast as it passed a few hundred yards to the north, its occupants completely oblivious to her waves and cries for help.

After watching the tail rotor disappear behind the mountains, she succumbed to an overwhelming feeling of desperation. Collapsing, she slumped to the ground and wallowed in self-pity for several minutes. *Who am I? Why am I here?*

Slowly, a vague sense of self-recognition began to wash over her. With it came a cognitive awakening, as though the gears in her brain were finally falling back in synch. First she became aware of her past — of who she was, where she belonged, and what must have happened. Memories rushed back, some brought tears to her eyes, while those of the recent months spent with Max made her smile.

In spite of the intentions of the Natural Killers, she found a reason to rejoice. She'd seen enough of the helicopter to know that it was Cal's Bell 427, which meant that Max was close by, already searching for her. They had found the last two victims alive, and they would find her, too. Taking a deep breath, she wondered what she should do to make certain that happened as quickly as possible.

Although she and Max had only been together for a couple of months, she felt as though she had known him for years. During the winter, it hadn't been unusual for them to sit from dusk to dawn snuggled in front of a roaring fire, discussing their past and planning their future. Since search and rescue work was a major part of Max's life, she had found the stories he shared both fascinating and educational.

Hug A Tree and Survive, Kaycee remembered, thinking of the night that Max described the program designed to educate children about what to do if they got lost or separated from their family or friends while in the woods. Perusing the surrounding trees, she tried to find one that fit the plan's standards. "Lost people are supposed to find a tree and stay put. It should be one near a clearing where they can be spotted from the air, and if possible, they should make a large X with rocks, sticks or in the dirt." With a sigh, she added, "I guess I already blew that chance."

Since the trees were so thick, she decided to hike to the top of the slope, hoping to find a place with better visibility. As she walked, she poked her hands in the front pocket of her sweatshirt and abruptly stopped. Her heart pounded as she remembered cramming half the stuff in her purse into that pocket.

Closing her fist around the treasures, she dropped to her knees and carefully spread them on the forest floor. There was a pair of needlepoint scissors, a roll of wintergreen Lifesavers, a plastic tube of aspirin, a metal fingernail file, a compact, a small packet of Kleenex, and a granola bar. Frantically checking the pockets of her jeans, she cried, "The phone! Where's my cell phone?"

Remembering her terrorized escape from Dakota's ghost, she knew that at least part of it had been real. As she ran, her phone must have fallen out of her pocket. Looking around, she knew that it could be anywhere.

« « «   » » »

Max and Stagga had searched all afternoon without any luck. As the sun began to slip beneath the horizon, he glanced at his watch. Realizing that they were overdue for a rest period, he called Stagga and rewarded the dog for his hard work. Sloughing off his backpack, he dug out a pouch of dog food and waited while Stagga happily consumed it.

Using his camelback of water, he squirted some in the side of Stagga's mouth until he was sure the dog had quenched his thirst. For himself, Max retrieved a slab of beef jerky, a package of peanut butter crackers, and a Snickers bar. Always conscientious, he gathered all the trash and stuffed it into a different compartment of his pack.

It had been a very calm afternoon, which Max hoped accounted for their lack of progress. Without a little wind to spread the scent, Stagga would have to find Kaycee's actual trail — a more difficult challenge in such a large search area. Radioing the base camp, he quickly filled in Agent Collier on his progress and exact location.

In response, she said, "There may be some good news next time you check in."

"Really, what?"

"A truck and trailer that matches what we think the Sandersons are driving, complete with an ATV, has been located. It has stolen license plates, but that's to be expected. The forensics team is on its way there."

"Where is it?"

"Not too far. It was parked on a dirt road between here and Poteau. The farmer got suspicious and called the sheriff."

"Let me know what happens."

"I will."

"Is Cal around?" Max asked.

"He's right here."

Cal said, "Hey, buddy. What can I do for you?"

"I've been worried about Joan all day. Has she checked in lately?"

"She's fine. We've got all the LaSAR teams in the field, plus confirmations of teams responding from Fort Smith, Texarkana, and Dallas. Since reinforcements are here, Randy and Joan are on their way back to base camp. As soon as he's had a few minutes to eat and rest, I'm going to ask Randy to start flying grids with me using the FLIR."

"Good idea. It worked with Aubrey. What about Joan?"

"She can stay at the base and rest with D.C. and Smokey."

Max shook his head. "I doubt she's going to take that very well."

"Collier isn't planning to give her a choice."

"I agree. She shouldn't be taking chances. It feels like the winds are picking up a little. What's your weather guru have to say?"

"I talked to him twenty minutes ago. The front is on schedule, so expect a steady increase until midnight."

Standing, Max ruffled the fur on the dog's head. "Then Stagga and I need to get back at it before the scent scatters too much. Any word on Aubrey?"

"She's still unconscious, but the doctor says her vital signs are very strong. He's upgraded her condition from critical to guarded."

"Thank God."

Cal said, "Hang in there, buddy. We've got some of the best SAR teams in the nation on our side. We will find her."

"Thanks, Cal. Be careful up there tonight. These mountains may not be as tall as the ones in the Rockies, but I'm sure they have some tricks all their own."

"Without a few challenges this job would get boring. Besides, Randy's long overdue for a thrill ride."

"That he is!" Max replied.

"Take care."

"You, too." Max stuffed the radio into its pocket on the front of his right thigh. With his flashlight in hand, he gave Stagga the scent again and they went back to work. As if he knew what was at stake, Stagga seemed to be more alert than ever.

Darkness quickly descended, and each step heightened Max's awareness of Kaycee's vulnerability. Seconds seemed to slip slowly by, yet before he knew it hours had passed. Punching the button on the side of his watch, Max realized it was time to give Stagga another break.

When he called the order for Stagga to return, the dog immediately obeyed. Stagga was loping toward him in his usual carefree fashion, then abruptly stopped. Turning slightly into the wind, he cocked his head and stiffened.

Watching in the halo of the flashlight, Max witnessed the exact moment when Stagga caught Kaycee's scent. Unwilling to waste a second, he shouted, "Find her, boy. Find her!"

« « «   » » »

Craig and Pam had picked up their spare car from its hiding place in the parking lot of the 24-hour Wal-Mart in Ft. Smith, then abandoned the pickup early in the afternoon. In spite of Pam's insistence that they needed to distance themselves from the crime, Craig had demanded that they take the scenic route to Hot Springs. They spent the rest of the day traveling the beautiful country roads that crisscrossed the Ouachita National Forest in complete silence, Pam growing more certain with each passing minute that he was throwing away their future.

That evening when they were settled in a motel room, Pam felt as though the weight of the world was finally off her shoulders. As Craig started to shower, she switched on the late news, hoping to relax. Over the last few months she had grown accustomed to the daily updates on the infamous Natural Killers, but that night's lead story caught her completely off guard.

As the anchorwoman declared that a new search was underway, she felt her stomach tighten. She was shocked to see Kaycee Miller's Lexus backed into the parking place at the recreation area, exactly as she had left it early that morning. One hand flew to her mouth. Her eyes darted to the empty bed as she whispered, "You were right, Dakota." Louder, she called, "Craig! Come quick!"

Dripping wet, Craig rushed angrily out of the bathroom. Grabbing his gun off the dresser, he darted to the window and peeked outside. "What's wrong?"

Nodding toward the television, she seethed, "They've already started the search!"

The anchorwoman declared that the authorities were launching two of the largest manhunts in recent history — one for Kaycee Miller, the latest victim, and the other for the people suspected of being the Natural Killers. Pam gasped as she saw her own picture plastered on the television screen, followed by an equally unflattering one of Craig. As the FBI's special hotline number was flashed beneath their faces, the woman declared, "Anyone with information on the whereabouts of Pamela and Craig Sanderson should contact the authorities immediately. They are considered armed and extremely dangerous."

When the newswoman switched to the next story, Pam stormed across the room to shut off the television. "I told you this would happen! They're going to find her and we'll spend the rest of our lives rotting in jail."

A vein in Craig's forehead pulsed as he snapped, "And I told you that I had everything under control. No one is going to recognize us from those old pictures. Both of us have gray hair now and I've almost grown a full beard. Stop worrying!"

Wide-eyed, she asked, "How could you possibly have predicted this? They've *never* organized this fast before! There's no way to keep them from finding the Miller woman in time!"

Like a first grade teacher rapidly losing his patience with a slacking student, Craig shook his head. "Sure there is. How does God punish sinners?"

Pam's brows furrowed. "Forty days and forty nights of rain?"

He laughed. "Think more along the lines of something that's actually possible. I may not be able to send them straight to hell, but I can certainly make their last moments on this earth as tormented as they'll be for eternity."

A smile slowly spread across her face. "Fire?"

He nodded proudly. "I planted sets of incendiary devices that are controlled with timers. The first six are randomly spaced throughout the entire Ouachita National Forest. That's why I kept stopping today and hiking into the woods. I wanted to be certain the initial fires spread the first response teams as thinly as possible. In this part of the country, manpower will be scarce anyhow. The more fires there are, the fewer people they'll have at each location."

"When are they set to go off?"

"All hell will break loose at eleven o'clock tonight."

"Are you sure it won't just draw more people into the area?"

"Of course it will, but they'll be too focused on the forest fires to care about anything else. Once the first fires are going strong, the second set of devices will discharge. They form a mile wide circle around the spot where I dumped Kaycee Miller."

"A mile isn't very far. She could have easily hiked out of that area by now."

He shook his head. "The drug has always incapacitated the targets for the first forty-eight hours. Most of them can't even walk a straight line after three days, and we gave her a double dose before the first shot had even worn off. She may not be in the exact spot where I left her, but she won't have wandered far."

"What time will the second set start?"

"I left time for the distraction fires to get going first. With these dry conditions and high winds, that shouldn't take long. Thirty minutes after those are ignited, Kaycee Miller will find herself in a ring of fire. Even if she's coherent enough to save herself from the flames, the smoke will kill her in a matter of minutes."

Pulling Pam into his arms, Craig added, "There's no way she'll survive. No way."

Kaycee climbed to the top of the nearest ridge and chose a spot beneath a large oak tree for shelter. She had spent the pre-dusk hours gathering rocks to make an X in the small clearing by the tree. Once that mission was accomplished, she searched for a broken branch that she could use as a weapon.

As darkness began to steal the last of the light, Kaycee realized that she would have to quickly settle in for the night. For the first time since her ordeal had begun, Kaycee remembered her *retinitis pigmentosa*. With mild amusement, she realized that she had been thinking of it on a regular basis for months, and how nice it had been to forget it for awhile.

After scraping together a large pile of dry leaves under her special tree, she plopped down on top of them. The brush crunched and snapped beneath her as she watched an iridescent beetle skitter away for his own protection. She had no idea how cold it would be that night, but she didn't want to take any chances. Max had described victims who lost body heat because they had lain directly on the ground. Covering with leaves and brush was supposed to serve as insulation as the temperature fell. Unfortunately, as the wind started to blow harder, only the leaves directly beneath her were safe from its influence.

Speaking aloud, she said, "Find the positive side. Let's see, snakes are cold-blooded. Being cold is bad, but being snake free is good."

It seemed like every part of her ached, from her toes to her hair, so she rewarded herself with a wintergreen Lifesaver. Since she had learned that she was going blind, she had spent many hours talking with her friend and mentor, Ellen Henderson, who had encouraged her to begin developing her other senses, especially the two she would need the most: hearing and touch. Kaycee had been a diligent pupil, practicing the basic skills every day in spite of her rigorous schedule.

As the creatures of the night brought the forest to life, Kaycee wished she hadn't been quite so tenacious. Every new noise brought a shiver of fear. The growing wind made the trees creak and bend, which seemed to be an invitation to the forest's nocturnal inhabitants to chirp even louder.

Hoping to muffle the unnerving sounds, she cinched the hood of her sweatshirt around her face and tried to relax by taking long, deep breaths. Feeling a little better, she allowed herself another bite of the granola bar. Exhausted, she leaned against the tree and dozed off for a few hours.

Kaycee awoke in the dark, completely terrified. Every joint throbbed, and every muscle was so stiff that she wondered if she had miraculously aged twenty years like Rip Van Winkle. The wind was blowing even harder, amplifying the creepy noises to a level that made her skin crawl. Certain that every insect within a hundred miles was swarming toward her, she frantically swatted the imaginary bugs away, then tugged her arms out of the sleeves so that they were inside the sweatshirt next to her body. Bending her knees, she tucked her legs inside it, too, hugging them as she began rocking back and forth.

Logically, she knew the images that began taunting her couldn't be real, but that made no difference. It was only after the fact, when one vanished and another appeared that she could grasp reality for a few moments. During those fleeting bits of sanity, she cursed the Sandersons and the effects of their horrible drug.

When the last of the hallucinogen took control of her mind, Kaycee was certain that a pack of wolves was slowly closing in on her. A life-size image of Joan appeared a few feet away, her pleading eyes warning of the peril they faced. The moment Kaycee reached for Joan, she saw that the tender flesh of her neck had been torn completely asunder. Before her eyes, Joan's canine teeth began dripping blood and hair started to appear on her face.

Screaming, Kaycee ran blindly into the night.

« « «   » » »

Randy was diligently watching the screen of the FLIR when Cal said on the intercom, "We're running low on fuel. Once we complete this grid we'll need to go back to base."

Responding with a thumbs up, Randy's gaze never left the small display on his lap. "This is truly a fantastic contraption."

"No kidding. I'll have to see what we can do about getting one to keep."

The screen of the FLIR suddenly came to life. "What the hell was that?" Randy exclaimed.

"Need me to swing around for another look?"

"You bet. I know I haven't been at this very long, but I think it was something really strange."

"Such as?"

"Maybe an explosion. From the upper right corner, the whole screen flashed white. But the display looks normal now."

Cal replied, "Could be a malfunction."

"I'm sure it was, but let's swing around to double check just in case."

As Cal maneuvered the helicopter back into position, Randy asked, "Wouldn't the upper right quadrant be northwest?"

"Affirmative. Coming up on it now."

"Oh, my God. Look." Randy tilted the display so that Cal could see it. Even though the image was in black and white, it was clearly a tree going up in flames. Taking their eyes off the tiny screen, they looked down at the ground in time to see the fire jump to three different trees. Tiny white spots on the screen began to appear as ashes were scattered by gusts of winds. They had witnessed the birth of a living, growing triangle of fire.

Randy's concern was obvious as he asked, "Could Kaycee have started it?"

"I doubt it. Did you see any image that could've been human?"

"No. One minute there was nothing, the next the screen was white. There was never any indication of a person in the vicinity. But then again, fires don't just start themselves." As Cal turned the nose of the helicopter into the wind, it became painfully clear how fast the blaze would spread.

"Is there anything we can do to stop it?" Randy asked.

Cal swung around hard, "Not from here. I don't have the equipment to do a water drop, and we don't have anything on board large enough to even make a dent in it."

Switching to his radio, Cal alerted the proper authorities, then climbed to a higher altitude to return for refueling. He had just radioed Joan when Randy signaled for him to look to the east. The new altitude had exposed two more fires dotting the horizon.

Cal immediately radioed the base. Joan answered, "Base Station Command. Go ahead, Cal."

"We have an emergency. Call back all SAR teams immediately. We've now spotted a total of three . . . No, four! fires in the search zone. In these winds, they're spreading rapidly. Have you heard from Max?"

"He checked in half an hour ago. Stagga's hot on a trail."

"They're the farthest from the base. I'll need to pick him up in about fifteen minutes, so find out where he's going to be."

"Will do."

"I need Larry to get ready to refuel us, is he nearby?"

"Hold on while I find him."

A minute passed before he heard Larry ask, "What can I do to help?"

"We'll need to refuel in a hurry. There will be a lot of spot-overs from the initial fires. Without air support they'll be devastating. Get on the phone and call in everyone we know who has a bucket and is willing to help. Tell them to call their friends, too."

"Will do. What's your ETA for refueling?"

"Five minutes."

"See you then."

Once Cal had signed off, Randy asked, "What's a spot-over?"

"In winds this high, they're our worst enemy. A gust of wind can pick up an ember and carry it for miles. If it lands in more dry brush, then a new fire starts. In a matter of minutes there can be hundreds of hot spots. One of the most effective uses for helicopters is controlling spot-overs. A bucket dropped on the newly started fire can stop it before it has time to spread."

"How much water do these buckets hold?"

"It varies. There are Bambi Buckets that hold anywhere from 1300 to 2600 gallons and can be filled in less than a minute."

"Filled from where?"

"Usually the closest lake or pond. In a well-organized effort, an air racetrack is formed using multiple helicopters. The pilots fly an oval from the lake to the hot spots. They make their water drops, then repeat the cycle. In a perfect world you could have enough helicopters to keep a constant water flow along the front line. Unfortunately, with the multiple fires we're looking at, plus the limitations of both equipment and manpower, this isn't going to be pretty."

"I don't suppose you have a bucket handy right now?"

"There's one back at R.R.M. If I know Larry, he's got everyone scrambling already."

For a couple of seconds Randy was quiet. His voice was soft when he finally asked, "Any chance that Max and Stagga will get trapped in this?"

Cal sighed. "There's always a chance. Flying in the dark in heavy smoke isn't exactly a smart thing to do. The sooner we get them out of there, the better."

"What about Kaycee?"

After a long silence, Cal replied, "She could use a miracle about now."

« « «   » » »

Although the winds were obviously playing tricks with Kaycee's scent, Stagga diligently led Max through the forest at an impressive pace. With each step, Max's expectation of finding Kaycee alive soared. They were maneuvering down a particularly steep embankment when he heard Joan's voice calling, "Base Station Command to Rescue One. Come in Rescue One. Come in."

After giving Stagga the order to halt, Max slid a little farther down the hill until he came to a spot where he could brace himself against a sturdy tree. Taking out his radio, he replied, "Rescue One."

In a flat voice, Joan stated, "I'm sorry to have to break this to you, but the search has been temporarily called off. Cal will be picking you up in about fifteen minutes. We need your exact location."

Allowing his knees to buckle, Max slid down the tree until he was on solid ground. Still winded, he keyed the radio and muttered, "Why?"

"There are six confirmed forest fires scattered throughout the park at this time. We need all personnel accounted for at the base station until the fires are under control."

"What about Kaycee?"

Joan's voice cracked. "Max, we're all aware that you're on her trail. As soon as the danger passes, we'll flood the area with SAR teams. Right now, we need to protect your life, too. We both know that once the smoke gets too thick, a long-line pickup will be impossible."

As if the mere suggestion of smoke made it a reality, Max caught the first whiff. Slipping off his backpack, he took out two bandanas and soaked them with water.

"Max, are you there?"

"Yes."

"I need your coordinates."

"Sorry, my GPS seems to be broken."

Randy broke in to say, "Don't do this, pal. We know your GPS is fine. What's more important is that the smoke is going to mask Kaycee's scent. Even if you do manage to find her, you'll both be trapped."

"That's a risk I'm willing to take."

"Dammit, Max. Be sensible! Kaycee wouldn't want you to sacrifice yourself."

"Listen. Stagga's close. I can feel it. The smoke has just reached this area, so I can't waste another second. I'll call you when I find her. Thanks for caring, but don't try to stop me. I've made up my mind. Rescue One out."

He stuffed his radio in his pocket and tied the wet bandana around his face. Hugging Stagga, he gave him a drink and said,

"We've got to work fast, boy. Give it all you've got."

Max unzipped the front pocket of his backpack and took out Kaycee's pillowcase. He gave Stagga the scent one more time and they were back in business. If the smoke was affecting his trailing abilities, it didn't show.

Three minutes later, Max stopped when a sudden *crack!* pierced the air. Turning toward the sound, he watched in disbelief as sparks flew out of a small device nailed to a tree. The sickening reality struck home as, one by one, the leaves scattered on the ground nearby began to ignite. He called Stagga to his side and ordered him to sit. Rushing to the fire, he spent several minutes stomping out the largest spots.

As he kicked dirt across the smoking embers, he dug out his radio and called, "Rescue One to base, come in."

Agent Collier's voice carried her anger as she replied, "What's your location, Rescue One?"

"Unknown. Tell the fire chief that the fires are being started by crude incendiary devices that are on timers. They're nailed about a foot off the ground and spray sparks in an arc about five feet long."

After a couple of seconds, she replied, "Affirmative on the arson. Is it possible to recover one of the devices?"

"I'll try. Rescue One out."

As he stuffed the radio back in his pocket, Max could hear Collier's angry demands that he continue their conversation. Ignoring her, he carefully touched the metallic device through the extra bandana and instantly recoiled. It was extremely hot, so much so that it might still pose a fire threat.

Unwilling to waste precious time, he stepped back and landed a solid kick on its side. It flew off the tree, rolling onto the ground a few feet away. Since it was still too hot for him to carry in his backpack, he decided to bury it. Unfastening the small collapsible shovel from the side of his pack, he dug a shallow hole, kicked it in, then covered it with dirt. Grabbing his GPS, he logged the exact location so that it could be recovered by the police after the crisis had passed.

Satisfied that the area was temporarily safe, he gave Stagga the scent again and they took off. The smoke was growing so thick that his eyes were beginning to burn. Although he tried to keep a close eye on Stagga, it was next to impossible. His flashlight was rapidly becoming useless, its strong beam reflecting back at him because of the smoke.

Max almost tripped over Stagga when he abruptly stopped. Squatting at his side, he held the extra damp bandana over the dog's nose and mouth, allowing him to breathe the filtered air. Stagga was starting to shake from instinctive fear. Max wrapped him in his arms and tried to soothe him. In a few seconds, he had calmed down.

"I know that I'm asking a lot, boy. Let's try one last time." Taking out Kaycee's pillowcase again, he took the bandana off Stagga's muzzle and urged, "Find her, boy! Find her!"

Rejuvenated, Stagga took off again. Less than a hundred yards later, he stopped so quickly that he actually slid on the forest floor. Turning back toward Max, he hoarsely started to bark.

« « «   » » »

Cal was pacing outside the recreation shelter that had been designated as the SAR base. He was emitting so much nervous energy that he seemed close to the point of exploding. "We can't just sit here and let them burn to death. We have to do something!"

Randy sighed with frustration. Angrily throwing the bag of ice off his swollen leg, he asked, "How much longer until your friend gets here with that water bucket for the helicopter?"

Glancing at his watch, Cal snapped, "An hour. It'll be too late."

"Is there any other way to rig a water drop? Couldn't we just find a big container and hook it to the cable?"

"There wouldn't be a way to dump the contents. And even if we did attempt a one-shot wonder, the water and container would hit like a bomb — uneven dispersal, no accuracy. The coverage area would be too small to be of any benefit and if it happened to hit a person it would probably kill them."

Joan had been sitting with her eyes closed, eavesdropping on their conversation. Bolting up, she said, "I just remembered! We need Agent Collier to call Kaycee's cell phone!"

Looking at her as though she'd lost her mind, both men simultaneously asked, "What?"

"We couldn't risk calling it earlier because if it rang it might've endangered her life. Apparently, the Sandersons started the fires to be certain she didn't get out alive. If that's the case, then they're long gone by now. Supposedly, the cell phone company can triangulate a position from the transmission towers." Reacting to their unenthusiastic responses, she added, "I'll admit, it's a longshot, but at least it's better than sitting here waiting for a miracle to land in our laps."

Randy agreed, "You're right. It's worth a try. If they can narrow down the area, at least Cal can be in the air, waiting to hear from Max."

Standing, she said, "I'll find Collier and get the ball rolling."

Cal and Randy watched her leave, then resumed pacing. After a few minutes, Joan returned. "They're working on it." Holding up a file, she said, "This is the official report on the search and recovery of Dakota Sanderson. Collier noticed a couple of minutes ago that tomorrow is the anniversary of his death." Tapping her wristwatch, Joan said, "It's almost midnight. They calculated exactly when all of this had to happen. Collier wants us to review the report one more time and see if there's anything even remotely helpful that might have been missed."

Cal declared, "I can't do this. At least if we're in the air we have a chance of spotting them. Maybe Max will shoot a signal flare, or he'll radio his position."

"I agree. Joan, you're the bookworm. Why don't you read the report? If you find something, we'll be able to respond faster if we're already in the air," Randy said.

Hugging them both, she replied, "I understand. Just be careful."

Within five minutes they were in the air again, but it was the strangest night either of them had ever encountered. Instead of looking at the world in the glow of moonlight from above, it was lit by growing lines of light dancing on the ground. In silence, they watched and mourned nature's tremendous loss.

Joan's voice filled their headphones as she radioed, "Base

Command to Air Support One."

"Air Support One. Go ahead."

"I found something buried in the back of the file that might be pertinent. At any rate, it's worth a try. The Sandersons obtained a special permit to place a small memorial marker on the exact place where Dakota was found." She rattled off the coordinates. "If they really do want this to end where it began, that might be where they left Kaycee."

Banking hard, Cal headed that way. "Good work, Joan. Let's hope you're right."

As they approached the area, Randy keyed the intercom and said, "Jesus. Just when you think that things can't get any worse . . . "

Cal's voice cracked as he replied, "I've never seen anything like it. Except for the break on one edge, it's almost a perfect ring of fire. God help us."

« « «   » » »

After seeing themselves on television, it hadn't taken long for Pam to convince Craig that they should put as much distance between themselves and the Ouachita National Forest as humanly possible. They quickly packed and headed east, planning to regroup in Memphis the next morning.

Shortly before midnight they were on Interstate 30, just west of Little Rock. Reaching over, Craig patted Pam's hand and said, "All of the fires are burning by now. In a matter of minutes Dakota's death will be completely avenged."

Fidgeting, she asked, "Can't you drive any faster?"

"No! The last thing we need to do is draw attention to ourselves. We'll do the speed limit and obey every traffic law."

She was nervously scanning the area. "I think we should get off this road. I've seen two patrol cars in the last few miles."

"If we don't stick to the Interstates, it'll take us twice as long to get out of here." Squeezing her hand he added, "We've been through so much to get this far. In a few hours we'll be headed to the Cayman Islands. There's enough money in our account there to last us twenty years. We'll be living in paradise, finally free of that horrible day's grasp."

Clutching his arm, Pam's eyes went wide. "Look!"

Orange construction cones had been established to force the traffic down to one lane by the right shoulder. Half a mile up the road, three police cars were parked end to end to form a roadblock. As they slowed to accommodate the funneling traffic, it was clear that the police were only letting one vehicle through at a time.

Slamming his fist against the steering wheel, Craig muttered a string of obscenities.

Starting to cry, Pam asked, "What are we going to do?"

Frantically scrutinizing the slight embankment on the side of the road, he replied, "Just keep quiet and try not to look upset. Open the glove box and hand me the gun."

She did as he asked. Turning off his lights, he pulled onto the grassy shoulder where the headlights from the passing traffic illuminated them as little as possible. Taking a deep breath, he shut off the engine and tucked the gun into his waistband.

Climbing out of the car, Craig walked to the front of the vehicle and propped open the hood. Casually moving to the trunk, he grabbed a rag and a container of oil and headed back toward the engine. As he walked in the cloak of darkness, his free hand rested on the butt of the gun.

At first, Craig thought that the approaching helicopter had been called as backup because they had somehow recognized his car from a distance. As the noise level increased, he calculated the odds of taking out the state trooper walking toward him. It was an easy shot, but there would be little hope of escape. Firing at the helicopter might temporarily make it move higher, but disabling it would be next to impossible.

Taking a deep breath, he looked up as the helicopter zoomed past without hesitation. A smile curved his lips as he realized that it was probably on the way to help fight the fires.

Certain their only hope was to slip past the road block unnoticed, he turned his back to the approaching officer, pulled out the dipstick, then pretended to inspect the depth of the oil. By the time he reinserted it, the quiet of the night had returned.

"Need help? A tow truck?" the trooper called.

With a friendly smile on his face, Craig turned and replied in a heavy southern drawl, "No. She's just a little low on oil." Holding up the container, he added, "Once I add this quart we'll be back on the road. See you in a couple of minutes."

The trooper was still about twenty yards away. Stopping, he asked, "You sure?"

"Yep. Sorry you had to go to so much trouble. If you want to wait, we can give you a lift back to where you folks have the road blocked up there."

"No thanks. It's a great night for a walk." Turning, the trooper called over his shoulder, "Promise not to leave that empty oil container on the shoulder!"

Raising his voice, Craig called back, "I won't! Thanks again!" To complete the charade, Craig held the container upside down so that it would look as though he were adding the oil. By the time he climbed in the car beside Pam, the Trooper had rejoined his coworkers.

"Now what?" Pam asked.

Craig started the car and said, "Just watch." Shifting into drive, he left his headlights off as he very slowly drove up the embankment, over its crest, and into the small field next to the road. Bumping through the uneven grass, he wound around several trees until he emerged on a narrow paved road. Rolling down the window, he waited to hear the sound of sirens, but none ever came.

Turning to Pam he smiled and said, "See? You just have to have faith. Once they determined that I wasn't a problem, they quit watching me so carefully. When they realize I'm gone, they'll think I pulled back in traffic."

Pam nodded. "Dakota says that you're pretty clever and that he's glad you didn't use the gun."

Craig started to reply, but changed his mind. In silence, they drove.

« « «   » » »

Stagga continued barking as Max ran to him. Although it was a hoarse version of the bark that indicated he had found his target, Max couldn't see anyone. Kneeling at the dog's side, he covered his nose with the wet rag again, giving him a chance to breathe more clean air.

While he waited, he noticed that Stagga was sitting in a large pile of leaves beneath an oak tree. Using the flashlight, he scanned the area and spotted the X made of rocks. Hugging Stagga, he said, "Good boy!"

Max called, "Kaycee! Can you hear me? Kaycee!"

Listening with all his heart, he heard only the wind. The smoke suddenly grew more dense. Certain he could no longer keep track of the dog from a distance, he snapped on his leash and said, "Come on, Stagga. Find her, boy! Find her!"

With his head held high, the dog started in one direction, then hesitated. Circling, he whimpered. Max realized that the smoke was wreaking havoc with his senses. "Come on, boy! Try hard. Find her!"

Although he started three times before kicking back into high gear, Stagga finally found her scent again. Max had to run to keep up as the dog dashed between trees and under low limbs. Time and again he ran into branches that tore his flesh, but he didn't feel any pain.

Out of the blue, Stagga started barking as he ran. Max had never seen him act so confused. Lunging, the dog pulled fiercely against the leash as though he were desperate to be free of it. Leading Max in a semicircle, he actually stopped at one point and turned to bite the leather. Ordering him to halt, Max knelt at his side.

As he checked Stagga for injuries, Max heard a *snap!* followed by a muffled cry. Realizing that Kaycee must be very close, he took the leash off of Stagga and gruffly said, "Find her, boy!"

As the dog bolted off, Max followed — listening and praying. In less than a minute Stagga's barks were joined by ear-piercing screams. Following the cacophony, Max made his way through the smoke and spotted the problem.

Kaycee was terrified, huddled against a tree and holding a stick as though she were going to smack Stagga if he dared to move. "Quiet, boy! Come!"

The dog immediately hushed and returned to his side, but it was clear that Kaycee was still paralyzed by fear. Walking slowly toward her, Max calmly called, "Kaycee, it's okay! It's me, Max. You're going to be fine now."

Shaking her head, she waved the stick, coughed, then shouted, "You're not real! None of this is real! Joan's dead!"

"Kaycee, you're okay and Joan is just fine. I know you've been though a lot. I swear, I'm very real and so is the forest fire. We've got to get out of here." He took a few steps toward her.

She seemed to stare through him before screaming, "No!" Backing away, she bumped into a different tree and stumbled. Clinging to it, she crawled back to her feet and yelled, "Get away from me! Leave me alone!"

Realizing Kaycee couldn't see him well because of the combination of darkness and smoke, Max knew what he needed to do. "Stagga, stay!" Max ordered, then began walking toward her. Instead of using the flashlight to illuminate the way, he held it in front of him so that she could see his face.

The entire time he advanced, she continued to shake her head and cough. When he was within a couple of feet, she charged him, swinging the stick like a baseball bat. Had he not ducked at the last moment, she might have broken his arm or a few ribs.

Knocking the weapon out of her hand, he pulled her against his chest. She continued to struggle for several seconds as he soothed, "You're okay, Kaycee. Everything is going to be all right." Finally, she began to relax.

"Are you sure you're real?" she sobbed, her fingers gently touching his face.

"I'm sure."

"I couldn't see you. It looked like you were floating."

Max wrapped her tightly in his arms. "That was just the way the light was reflecting off the smoke. I really need to radio for help right now. Do you promise you won't try to run away if I let go of you?"

Her reply was a soft nod. "I don't know what's wrong with me. I keep seeing crazy things."

"They gave you a drug that has long lasting hallucinogenic effects." Easing his grip, he watched her intently as he pulled the radio out of his pocket and said, "Rescue One to Command Base."

"Go ahead, Rescue One," Joan replied.

"I've located Kaycee. We're in heavy smoke. Stand by for our exact coordinates."

In the background he heard everyone cheering as she replied, "Great job, Max! Well done!"

Shrugging off his backpack, Max found his GPS. After dictating the exact location, he said, "Any chance of a long-line pickup under these conditions?"

"Cal is in the air and en route to your location. He's requested you deal directly with him from this point. Base Command, out."

Max waited a second, then asked, "Cal are you there?"

"I'm here. Everyone okay?"

"Ten-four, but this doesn't look good."

"I'm going to drop my altitude and see if there's any better visibility."

"We'll stand by." For the first time, Max looked around. The blowing smoke made it impossible to assess their situation. Taking out his water, he told Kaycee, "You need to take a small drink, okay?"

She didn't reply, but responded as he squirted the fluid on her lips. Afraid to startle her, he soaked another bandana and explained, "I'm going to tie this around your face to filter the smoke."

"All right. Can Stagga come here?"

Max smiled. "Sure. Stagga, come!"

Stagga's tail was tucked between his legs as he approached them and sat down next to Kaycee. Wrapping him in her arms, she said, "Thanks, boy."

Max asked, "Are you feeling well enough to help?"

Eagerly nodding, she said, "I'll try."

"I need you to hold this damp rag over Stagga's nose and mouth. It can't be too tight. He's been pretty good about letting me do it."

"Okay." Very gently, Kaycee did as he asked. The sound of the helicopter seemed to float all around them. It grew louder for a few moments, then more distant again.

Sweat burned Max's eyes and for the first time he realized that the temperature was rising rapidly. Keying his radio, he coughed, then carefully worded his question so that Kaycee wouldn't be alarmed. "Hey buddy, things are getting really tight here. Any tactical suggestions?"

Cal replied, "Can you move to a different location?"

"How far?"

"We can see one exit corridor, but you're a good half mile from it."

Max thought for a few seconds, and knew that there was no way the three of them could make it that far under the circumstances. "Not possible in this smoke. What's it look like from up there?"

"Code red."

"How close?"

"Unless there's a drastic wind shift, it'll be on top of you in less than ten minutes. You're near the north side of an almost perfect ring of fire. We have helicopters flying in from Little Rock with water drop capability. They'll be here soon, but probably not soon enough." With a mixture of anguish and frustration, Cal added, "The visibility is too limited to attempt a long-line rescue."

Max sighed. "I understand."

Max took Kaycee's face in his hands and said, "In order for us to survive, you're going to have to trust me. It isn't going to be easy, but I know it will work. Promise to do exactly as I ask?"

She nodded.

Dumping the contents of his backpack on the ground, he said, "I need you to sit still and keep that rag over Stagga's mouth while I get everything ready. We're going to dig in. This fire is moving so fast that it will flash burn right over us."

Kaycee's eyes went wide. "Can't Cal just pick us up?"

Max spread out two pieces of rectangular material that looked like something from a spacesuit. "Not this time. Too many trees, too much smoke. But don't worry, everything will be fine."

"What are those?"

"They're thermal blankets. I'm going to dig a place for us to wait out the fire. As I dig, I'll pile dirt on top of the blankets. When the fire gets really close, we'll lie in the hole and pull the dirt-covered blankets over the top of us."

"We'll suffocate!"

"No! We'll be fine. Remember, you promised to trust me."

She nodded, then called, "I want to help dig, too!"

Grabbing his shovel, he began digging. "I only have one shovel. If you really want to help, just take care of Stagga and stay out of my way."

"I still don't understand how this will keep us alive."

Coughing, Max worked as fast as he could as he explained, "Fire travels quickly up the windward side of a hill, then slows down over the crest. We'll dig a shallow pit here, cover ourselves with dirt, and wait until it burns past us. Once the smoke clears a little, Cal will pick us up in a matter of seconds. He has our exact location, but can't get close enough because of the smoke."

A gust of hot wind carried a heavy wave of sparks and burning leaves. "Right."

Max raised his voice to ask, "What's your sweatshirt made of? Cotton?"

Looking at him as if he had lost his mind, Kaycee replied, "I have no idea. Why?"

"The jeans are cotton, so they're okay, but if you're wearing anything that has synthetic fibers in it you need to take it off."

"Because?"

"It could melt to your skin, plus some synthetic fibers flash burn."

Kaycee froze for a second, then began taking off her bra from underneath the sweatshirt. Tossing it away, she called, "Should I take off Stagga's collar and rescue vest? The collar has a metal buckle!"

"Yes!"

Max took off his flourescent orange vest and laid it next to her discarded bra and Stagga's things. As he dug, they were quickly covered with dirt. The fire was growing so close that they could see the flames jumping from tree to tree. The pit slowly began to take shape.

After a few more minutes, Max signaled for Kaycee and Stagga to move closer. Coughing, he said, "I think it's time. Lay down on your back, right in the center."

Glaring at what looked like a shallow grave, then at him, she asked, "What about you and Stagga?"

"Trust me!"

Another gust of wind carried even larger chunks of burning debris. Instinctively cowering, Kaycee was stunned when Max suddenly threw her to the ground and began pounding her hair into the dirt. When he finally stopped, he wrapped her in his arms and said, "Sorry. Your hair was on fire."

"Oh, my God!"

"Did it burn you?"

"I don't think so."

"Good. Now stretch out flat. Stagga, come!"

As if he knew his life was in Max's hands, Stagga sprang to attention. Squatting next to Kaycee, Max patted the freshly exposed dirt at her side and commanded, "Stagga, down!"

Stagga snuggled close, resting his nose in the crook of Kaycee's arm as she wrapped it around him. Max took off his lightweight jacket and placed the stick that Kaycee had been using as a weapon across the top part of the hole. He quickly explained, "This jacket is flame retardant material. The stick will help trap air underneath it. We'll put it over our faces so that we can still breathe. I'll pull the first dirt-covered blanket over the two of you from above, then jump in right next to you at the last moment. Once the blanket is in place on top of you, try not to move at all. Understand?"

"Yes. Hurry!"

From the intense heat and the roar of the fire, they both knew they didn't have much time. Kaycee squeezed Stagga close as Max placed the jacket over their heads. She started shaking violently and could barely contain the urge to flee. Tears ran freely, absorbed by the damp cloth across her face.

Moving as fast as he could to keep the dirt from spilling over the sides, Max pulled the first covered blanket over Kaycee and Stagga. When it was perfectly positioned, he sat in the hole next to Kaycee and picked up the narrow end of the second blanket. As he pulled it forward, he eased his body down until his head was just above the jacket propped up by the stick.

Max wiggled until his head was beneath the protected area and he was lying next to Kaycee. Although he wanted to hold her in his arms, the best he could do was carefully shift his arms so that they were at his side. Much movement could expose one or both of them to the fire's intense heat, so he had to settle for simply being close.

Even though he was gasping from working in the heavy smoke, he tried to keep from breathing hard as he wrapped her hand in his. "You're doing great. Just hold really still. We shouldn't have to stay here for too long."

"I thought . . . " she coughed.

It broke his heart to feel her entire body trembling. He said, "Everything is going to be okay now, Kaycee. I know that being under here is really unnerving, but it'll be one of those things you tell your grandkids about someday."

She sighed, then coughed. "I feel like this is the second time I've been buried alive lately. I swear they brought me here in a casket."

"Not exactly. It's more like a large metal box filled with a very pungent mixture. We think they were trying to throw off the tracking dogs by making sure your scent was masked. The police recovered the box and something like compost with the Sanderson's truck."

"I remember being wrapped in a blanket, and then they started dumping stuff on me that smelled horrible. Actually, I can still smell it right now, but it doesn't seem quite as strong. I think the smoke is overpowering it."

"Me, too. However, I'll vouch for the fact that the underlying," he paused, groping for an appropriate word, "fragrance is still there. It's very distinctive."

"Was that supposed to be a polite way to tell me that I stink?" she asked.

"Well . . . yes. As a matter of fact, Cal may make you ride back on the skids. Since he's been helping find the victims of the Natural Killers, the passenger area of his helicopter has developed a distinctive smell all its own."

"Tell him I'll happily pay to have it sanitized. Probably the only thing worse than being buried alive would be dangling over a forest fire from a helicopter."

"No way! Long-lining is fun. You'll love it."

"Please tell me that I won't have to find out. Once this passes, he'll be able to land and let us walk on. Right?"

"That depends. There would have to be an area big enough to land. Most of the trees aren't burnt to the ground after a forest fire. Besides, wind currents will impact the decision." He nudged her with his leg. "If we have to long-line, I'll be right at your side. You'll never be alone."

She sighed. "When I woke up in the forest I felt like the last person on earth. I didn't know who I was, or how I'd gotten here. It was one of the worst feelings I've had in my entire life. Is their son,

Dakota, buried where they left me?"

"I don't think so."

"Do you know what happened? Once those horrible visions started it became impossible to tell what was real. I guess I imagined seeing his tombstone, but it didn't seem like it at the time."

"Actually, you probably ran into Dakota's memorial marker. If you start to hallucinate again, just remember I'm right here."

"I'll try, but logic runs and hides when these visions attack. No matter how many times I told myself that Joan hadn't grown fangs and fur, I would've sworn she had."

"Maybe you saw too many werewolf movies as a kid."

"I never want to see one again!"

He gently squeezed her hand. "Listen, I'm very sorry, Kaycee. Hopefully, the people who did this to you won't get away with it."

"They never told me why. I know it had something to do with retribution and ineptitude, but my muddled brain hasn't quite fit the pieces together. What does the book have to do with this? They made me touch it."

"As far as we know, it started out as their cover. They thought the authorities would accept the suicide story. And at first, they did. But like most criminals, the Sandersons began following the same pattern even though it didn't fit each situation perfectly. By the time they nabbed you, I think the book had become more of a symbol, a kind of trademark signature like serial killers use."

"But why did they choose me?"

Max closed his eyes. "Revenge. They've been systematically avenging their son's death."

"I never knew their son!"

"Neither did I. He was lost in this area and a SAR team found him shortly after he died of exposure. According to the FBI profilers, the Sandersons are exhibiting something called induced psychotic disorder, or shared psychosis. Most likely one of them went off the deep end when their son died and the other one eventually bought into the psychotic beliefs of the spouse. Apparently, they think that by killing people close to the members of the SAR teams who failed to find their son, they'll avenge his death. I'm so, so sorry that they hurt you. In a way, this is all my fault."

"Even exhausted and drugged I know that's not true. You saved me. And I don't just mean by digging this hole. You brought me hope when I needed it the most."

"You did the same for me, except I hadn't even realized how much I'd shut out the world. I feel like the luckiest man alive to be holding your hand right now."

Kaycee laughed. "You are quite a catch, Max Masterson. What other guy would feel lucky to be buried just inches below a forest fire?"

"If nothing else, the past few months have taught me not to take what I have for granted."

"I'll second that." Sweat ran from her brow as Kaycee added, "I seem to remember from basic chemistry that fire consumes oxygen. You can tell me the truth, Max. Is this going to be our grave?"

Max confidently replied, "We've got our own little supply of oxygen trapped in here with us. Because the area is so dry, the winds will kick the fire past us in record time. I'd guess from this heat that it's either right overhead or already moving away. We'll be fine."

Her voice was low and soft as she replied, "If we're not, I want you to know that I love you and that the last few months have been the best of my life."

A fresh wave of tears burned his eyes. "I love you, too." Chuckling, he added, "I was hoping to say that to you for the first time under better circumstances, but I suppose that this will have to do."

"Reminds me of our first date."

"Exactly."

Kaycee laughed lightly. "You do realize that there is one thing seriously wrong with our relationship, don't you?"

"What's that?"

"Until I met you, I'd never been kidnapped by a psychotic killer. Now it's happened twice!"

"And twice we've made it through. Together. Sounds like our relationship is strong enough to make it through anything."

"Let's try not to test it again for awhile, okay?"

"When we get home, I'll spray you with a can of Psychopath Repellant."

"Let me guess, it'll probably reek to high heaven. Then again, anything would be better than smelling like this."

Stagga whimpered, and Max soothed, "It's okay, boy. Hang on." It was obvious that he was panting. "I'd guess it's over a hundred degrees in here. Can you tell if Stagga's okay?"

"He's hot, but . . . all right. I've been scratching . . . his side and softly . . . patting him . . . to keep . . . him . . . calm."

"Kaycee, are you okay?"

"Getting . . . really . . . sleepy." She yawned. "Mind if I . . . take a quick . . . nap?"

Max realized that he, too, was starting to get lightheaded. Since Kaycee had been exposed to more smoke for a longer time, her lungs were probably not functioning as well as they should be. Unwilling to risk her life, he decided to try to see if the fire had passed.

Shifting slightly, he raised the side of the blanket with his left hand. Clods of dirt fell inside, followed by a wave of heat. With relief, he realized that his hand wasn't burned, and that the flicker of light in the distance was on the opposite side of them. Pushing the rest of the blanket off, he stood and pulled back the one covering Kaycee and Stagga.

"We made it!" he declared, and Stagga replied with a bark. Staying close to Kaycee, he pawed at her arm but she didn't respond. Kneeling at her side, Max tugged off both their damp bandanas, then leaned close to see if she was still breathing.

Her lips were slightly parted, but no air flowed from them.

« « «   » » »

The helicopter hovered a safe distance above the area while they watched the flames consume the trees where Max and Kaycee were trapped. As the fire marched on, Randy's eyes were glued to the FLIR, hoping to spot any sign of movement that wasn't a flame. When he finally saw the vague outline of a man, he screamed, "Thank God, they made it!"

Cal radioed, "Rescue One. We see you! I've lined up a water drop to cool your location in thirty seconds. Please confirm and prepare yourselves."

The radio was silent. Finally, Randy keyed the intercom to tell Cal, "The ground is still so hot that the images are really blurry, but it looks like only one of them is moving. Do you think the water drop would help, or hurt?"

"It'll knock the ground temperature down, reduce the smoke in the air and minimize the blowing embers. If one of them is in trouble, we don't have time to wait." Switching to the radio, Cal contacted the other pilot, then maneuvered away so that the airspace directly above Max and Kaycee would be free.

« « «   » » »

Max heard both his radio and the sound of the helicopter, but didn't have time to respond. Instead, he lightly touched Kaycee's neck to check for a pulse. Her heart was barely beating, but it *was* beating. Leaning over, he covered her mouth with his and gave her three short puffs of air.

He thought his own heart was going to stop as he waited, hoping to feel her breathe on her own. When she didn't, he tried another three breaths and said, "Come on, Kaycee, breathe for me. Please. Just take a breath." On the third attempt she abruptly began to cough, and he wrapped her in his arms.

After coughing for a few seconds, she opened her eyes and whispered, "Is it over?"

"Almost."

"Are we in the golden hour?"

Max replied, "It's nice to know you pay attention when we talk."

"It's why I hugged a tree."

Smiling, he gently kissed her. Although he had heard Cal tell him to prepare for a water drop, by the time he realized that it was about to happen it was too late to do anything. As the large military helicopter swooped low, he commanded, "Stagga, down!" Covering Kaycee with his own body, he braced himself as he whispered, "Hang on, we're about to get soaked."

The words had barely escaped his lips when the blast of water hit them like a miniature tidal wave. Although he thought he was ready, the weight and intensity of the stinging fluid knocked him off of Kaycee and crushed the breath from his lungs. Momentarily dazed, he sat up in the black muck and sucked in a long, deep breath of clean air.

Kaycee had been spared from most of the impact by his body, but she was confused and frightened. "Max! I can't see you! Max!"

"I'm right here."

"Are you okay?"

With a half-laugh, he pushed himself up and replied, "Never better." Spotting Stagga's collar and vest, he grabbed them.

Wiping the dripping soot out of her eyes, Kaycee sighed and asked, "Was that supposed to help us or kill us?"

"At this point, I'm not sure. Stagga, come!"

Stagga stood and shook himself from head to toe, drenching Kaycee and Max one more time. It was her turn to laugh as she said, "You knew he'd do that! I think you did it on purpose."

"I'm not that devious," Max replied as he checked to be certain Stagga was unharmed. Comforting him as he worked, he slipped the wet collar and vest back on and gave him a hug.

As though a star had dropped from the sky directly above them, the area was suddenly illuminated by the helicopter's powerful light. Having ignored Cal's voice on the radio for several minutes, a wave of guilt hit Max when he heard him practically beg, "Rescue One, come in!"

Digging out the radio, Max knelt at Kaycee's side as he answered, "Air Support One, sorry for the delay. Thanks for the heads up on the water drop and the spotlight to show us exactly how ridiculous we look. We'd love a ride out of here."

Cal replied, "Good to hear your voice, old pal. You had us worried. Randy is on board and ready to descend."

"No need. I'm good to go."

"You've had a rough night. Are you sure?"

"Positive. Time is critical."

"Okay. The Bell stretcher is ready and will be on its way down as soon as you give us the go ahead."

Kaycee's eyes widened and she shook her head. Coughing, she rattled, "Stretcher? I don't need a stretcher."

Taking her hand, Max keyed the radio and said, "The patient would prefer that you land to pick her up. Is that possible?"

"Negative. The closest clear spot is a third of a mile away and the ground is still glowing. Tell the princess that we've made sure there aren't any peas in the bed on board, and that we'll make the ride up as pleasant as possible."

Max leaned over and kissed her. "You promised to trust me."

She nodded. Max radioed, "The princess is awaiting her chariot. Ready here to receive the stretcher." Turning to Kaycee, he said, "For a couple of seconds you'll be alone in the dark. Can you handle it?"

Another nod.

Max quickly stepped to the opening where the stretcher was being lowered. Quietly, so that she wouldn't hear, he radioed, "Cal, she stopped breathing while we were dug in, so I don't want to waste any time getting her to the hospital. The three of us will be coming up together. Throw in a portable oxygen tank and extra blankets, okay?"

"Already done. We'll stand by for your signal."

When he returned with the stretcher, Kaycee eyed him as though he were insane. "Can't I just hold onto you?" she asked, trying to stand.

Putting a hand on her shoulder to stop her, he replied, "Stay still. From this moment on, I want you to be quiet and relaxed. It would be too dangerous for me to try to carry you up. If it makes you feel any better, Stagga will be strapped in the stretcher with you."

"Where will you be?"

"At your side. And I thought I asked you to be quiet," he scolded as he swept her in his arms and gently placed her in the stretcher. After positioning the oxygen tank and turning it on, he took a couple of long breaths, then placed the mask over her face. "This should make it a little easier to breathe."

"Thanks."

Pretending to lose his patience, Max held a finger to his lips. Once she was settled into position, he patted the spot between her legs and ordered, "Stagga, come! Down!"

Stagga hopped aboard with his tail wagging, apparently as eager to get out of there as they were. Max tucked one of the extra blankets over Stagga, leaving only his head exposed. By the time he finished wrapping up Kaycee like a papoose, her face was all that showed. Giving her a gentle kiss, he winked as he strapped them in and asked, "How does dinner at my house on Friday night sound?"

"Like heaven," she muttered, then playfully added, "If you don't want me to talk, stop asking me questions!"

"Good point." Confident they were ready, Max attached the cable and signaled Cal. He said, "We'll be inside the helicopter in a few minutes. Just stay still and let us do all the work. It's pretty windy, so it's not going to be the smoothest ride, but we'll be fine. To keep the motion from bothering you, find something close to you to stare at on the way up. Here we go."

As the winch tightened the cable, Max took his position, standing with one foot on each side of the stretcher. They began the ascent. Although the wind kicked and spun them, it was clear that Kaycee had chosen him as her focal point. He was relieved to see her intent gaze remain confident the entire way. When the last of the cable had been recoiled, Randy gave Max a hand and together they positioned the stretcher onboard and locked it in place.

Before Max buckled in, he kissed Kaycee one more time and leaned close so that she could hear him over the engine noise. "You did great. That wasn't so bad, was it?"

She smiled and softly shook her head. Seeing Randy, she mouthed, "How's Smokey?"

Randy yelled over the din, "He's fine, back to one hundred percent. Right now, you need to rest."

As if she had been waiting for permission to relax, she nodded and closed her eyes. Max settled in and Randy handed him an oxygen mask, then held up a special one that had been made by cutting the end off of one and duct taping it to another. Leaning close, Randy said, "Custom made for Stagga."

Grinning, Max placed it over the dog's muzzle, then said, "Thanks. You're the best." Breathing the pure air was practically intoxicating. As they soared toward the hospital, Max looked at his watch. Even though they would barely reach the hospital within the golden hour, he had a good feeling for the first time in weeks.

« « «   » » »

Craig drove the side streets of Little Rock, seemingly without a plan. After thirty minutes, Pam impatiently asked, "What are we going to do? We can't just drive all night."

"I think we're going to have to change our plans. With every cop in this part of the country looking for us, we don't stand much of a chance of booking a flight to the Caymans from here. Maybe we should head down to the Gulf of Mexico. We could take a cruise."

"They're still going to want identification. The police know our names."

"Okay. If you have a better idea, I'm open to suggestions."

"Dakota says we should head west, back into the Ouachita National Forest. He thinks that the police will be so busy helping fight the fires that they won't be paying attention to anything else."

Craig shook his head. "They'll probably have all the roads closed."

"The wind is blowing from the north. If we stay north of the fires, then the roads should be open. We could go to Oklahoma, then down to Houston. Maybe there we could find one of those sleazy people who make fake ID's. It's worth a try."

He hesitated. "I don't know . . . Sounds pretty risky to me."

"At this point, everything has its risks. So far, Dakota's ideas have worked really well."

Exhausted, Craig ran his hands through his hair. "Okay, but I've got to get a couple of hours of sleep. Once we get out of town, you'll have to drive."

"No problem. I'll take a little nap now, then I'll be ready to go."

Shooting a U-turn, he headed west once again. Pam propped a pillow between her head and the window and promptly drifted off to sleep. To help him stay awake, Craig turned on the radio and flipped through the channels until he found one with 24 hour news. He'd been driving half an hour when they broke in with a story about the forest fire.

Cranking up the volume, Craig listened intently: *This is a live update from 103.7, The Buzz in Little Rock. The governor has declared a state of emergency due to the extensive wildfires that are currently threatening over ten thousand acres of the Ouachita National Forest. He has authorized the National Guard to respond to help fight the fires, protect the property of those forced to leave their homes, and to provide support to the other local agencies that are involved in the crisis. An anonymous source has confirmed that the fires are currently believed to have been associated with the latest kidnapping by the Natural Killers. Kaycee Miller, the woman the Natural Killers are believed to have abducted from her Tulsa residence, has been admitted to a local hospital. We have reporters standing by both in the field and at the hospital, so stay tuned for most accurate, on the spot news.*

Craig took the next exit ramp and stopped so fast that Pam was thrown against her seat belt as it locked in place. Flipping on the map light, he was searching for a route as Pam asked, "What's wrong?"

He seethed, "Kaycee Miller is alive."

Pam shifted slightly in her seat as though she were listening to someone, then coldly replied, "Not for long."

C H A P T E R **14**

It was almost five in the morning when Kaycee was finally wheeled into a semi-private room. The moment the nurse allowed them to enter, Max, Randy, Joan, Cal and Stagga were at her side. Max happily noted that she was sitting up in bed, alert and practically beaming.

Although most of the soot had been washed away, Kaycee's dark hair was twisted in a bun sprinkled with a mixture of twigs, dirt, and ash. She was dressed in a hospital gown that was the same blue as her eyes, and her smile was the prettiest thing he'd ever seen.

Max gave her a quick kiss, then said, "Dr. Gillock says that you're going to be fine. I've been checking around and he's one of the top men in his field."

"What about you? Are you okay? Why aren't you stuck in a hospital bed?"

Winking, he said, "I know who to bribe." Giving her another kiss, he added, "Seriously, I'm good. The doctor's going to keep an eye on me for the next twenty-four hours. As I'm sure you've noticed, I'll be hoarse for a few days, but the smoke inhalation doesn't appear to have caused any long-term damage."

"And Stagga?"

"Dr. Gillock has a friend who's a vet. Believe it or not, he's such a nice guy that he drove here in the middle of the night just to check him out. Stagga will need to rest for a couple of days, but then he should be back to his old self."

Beaming, Kaycee replied, "That's great news."

Joan said, "We just wanted you to know that if you need anything, all you have to do is ask."

Kaycee smiled at Cal, Joan and Randy. "Thank you all for helping Max and Stagga find me." Motioning for him to lean close, she eyed Joan and whispered, "It's not a full moon, is it?"

He laughed, then realized that the doctor had warned him there were still trace amounts of the hallucinogen in her bloodstream. Looking her in the eye, he asked, "You're kidding, right?"

"Of course! Joan, did Max tell you that I thought you were a were-wolf?"

Tapping the white cervical collar, she replied, "Well, you know it's only been a couple of days since I was bitten. The next full moon isn't for another week or so . . . "

Randy held up a string of garlic and placed it on the bed tray in front of Kaycee. "I ran to the grocery store a few minutes ago. I figured you might want to have some handy." Winking at her, he added, "I got some for myself, too. You can never be too careful around a *tsv-s-gi-no wa ya.*"

Although the others shared curious glances, Kaycee grinned. "Oh, yes, the devil wolf. That story is probably what triggered my hallucination. Now if you could just explain the one I had where the sky ripped open and bled, I'd say you were brilliant."

Cal asked, "You know how you said that you could tell people's deep dark secrets by analyzing their handwriting? It sounds like your hallucinations might reveal more than you think."

"You really should've been a psychologist. I'd guess the sky was symbolic of my life, and the fact that it was torn asunder pretty much fit the situation I was in. I'm just happy that, thanks to all of you, my sky is in one piece again."

Squeezing her hand, Max asked, "Seriously, besides lots of rest and some food that doesn't come from a hospital cafeteria, is there anything you need?"

"What I'd really like is a shower, but they said I'll have to wait until they take out the IV later today. You should've seen the looks I got when they were rolling me down the hall! I almost pointed at the nurse and held my nose, but I was afraid she might push me out the window."

Randy shook his head. "You've got to give those horrible people some credit. They've invented the only thing that smells worse than a skunk and lasts just as long."

"I know my helicopter will never be the same," Cal laughed.

"Since you gave the princess in need a ride on your noble steed, the least you can do is let her pay to have it fumigated."

"Actually, I think it's about time to upgrade anyway. I may sell the 427 and buy me a new, improved toy."

"And I'll bet a hundred bucks that the new one will have a state-of-the-art FLIR," Randy added.

Cal winked and nodded.

"How's your sister, Cal? Is she going to be okay?" Kaycee asked.

"I talked to my mother right after we arrived here. Aubrey's still unconscious, but apparently that's not necessarily a bad sign. The doctor is still very optimistic and says that the coma may just be her body's way of dealing with the trauma."

"Did you ever find out what she was so afraid of?" Shivering, Kaycee added, "I can still feel the impact it had on her emotional state of mind. Very intense. Very personal."

"Not yet. Hopefully, she'll wake up soon and tell us exactly what happened."

Wrinkling her nose, Kaycee said, "Well, if I ever figure out the antidote for this disgusting odor, I'll share the secret with her. The victims of the Natural Killers have to stick together you know."

Max, Cal and Joan all froze, each of them realizing the same thing. Max softly said what the others were thinking. "Aubrey didn't reek from being transported in the Sanderson's metal box. All the other victims were saturated with that horrible odor."

Randy said, "Since you guys were directly involved with searching for the Natural Killers' victims, I followed the news coverage very closely. Nothing about the peculiar odor was ever made public."

"Which means that a copycat killer wouldn't have known about it," Max replied.

"You know, I overheard those horrible people talking when I was rolled up in a blanket in the back seat. They said that Solomon, Roegiers, and Newsome had all paid, and that it was Masterson's turn."

"Technically, those were the only SAR teams on Dakota's rescue. Cal just gave me a lift to the scene. I ended up riding back to Shamrock with a State Trooper who happened to be headed my way. Come to think of it, the Sandersons weren't around when I arrived at base camp that day. They wouldn't have known that Cal helped me at all."

Cal was softly shaking his head. "That also might explain why the book wasn't clean like the others. It wasn't that the Natural Killers were getting sloppy, someone wanted us to blame them but didn't know that the books had always been specially handled."

"Did they find any of the hallucinogen in her blood?" Kaycee asked.

"Not a trace," Cal replied.

"What about her diary?"

Max declared, "Just before you called my cell phone, Phoebe was looking for it. She said Peter asked her to check the master bedroom closet, so she was searching on a high shelf near where Peter said your mother's old journal was stored."

Cal shook his head. "That's not possible. I'm almost certain that my mother didn't keep one. She's had arthritis most of her adult life and has always been really self-conscious about her poor penmanship. Even in this age of computers, she has an old manual typewriter that she uses every day. She even types her checks and only writes long-hand when absolutely necessary."

Holding up her hands, Joan said, "Let's not jump to any conclusions. We really need to get Agent Collier and her team involved again."

Growing more agitated every second, Cal asked, "How could we have been so blind? When we found Aubrey, she was wearing hiking clothes. The other victims were dumped wearing the same clothes they had on when the Sandersons jumped them. Plus, from the extra food she packed, I'm sure Aubrey knew that she was going hiking and wanted to be sure she could handle any complications that might arise from her diabetes."

Max looked him in the eye and said, "That trail was too far from her house to make a round trip hike in one day. She had to have had a ride, which means she knew and trusted the person who attacked her."

"I told Mother to be careful and never leave her sight. Even so, I'll call to warn her that Aubrey is still in danger."

"Be sure to tell her not to mention it to anyone else — especially Phoebe. If that was Aubrey's journal, and it had anything in it that might incriminate her, she's probably already destroyed it. You might ask your mom whether it could have been hers, then look for it as soon as you get back there."

Cal crossed the room to stand at Kaycee's side. Giving her a gentle hug and a kiss on the forehead, he said, "You're definitely off the hook for fumigating the 427. Thanks to you, we might be able to catch the person who tried to kill my sister."

"When are we leaving?" Randy asked.

Cal snapped, "I'm leaving as soon as the helicopter is refueled. You're not going anywhere."

Grinning, Randy merely shook his head and looked at Joan.

She gave Cal a stern look. "When are you going to stop being so stubborn? You know we're not going to let you go alone. Max and I are on the injured list, which means you're stuck with Randy. Like it or not, he's going. Why fight it?"

With a sigh, Cal replied, "I don't know what I'd do without you guys."

« « «   » » »

Before sunrise the Sandersons were back in Little Rock, searching for the hospital where Kaycee Miller had been admitted. Since they were unfamiliar with the city, they stopped at a convenience store on the outskirts of town and told the clerk that their son was a firefighter who had been injured fighting the forest fire. Claiming that they had only been notified that he was being taken to the closest hospital, they asked the clerk which one was most likely to treat victims from the wildfires. He not only gave them the obvious choices, he even sketched maps of the easiest ways to drive to them.

Back in the car, Pam said, "I think we need to get some sleep before we do this. We're both tired."

To her surprise, he replied, "You're right. Let's find a hotel and get some shuteye. Considering the amount of toxin I gave her, there's no way they'll let her out of the hospital anytime soon." Laughing, he added, "She's probably locked in the psychiatric ward in a straitjacket."

Leaning close to him, Pam asked, "Are you going to miss it?"

"Miss what?"

"Teaching botany. Playing with the extracts of all those exotic plants you've got growing in the basement. It's been your life for thirty years."

He shrugged. "I've been on automatic pilot at the college for a long time now. Actually, I'm looking forward to studying the plant life in the Caribbean. It will be fascinating."

"Just imagine. No alarm clocks, no spoiled rotten students expecting you to let them make up tests at all hours. It'll be heaven."

Holding her close, he replied, "You know, we could just leave without killing the Miller woman. We can buy a boat in any city on the Gulf and sail to the Cayman Islands at our leisure."

Pam instantly recoiled. "No! We have to finish this or everything will be ruined. Come to think of it, sleeping will just delay the inevitable. Let's go straight to the hospital." Opening the glove box she pulled out a needle and a vial of the mushroom extract. "A generous dose of this in her I.V. ought to do the job once and for all."

« « «   » » »

As Randy, Cal, and Joan were leaving, Kaycee squeezed Max's hand and said, "Please stay a little longer."

Waving his friends on, he called, "Keep in touch. You know where I'll be."

Once they were gone, Kaycee admitted, "I'm sure I sound crazy, but I really don't want to stay here alone. Most of the time I feel okay, but every once in awhile I get really paranoid."

Grinning, he asked, "Did you honestly think that I was going to just walk out of here and leave you by yourself? Wild horses couldn't drag me away from you right now. Believe it or not, I have Dr.

Gillock's blessing to stay. Under one condition, of course."

"What?"

"He made me promise that we'd both get lots of rest." Nodding his head toward the empty bed, he added, "I'll hold your hand until you fall asleep, then I'll be right over there."

"What about Stagga?"

"The nurse supplied an extra blanket for him. Since the vet gave him a sedative to be sure he didn't overdo it, he's been asleep over in the corner ever since we arrived." Max walked to where he could see him and added, "He could barely walk before and now he's definitely out of it."

"I can't believe they let a dog stay in the hospital."

"He's not exactly an ordinary dog. Besides, your instant fame has increased their level of cooperation a few notches."

Her eyes narrowed. "What do you mean by fame?"

"There are camera crews set up at every entrance. Being a survivor of the Natural Killers makes you the target of all the news shows on the air. The hospital had to call in their Director of Publicity just to handle your case, and Dr. Gillock is holding a press conference in a couple of hours."

Horrified, Kaycee asked, "Surely they don't expect to talk to me?"

"I'm sure eventually they will. But for now, Dr. Gillock has made it very clear that you're completely off limits."

"Good."

Max sighed. "I don't know about you, but I'm exhausted. Let's get some rest, okay?"

"Thank you again for staying."

"There's no place in the world that I'd rather be."

Kaycee yawned, then asked, "How long was I out there?"

"Around thirty hours."

"Is that all? How did you find me so quickly?"

"I wish that Stagga and I could take all the credit, but in reality it was your new assistant, Tamara, who actually put the rescue in motion."

Kaycee's brow furrowed. "Really? How? She barely knows me."

"She reported for her first day of work to find you'd been kidnapped. She's a very perceptive young woman. It was her idea to use the OneEarth satellite system to find your car. Once we knew where to look, the rest was easy."

Kaycee's smile was contagious. "Tamara is perceptive, enthusiastic, and downright bubbly. How in the world did she know that I had *OneEarth*?"

"She figured it out from the board in your garage where you keep your car's maintenance schedule."

Nodding, Kaycee replied, "Tamara may be the first person in history to get a raise before she even starts work. I can't wait to tell her thank you."

"I called her once you were being treated in the emergency room. I swear, I think that girl has enough energy to fuel an entire city."

"No kidding. I just hope she can funnel it into her job."

"Listen, if you don't get some rest, they're going to kick me out of here." He softly kissed her. "So, my princess, sweet dreams."

She closed her eyes, but murmured, "I refuse to be nicknamed princess."

"Whatever you say, princess." Kaycee's eyes flew open, but Max quickly placed his finger on her mouth to keep her quiet. "Go to sleep!" he ordered. Pulling a chair next to the bed, he took her hand in his. In a matter of minutes, the regular rhythm of her breathing made him certain she was asleep.

Standing, he stretched and checked on Stagga. Stooping next to him, he gently stroked his neck, but the dog was completely oblivious to the world. After kicking off his hiking boots, Max sprawled on top of the spare bed's creaseless sheets and allowed himself the luxury of closing his eyes. Less than a minute later, he had fallen into a deep, dreamless sleep.

« « «   » » »

Cal was going through his pre-flight checklist when Randy asked, "How did your mother take the news?"

"Better than I expected. For a woman in her seventies, sometimes

I think she has more energy than I do."

"Must be where you inherited that stubborn streak."

With a grunt, Cal replied, "I asked her who had tried to come see Aubrey. She's started a list of everyone who's stopped by her hospital room. So far, they're all neighbors and co-workers."

"What did Agent Collier have to say?"

Cal shook his head. "Believe it or not, she's got to get permission from her supervisor to go back. Now that it appears that Aubrey's accident wasn't caused by the Natural Killers, it doesn't fall under her current assignment. I think she may be in over her head. Don't get me wrong, she truly wants to help, it's just that she has to go through the bureaucracy's proper channels."

"Which will take time . . . "

"Of course!"

"Did you get any sleep last night?" Randy asked.

"No, but I slept the entire time I was waiting at R.R.M. for Max to call, plus I napped a couple of hours yesterday afternoon while everyone was in the field. Don't worry, I'm quite capable of making this flight."

"I know you are. It's just that we've all been under a lot of stress lately."

"Aren't we always?" Cal laughed.

With a wide grin, Randy replied, "I suppose so, but you have to admit this is one of the longest streaks — "

" — of wobbling moons?"

"I couldn't have said it better. Do you have a plan of attack in mind for when we arrive in Colorado?"

"Actually, I do." Reaching down by his feet, he handed Randy a thick, black leather case. "That's exactly why I borrowed Max's laptop. I hope he doesn't mind."

"I have a feeling that you could take all his worldly possessions right now and he wouldn't even notice. I don't think I've ever seen him so happy."

« « «   » » »

Craig whispered, "Hurry up! It's almost time for shift change. Everyone will be too busy to notice what's going on."

Pam emerged from the closet dressed in the hospital's standard-issue, blue scrub uniform. Craig was wearing a similar outfit, although his was so large that the pants dragged the floor. For the last hour they had been roaming the floors, in search of idle equipment and supplies that could easily be taken.

Their scavenger hunt had yielded two stethoscopes they had found lying at nurses stations, and ID badges that had been removed from jackets hanging on the coat rack in the cafeteria. Craig easily located the area where the off-duty respiratory technicians stored their carts. Taking one from the back of the line, he carefully placed his gun and the hypodermic in a tray where they were easily accessible.

Not once did an employee question their presence as they sauntered around, acquainting themselves with both the layout of the hospital and the computer system. With a few simple keystrokes, they found Kaycee Miller's room number, as well as the exact times of the tests and treatments that she was scheduled to undergo.

Tapping the screen, Craig said, "She's alone in a semi-private room on the sixth floor. Shift change is in ten minutes. Respiratory therapy is scheduled for nine a.m., so we'll fit right in. That not only gives us plenty of time to put the extract in her IV, it'll have long enough to take effect before anyone finds her."

Pam replied, "You can guard the door while I give her the injection."

"Fine." Glancing at his watch, he declared, "There's not much time. Let's do it."

« « «   » » »

Even though she wasn't on duty yet, Angela Bowers quietly slipped into Kaycee's dimly lit room, careful not to wake her. Angela had only been out of nursing school for four months, and she was eager and excited to be caring for Kaycee Miller, the woman being talked about on both the local and national news shows. Kaycee was the closest thing to a celebrity that Angela had ever been assigned to care for, and she wasn't about to let anything happen to her.

Dr. Gillock had given orders that the patient's vital signs be checked without disturbing her rest if at all possible. Standing next to the bed, Angela scrutinized the color of Kaycee's skin and the regularity of her breathing. The blood oxygen sensor on her left index finger was working perfectly, registering a reading of 95% on the digital display. Leaning close to the wall, she checked to be certain the oxygen was at the proper setting. With a broad smile, Angela was confident that Kaycee was doing very well.

After jotting down her findings, she softly crossed to the other side of the room. As she rounded the end of the bed, she came to an abrupt stop. The dog in the far corner had raised his head and was staring directly at her. Although Angela had known he was allowed to stay, seeing him had momentarily surprised her. She hadn't expected him to be quite so large, or nearly so intimidating.

For a couple of seconds his eyes locked on hers, as if contemplating whether she was worth crossing the room to sniff. Apparently he decided that she wasn't his type, because he slowly lowered his head, took a deep breath, stretched his hind legs, then went back to sleep.

Angela was also aware that the man sleeping in the spare bed was Max Masterson, the man who had rescued Kaycee. Since he, too, had been in the fire, she stopped at the side of his bed to check his condition as well. Although he wasn't wearing a blood oxygen sensor, his color was good and his breathing appeared normal. Quietly, she tugged the curtain that hung between the two beds so that they were separated.

Satisfied that they would both rest comfortably until her official shift check in an hour, she opened the door just as a woman was about to knock. Holding her finger to her lips, Angela stepped into the hallway and asked, "May I help you?"

Agent Collier reeked of smoke and had obviously not had time to change clothes or shower in awhile. Flipping open her badge, she replied, "I'm Special Agent Collier with the FBI. I'm here to check on Ms. Miller."

Shaking her hand, she replied, "Angela Bowers. I'll be her R.N.

this shift. She's resting comfortably."

"That's great. We're going to need to question her as soon as possible. Anything she can remember about her kidnappers may be critical in helping us capture them."

"The doctor wants her to rest until noon. At that time, he's going to reevaluate her condition." Seeing Agent Collier's frustration, Angela said, "I'm sorry. There's really nothing else I can do."

"These people aren't just kidnappers. They're directly responsible for several murders as well as for the forest fires that are destroying half the Ouachita National Forest. We need to get them behind bars."

Although she was trembling inside, Angela steadfastly held her position. "Ms. Miller is still suffering from smoke inhalation and the lasting effects of a drug they administered. I know that Dr. Gillock would want to help with the investigation in any way that he could, but without rest Ms. Miller's condition could easily take a turn for the worse."

"Can you give me his number?"

With a sigh, Angela declared, "Sure. I've got it at the nurse's station. Follow me. We'll call him together."

« « «   » » »

As Craig had anticipated, the nursing station was abuzz when they walked casually past it. Although he appeared to be looking straight ahead, he noticed three nurses huddled in front of a computer, and another off by herself. The loner was standing with her arms crossed, glaring at a woman whose face was smudged with soot. As he watched, the woman shifted, revealing the fact that her dark blue flack jacket had FBI boldly emblazoned in gold letters across the back.

Nudging Pam, he barely moved his head so that she would know to follow his gaze. A soft nod confirmed that she had spotted the agent as well. Consciously trying to maintain a nonchalant walk, they moved ahead.

In a stroke of good luck, Kaycee's room was at the far end of the hall, well away from prying eyes. Craig slipped his hand into the tray, removed the filled syringe, and placed it carefully into his wife's palm.

Whispering, he seethed, "You've got to hurry!"

Without knocking, Pam pushed open the door and walked inside.

Craig stayed in the hall. Although he was pretending to check his cart for supplies, his hand was wrapped around the grip of the pistol.

C H A P T E R **15**

At first, Max had no idea what was hauling him out of his deep sleep. Slowly he came to realize that his hand was being gently scratched. Instinctively pulling it away, he was irritated to feel an even more intense clawing on his forearm. Opening his eyes, he saw Stagga and realized that he was intently pawing at him.

Disoriented, Max saw the unfamiliar yellow curtain and had to search the room to establish where he was. When Stagga realized he had accomplished his goal, he lowered his paws to the floor, and tried to walk away. Apparently still under the influence of the sedative, he staggered and lost his balance, falling to his side.

Not wanting to wake Kaycee, Max quietly slipped off the bed and started to comfort him. He instantly realized that the dog was fighting to stand up, and that his lips were trembling as though he were trying to growl. Instantly on guard, Max placed his head close to the floor.

Only a pair of women's shoes were visible near the head of Kaycee's bed. Although she had on the type of surgical scrubs he was accustomed to seeing, the shoes were flat black slip-ons. At the same time he realized that something was wrong, he heard Kaycee claim in a scratchy voice, "You're not real. Go away. I want to sleep."

Max crept around the edge of his bed as the woman replied, "And you're not dead. But you will be soon. That's right, close those pretty eyes for the last time."

Peaking through the curtain, he saw her pull a large syringe out of her pocket and begin to insert it into Kaycee's I.V. line. Throwing back the curtain, Max grabbed the woman's wrist and wrenched it until the needle popped out of her hand and flew across the room.

She screamed, "Craig!" as she tried to break free of his grip. Max easily twisted both of her arms behind her back before the door flew open.

At the same time that Craig rushed in with his gun, Kaycee's eyes flew open. Looking for a way to keep her out of harm's way, Max dragged the struggling woman toward the opposite end of the room.

The door swung closed behind Craig. He pointed the gun at Kaycee and said, "Let go of my wife or I'll shoot."

Seeing that Stagga was no longer on that side of the room, Max knew that he needed to buy some time. Thinking fast, he declared, "Which will alert every person on this floor of your presence. Why don't you just put down the gun and I'll let you both leave. No harm, no foul."

Craig laughed. "You're not as smart as I thought you were."

"Every law enforcement agency in the nation is looking for you right now. Surely you know that there's no way you're going to get away with this."

"And yet we strolled in here without a single person batting an eye at us." He waved the gun. "Now, let her go."

Stagga had crawled under both the beds. His awkward emergence next to Kaycee's night stand knocked off the phone, causing Craig to jump back. Seeing his chance, Max hurled Pam against the windowsill. Her head hit the corner with a loud *crack!* and she appeared to be dazed.

Max lunged at Craig at the same time that Stagga managed to sink his teeth into the man's Achilles tendon. Although the dog didn't have the coordination to fight very well, once he latched on, it was clear that he had no intention of letting go. The impact slammed them both into the wall, with Stagga sliding across the floor throughout the struggle.

The gun discharged once as Max fought to wrestle it from Craig's hand. Screaming in pain from the dog's piercing bite, Craig viciously kicked him with his free foot while trying to break Max's grip on his wrists.

Max saw Craig's eyes go wide. Looking over his shoulder, Max realized that Kaycee had retrieved the needle and jabbed it into

Craig's upper thigh. Using the distraction to gain the upper hand, Max landed two solid punches to Craig's jaw.

Satisfied that he was no longer a threat, Max took a deep breath, then whipped around when Kaycee screamed, "Max!" Looking up, he saw Pam holding a chair over her head. For a moment it appeared that she was going to attack Kaycee with it, but then she suddenly stopped. Turning toward the window, she nodded as though she were listening to a voice that only she could hear. As if following instructions, she turned and hurled the chair through the window.

Agent Collier rushed in the door with her gun drawn at the exact moment Pam Adams Sanderson dove through the window. Even though they were six stories up, Agent Collier rushed to look outside. Turning back to face Max and Kaycee, she slowly shook her head.

« « «   » » »

When they arrived in Boulder, Cal and Randy went straight to Aubrey's hospital, hoping to find her awake. They found Cal's mother sitting in a chair next to the bed, reading aloud. Although the head of Aubrey's bed was tilted up and her hair was perfectly combed, upon closer examination it was clear that her eyes were closed and her head was held in position by pillows wedged carefully against the rails on each side.

Placing the novel on the bed beside Aubrey, Cal's mother crossed the room and gave them both hugs. Even though she barely topped five feet in height, she exuded confidence and strength. Smiling, she stepped back and declared, "You must be Randy. I'm Ruth Stevens. Better known as Mom."

Never the demonstrative type, Randy blushed and replied, "Nice to meet you."

Keeping his voice low, Cal asked, "How is she?"

"The same. You don't need to be quiet. I think it's good that she knows we're here. Just because she doesn't seem to be awake doesn't mean she can't hear us."

"Is that why you were reading to her?" Randy asked.

She nodded. "And I've been playing her favorite CD's. I want her to feel like she's at home."

Trying to be sensitive to his sister, Cal said, "Maybe we should go in the hall and talk about what we'd like to do."

"No need. I'm sure that Aubrey knows more about the evil person who did this to her than we ever will. If she can hear you, or sense your presence, it might be comforting to her to know that you're not going to let any harm come to her again." Motioning for them to sit on the sofa, she sat back down next to the bed and eagerly asked, "Okay, what's the plan?"

Cal filled her in on the discrepancies that they had uncovered with Kaycee's help, and asked, "Did you tell anyone I was on my way back?"

"Not a soul. Except Aubrey, of course."

"Good. Then we should be able to pull this off. By the way, have you ever kept a diary or journal?"

She laughed. "Surely you know better."

"I do. I just needed to be certain. You told me that you'd never left the room since you arrived, right?"

"That's correct. Peter wanted me to go sleep at their house, but I insisted on staying here. The nurses were nice enough to make the sofa into a bed for me, and they've been bringing me lots of food and snacks. I've actually been pretty comfortable."

"What about Phoebe? Has she come by?"

"Four times so far. Persistent, isn't she?"

The two men exchanged a wary look. "Has she offered to relieve you?"

"Every time."

"Do you think she'll stop back by?"

She glanced at the clock on the wall. "Around seven or eight tonight. She insisted on bringing dinner."

"Great. That gives us plenty of time to set up what we need," Cal said as he unzipped the laptop's case and slid out the sleek machine. Shaking his head, he added, "I sure wish Max were here to deal with this contraption himself."

Randy said, "I'm sure he could walk us through it on the telephone if we can't get it to work."

"True. But I'd really hate to have to admit that I wasn't technologically enabled enough to do something that he claims any six-year-old can do."

"Good point."

Ruth asked, "What are you going to do with that machine?"

"Set a trap. If Phoebe offers to stay here tonight, you need to take her up on it. In order to find out if we can trust her, she's got to be left alone with Aubrey. We're going to set up this computer in the room next door." He held up a small grey device that fit in the palm of his hand. "This is a wireless camera that will send a live video feed anywhere within 100 feet. When Phoebe is alone with Aubrey, if she tries to do anything, we'll not only be able to stop her, we'll have the digital proof we need to have her arrested."

Ruth softly shook her head. "I can't believe she might be the one who tried to kill Aubrey. I always just thought she was a little strange. Very lonely."

"If she agrees to stay tonight, we'll know one way or the other."

"Good. Is there anything I can do to help?"

Cal walked across the room and gave his mother another hug. "Right now, you can say a prayer that our plan will work."

« « «   » » »

Dr. Gillock leaned close, alternating between listening intently with his stethoscope and ordering, "Take a deep breath."

Kaycee willingly complied. Finally, he took a step back and gave her a curious look. Impatiently, she asked, "Well? Can I? Please?"

With a chuckle, he replied, "Your lungs are clear. You win. The I.V. is history and you can take your long awaited shower." Winking at Max, he added, "To tell you the truth, I think the rest of us are just as eager as she is."

Kaycee shook her head. "You know, in the last day I've heard that I stink in every way possible. Some comments were pretty tactful, others were downright rude. Do people really think that a person can't tell when they smell this bad?"

Stepping toward the door, the doctor grinned and said, "I'll go ask the nurse to come take out the I.V."

Swinging her feet over the side of the bed, she ripped the tape off her arm and slid out the needle. "Sorry. Can't wait that long!" Clutching the back of her hospital gown to keep it closed, she scurried across the floor and into the bathroom. Behind her, laughter filled the room.

Kaycee cranked on the hot water, slipped out of the gown, and stepped into the small steamy shower. As the smoke had cleared out of her system, her own disgusting odor had become impossible to ignore. She scrubbed every inch of her body, even the places that were bruised and swollen. The last thing she did was tilt her head under the stream of water so that she could wash her hair.

After squirting a generous amount of shampoo in her hand, she pulled her hair out of the pony tail it had been in since she'd arrived and began to lather it. Something was wrong. She smoothed down the dark sudsy strands and felt the back of her head. To her dismay, she found that a large chunk of hair was missing.

A memory flashed through her mind, one she had purposely avoided because she assumed it wasn't real. She broke into a sweat as she remembered flames so close that they seemed to be reaching for her, followed by Max throwing her to the ground when a blowing ember caught her hair on fire.

Tears rushed to her eyes, and she mentally scolded herself. *It's just hair! It'll grow back. Get over it.* But no matter how hard she tried, she couldn't seem to stop crying. The water and the tears kept flowing, until she heard Max at the door.

"Kaycee, are you all right? You've been in there a long time. Joan's here. Do you need help?"

Sucking in a jagged breath, she tried to keep her voice from shaking as she replied, "I'm fine. I'll be out in a minute."

Shutting off the water, she dried and slipped into the robe that was hanging on the back of the door. After staring at the brush on the sink for a long time, she finally worked up the nerve to brush out what was left of her hair. Throughly depressed, she quickly blew it dry and swept it back in a pony tail so that the damage wasn't quite so obvious.

When she opened the door, Max took one look at her and rushed across the room. Pulling her into his arms, he asked, "What's wrong? Are you hurt? Did you have another hallucination? Should I get the doctor?"

Burying her face in his chest, she shook her head. "It's nothing. Really. I just think that everything is finally catching up with me."

Joan said sympathetically, "The doctor warned us that the drug might take days to clear out of your system. You shouldn't expect to be back to normal in such a short period of time."

Looking up at Max, Kaycee said, "I want to go home."

"You will. Soon."

Setting her jaw, she declared, "I want to go right now. And I need an appointment with Connie."

"Connie?" Max asked.

Nodding, she replied, "She's done my hair for years. In case you hadn't noticed, a bunch of my hair burned off!"

With a sigh, Max smiled. "Is that what this is about? Your hair?"

Frustrated, Kaycee felt a fresh wave of tears. "It's not just that. I want my own bed, my own clothes. This may be a different room, but I keep seeing them here, and the needle, and . . . I just want to go home!"

Max looked at Joan as if begging for help. When she replied with a frown and a shrug, he explained, "Kaycee, your house was the scene of a crime. It needs . . . work."

Her eyes narrowed. "How much work?"

Trying to minimize her shock, he said, "There are a couple of broken doors . . . some painting . . . just basic repairs. It shouldn't take that long, but it will take a little time. As a matter of fact, I talked to Tamara while you were in the shower. She's lining up contractors to take care of it."

Looking at the two of them, she fumed, "You know, this isn't a prison, and they can't force — "

Kaycee's tirade was interrupted by a knock at the door. Joan quickly pulled it open to reveal Kaycee's sister, Niki. Rolling her wheelchair inside, she smiled and said, "I didn't mean to interrupt a perfectly good fight!"

Running to hug her, Kaycee said, "I can't believe you're here!"

"Considering I could hear you halfway down the hall, it sounds like I got here in the nick of time. Get back in that bed. Now!"

Kaycee sheepishly did as she was told. Max bent down to hug Niki and whispered, "Thanks for coming. I owe you one."

"Kaycee has never been a very good patient. Considering she's a psychologist, you'd think she could learn to be a little less controlling." Rolling across the room, Niki held out her hand and introduced herself. "Hi! I'm Niki Miller, Kaycee's younger sister. You must be Joan."

"That's right. It's nice to meet you."

"Well, I hate to be blunt, but I'd really like to talk to Kaycee alone. Why don't the two of you go get a cup of coffee and relax?"

Taking the not-so-subtle hint, they laughed and left.

Niki rolled to the side of the bed and looked Kaycee in the eye. "Are you okay?"

More tears sprang to her eyes, but she nodded. "First the kidnapping and the fire, then what happened this morning. It's just a little overwhelming."

Smiling, Niki said, "I can still see that look in Max's eyes. He's crazy about you."

"He won't be if I don't stop acting like a witch. I was really nasty a minute ago and I'm not even sure why. I can't explain it . . . He saved my life, and has been so supportive . . . "

"But you're angry. Not at him, but he's the easiest one to take it out on. Well, that's why I'm here. Who better to fight with than your sister?"

Kaycee laughed.

"Besides, I have something to show you that I know will cheer you up."

"Really? What?"

Niki rolled the wheelchair to the end of the bed. After locking the tires in place, she bit her lip and pushed herself to a standing position. Grinning from ear to ear, she took four carefully placed steps, then gently sat on the edge of the bed. Leaning over, she hugged her sister.

Kaycee started crying one more time, but they were tears of joy.

« « «   » » »

It took Randy and Cal the better part of the afternoon to set up the laptop in the storage room next to Aubrey's. Adjusting the wireless camera had been the toughest challenge, since they had to find a spot where it wouldn't be noticed.

There were surprisingly few places to hide things in the modestly decorated hospital room. After several failed attempts, they positioned the camera on top of the television that was suspended from the ceiling. From that angle, over seventy percent of the room was clearly visible, although everything along one wall was blocked. Even so, they decided that since Aubrey's entire bed could be seen, it was their best alternative.

Since they couldn't risk Phoebe seeing Cal, Randy left long enough to pick up dinner and bring it back to the closet. Sitting atop boxes of medical supplies, both agreed that the old fashioned hamburgers and onion rings were the best they'd had in ages. By the time Phoebe arrived at eight that night, they were getting mildly claustrophobic and downright anxious about the night to come.

On the small screen, they watched Phoebe hug Ruth, then walk into the area not covered by the camera. After a short time, she stepped back into the frame, but she was no longer carrying the small overnight case that she had brought along. As the two of them began having a quiet discussion, Randy commented, "This feels really weird."

Cal agreed, "Downright kinky. This would be a lot easier if we could hear what was going on in there."

Randy laughed. "Next time we decide to spy on someone, maybe we'll have time to plan a little better."

"I wonder if this is illegal?" Cal commented.

"Most likely. If the police did it, it would probably be considered entrapment."

"Then it's a good thing we aren't the police." After several minutes, Cal shook his head and said, "You know, half of me wants it to be Phoebe so that this nightmare will be over, but the other half is praying that we're wrong. After all, she seems like a nice enough person. And if it is her, then Aubrey may blame herself for not befriending her."

"It's definitely a no-win situation. Look, your mom's leaving."

Now that Phoebe and Aubrey were finally alone, both men's eyes were glued to the small screen. They watched Phoebe walk back and forth as if she were bored, then turn on the television. Cal chuckled. "It looks like she's watching us watch her."

"Think she'll notice the camera?"

"We should know in a couple of minutes."

The room fell silent as they waited. It quickly became obvious that Phoebe hadn't noticed anything out of the ordinary. She disappeared from the screen for a couple of moments, then reappeared with a bag of knitting supplies. Two hours later, she had added several inches to the afghan she was knitting when she stood to turn off the television.

For awhile, she slowly paced the room. At eleven p.m., she made a call on her cell phone. From her exaggerated gestures, it was easy to tell that it was a heated conversation. Finally, she hung up and walked to the side of the bed.

Both Cal and Randy were on their feet, ready to rush to Aubrey's aid. For several minutes Phoebe simply stared at her. Occasionally she would lift a strand of her hair, or gently touch the side of her face. The gestures seemed out of place, more like how a mother would caress her child.

For fifteen minutes Phoebe seemed deep in thought, as though she were trying to decide what to do. From the angle, they could only tell that she looked at the clock on the wall, said something to Aubrey, then sat back down.

Cal sighed. "I'm really beginning to think we were wrong."

"It's too soon to tell. Why don't you get some rest? I'll take the first shift," Randy replied.

Stretching out on a blanket on the floor, Cal went to sleep. Randy diligently observed Phoebe, fascinated by the woman's sudden changes. One minute she seemed as though she were on the verge of sleep, the next she would hop up and peek out the door. After nervously pacing, she would stop to take a series of yoga-like deep breaths. By one a.m., Randy was exhausted just from watching her.

Randy was on the verge of dozing off at one-thirty in the morning when he saw the door to Aubrey's room slowly open. Expecting a nurse, he was surprised to see Peter. His mouth actually dropped open when Phoebe rushed to into his arms and they exchanged a passionate kiss.

Softly kicking Cal, Randy muttered, "Wake up, buddy."

"Something happening?" Cal asked as he groaned and stretched.

"No doubt about it."

Together they watched Peter and Phoebe talk for a few moments before Peter slipped into the restroom. Phoebe immediately sat down in the chair next to the bed, pretending to be asleep. For the next five minutes, nothing happened. Finally, Cal whispered, "What the hell are they up to?"

"I have no idea, but it can't be good."

"Is there any way he could've crept out of the room without us seeing him?"

"No way," Randy replied, shaking his head.

"Look!"

The night shift nurse entered the room and began checking Aubrey's vital signs. Phoebe feigned sleep through the entire ritual, moving only after the nurse left the room. Jumping up, she rushed to the door and peeked out, no doubt making certain the coast was clear. Stepping back into the room, she crossed to the area that was out of their sight and didn't return.

"We'd better go now," Cal declared, ready to bolt.

Randy took him by the arm and said, "If you stop them now, you won't have any proof. No matter what they're getting ready to do, their lawyer will come up with some twisted reason why they were doing it. Just be patient a couple more seconds."

Cal sighed and returned to his spot in front of the laptop.

Peter finally reentered the screen, holding a two-foot-long black cylinder in his hand. Phoebe was a step behind him, one hand resting softly on his shoulder as if she were there for moral support.

"He put on gloves!" Randy declared.

Cal asked, "What could be in that tank?"

Randy cocked his head and leaned closer to the small screen. "I'd guess some sort of gas. Probably nitrous oxide."

"Laughing gas? The kind dentists use?"

"Yes. It's available on the black market. Kids buy it to get high. Dentists use about a 10% mixture, but inhaling it at 100% would be quickly lethal."

Randy and Cal watched in disgust as Peter disconnected Aubrey's face mask from the wall and connected the end of the tube to the tank. Before he had time to crank open the valve on the gas, they were crashing through the door.

Cal hit Peter with a tackle that would make any linebacker proud, sending him sprawling to the floor. Although Randy considered joining the fight, he had his own hands full when Phoebe tried to get past him.

Randy counted to ten as Phoebe pummeled him with her fists and kicked his shins. When his patience was exhausted, he simply grabbed her right hand and twisted her arm behind her back. After repeating the process, he pushed her into the room and used a roll of medical tape to bind her wrists.

Cal was straddling Peter, seizing him by the shirt collar as he screamed, "Why? Why did you try to kill her?"

Pretending not to know what he was talking about, Peter replied, "You're crazy. What are you doing here?"

Randy dialed 9-1-1 as Cal impatiently warned, "I want the truth! We know that one or both of you pushed Aubrey off the trail and tried to make it look like she was a victim of the Natural Killers. How long have you two been having an affair?"

As slick as ever, Peter stuck with his lies. "An affair? You really need a good night's rest. We're just friends."

"Sure you are. What are the police going to find inside that tank?"

"Nitrous oxide. I just wanted to be sure she wasn't in any pain. I wasn't going to give her much. Just a little. It's laughing gas, you know. I love Aubrey and want her to be happy. That's the only reason Phoebe and I are here — to help."

"Aubrey will be happy to have both of you out of her life. I'll bet you knew exactly how much gas it would take to permanently silence her." Infuriated, Cal hit Peter so hard that the sound of his jaw cracking filled the room.

Randy intervened, pulling Cal to his feet as a nurse and two orderlies barged in. Once they explained the situation, the orderlies restrained Peter and Phoebe until the police arrived to take them away.

When the room finally fell silent, Randy and Cal stood beside Aubrey's bed. Taking her hand in his, Cal said, "It's safe to come back now, Brey."

Max handed Kaycee a steaming mug of coffee, then sat down beside her on the porch swing. Kaycee loved everything about Max's ranch house, from the enormous front lawn to the way the last rays of sunlight reflected off the weather vane that topped the rustic barn. Kicking off her sandals, she tucked her legs to one side and snuggled close to Max.

Inhaling the aroma of the vanilla in her coffee, she said, "As always, your culinary skills are quite impressive." Placing the mug on the table, she added, "But I think I'll let this cool for a few minutes while we watch the sunset."

Pulling her even closer, he ran his fingers along the back of her neck, then sprinkled it with gentle kisses. "I think your new haircut has a few distinct advantages."

Giggling, she replied, "I suppose. But don't let it spoil you. I can't wait until it's long again. Believe it or not, I feel almost naked."

Playfully biting one of the narrow straps of her sun dress, he tugged it off her shoulder. "That could easily be arranged." Closing her eyes, Kaycee surrendered to the luxury of his touch. As if Smokey and Stagga wanted their share of attention, they ran across the porch, disrupting the intimacy of the moment by barking.

"What do you suppose has gotten into them?" Kaycee asked.

"I'd guess one spotted a rabbit and the other isn't about to be left behind."

Doing her best city girl impersonation, she asked, "They wouldn't hurt the rabbit, would they?"

"Only if they catch it, princess." Ignoring her threatening look, he said, "I wish your sister could've stayed longer."

"Me, too. Still, it was great to see her."

"It's funny. Sometimes the family resemblance is so strong that you seem like twins, then other times I don't think you're anything like her. But one thing is always there — that wicked sense of humor."

"We do know how to have a good time."

"And you're both very determined."

"With a few more months of hard work, she may never have to be in that wheelchair again. It's marvelous."

"Miracles do happen."

"Thanks to people like you. I've heard quite a few stories about how determined you were to rescue me. Have I mentioned lately how much I appreciate all you've done?"

"I believe you have. And as I told you before, it's going to take more than a little forest fire to keep me away from you."

"There's something I've been wondering about Craig Sanderson."

"What's that?"

"How did a botanist know how to build those devices that started the forest fires?"

"The FBI found the instructions in his luggage. He found them on the Internet."

"Sometimes too much technology is a *bad* thing!"

Leaning close, he whispered, "I can think of something that's been around forever and is as natural as can be." Max started to kiss her, but stopped when the phone rang. "Why don't we just pretend we don't hear that?"

"As much as I'd love to, we can't. My sister promised to call when she got home."

Hopping up, he went inside to answer the phone. Kaycee sipped her coffee and watched the dogs take turns chasing each other until he returned a few minutes later. Glancing his way, she instantly caught his contagious smile. "That must have been good news," she declared.

"Very good news. Aubrey regained consciousness. She's going to be fine."

"That's wonderful, Max. I'm sure Cal is ecstatic."

"He said the D.A. built such a strong case that Peter's lawyer is pushing him to plea bargain. He'd serve less time, but it would save Aubrey the agony of going through a trial. Since Phoebe has a long history of mental illness, she'll probably plead insanity and spend the rest of her life in an institution."

"Peter manipulated her, didn't he?"

"From what they have pieced together, he had Phoebe do the dirty work while he sat back and prepared to reap the benefits, both professionally and personally."

"If Aubrey didn't have anything to do with his company, why did she own half the stock?" Kaycee asked.

"Because he used her money to start the firm. It was just after they got married, and she called to ask Cal what she should do. Peter wanted all the stock in his name, but Cal insisted that she not allow that to happen. Apparently the company has been on the verge of bankruptcy for at least six months."

"Between having Phoebe next door and the business in trouble, it's no wonder her handwriting showed she was under stress."

"I'm sure it was like living with a black cloud over her head. It makes me wonder how long Peter had this in mind. The company took out a two million dollar life insurance policy on Aubrey just weeks after the corporation was formed."

"And with her out of the way, his financial worries would've been over," Kaycee stated.

"It always amazes me what people will do for money."

"Do you think they really believed they'd get away with it?"

Max shrugged. "They were counting on Aubrey's body not being found for a long time, if ever. And if the Natural Killers hadn't been captured, their scheme might have worked."

"Luckily, they were wrong about several things. Did I tell you what Agent Collier said about the book?"

He shook his head.

"It was co-written by one of Craig Sanderson's former botany students. In fact, several chapters were taken straight from the doctoral thesis he wrote for Professor Sanderson."

"They were very troubled people."

"I know the memorial marker I saw in the forest was real. Someday, would you hike there with me and we'll put flowers on it?"

"Why in the world would you want to go back there?" he asked.

"Closure. I think seeing it with you at my side would end the terror of the nightmare." Shivering, she admitted, "Right now, when I'm alone in the dark those fears are still very real."

He pulled her close, warming her with a kiss. "Then we won't waste any time. You just tell me when you want to go, and we'll put an end to this once and for all."

She whispered, "I love you."

"And I love you, too." Looking at the horizon he said, "The colors never cease to amaze me."

Kaycee sighed. "You know, I think that *the golden hour* should have a dual meaning."

"Such as?"

"Of course, the first will always mean getting a victim to a trauma unit in time."

"And the second?" he asked, moving closer.

Kissing him again, she replied, "That magic hour in the evening when we can hold each other and watch the sunset. Every day we could have our own golden hour."

"There's nothing I'd love more."

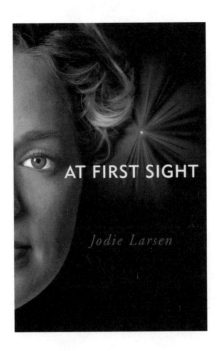
What would you do if you awoke in a strange motel
room to find a terrified child at you bedside?

At first, Kaycee Miller — a psychologist specializing in handwriting analysis — is certain she is dreaming. But one touch of
the girl's tear-streaked face convinces her the nightmare is all
too real. The door to the adjoining room is ajar; and the man
sleeping inside is armed. Kaycee and the girl flee — but soon
discover it is already too late to escape . . .